Greedy Givers

Greedy Givers

Jerri Williams

This book is a work of fiction. Names, characters, places, and incidents are either products of the author's imagination or are used fictitiously. Any resemblance to actual events, locals, organizations, or persons living or dead, is entirely coincidental and beyond the intent of either the author or the publisher. The opinions expressed in this book are the author's and not those of the FBI.

Cover design by Elizabeth Mackey / elizabethmackey.com

Formatting by Polgarus Studio / polgarusstudio.com

This novel is dedicated to my parents, Buford and Odessa Williams.
I'm blessed to have grown up in a loving home
where books were valued, and reading was encouraged.

"Every man has three characters: The one he shows, the one he has, and the one he thinks he has." (Alphonse Karr)

CHAPTER 1

A public stoning, that's what he deserved.

Any minute now, William Townsend would summon him before two hundred and fifty of the foundation's most strident supporters. Cuddy Mullins's eyes darted around the room and at the people at the head table, where he sat. Every face reflected back admiration and love, especially CeCe's. But he couldn't stop imagining them all with rocks in their hands, readying their aim to be among the first to bash in his skull.

He sank further into his chair and felt the Founding Fathers staring down at him from the priceless oil portraits mounted on the walls of the Philadelphia Union League's elegant banquet room. He wished he could place his hands over his ears and escape having to listen to Townsend, who was onstage, blabbering about his good deeds.

"...this young man's Foundation for New Visions in Giving has brought hope and stability...his fresh and innovative concepts have revolutionized the way charities and nonprofits access needed funding..."

Cuddy wondered what would happen if he refused to be dragged before the expectant crowd. He held a water glass to his forehead and tried to settle his nerves. But when Townsend trumpeted his name, Cuddy's heart raced even faster.

"Ladies and gentlemen, please stand as we welcome and honor Mr. Cuthbert 'Cuddy' Mullins III."

Everyone rose to their feet, and their thunderous applause unnerved him even more. He grimaced and glanced at CeCe. She probably thought he was upset because Townsend had used his full name. She knew how much he hated that. Jesus Christ, he wasn't one of them. He was Cuddy, just plain old Cuddy Mullins from Kensington. But that wasn't what was bothering him. He wished he could tell her. He wished he could warn her.

CeCe elbowed him. "Honey, get up," she whispered as she struggled to pull his chair out. She turned toward the audience and, with a silly grin, threw up her hands in mock exasperation. He rose on shaky legs. She playfully pushed him toward the podium and shouted after him, "I'm so proud of you, baby!"

As he walked toward the stage, he felt a pounding pressure in his chest as if the reverberant clapping of the crowd was messing with the biorhythm of his heart. He would go up and accept the award with a simple thank-you. No speech. Just take the damn award, smile, and walk back to his seat. As he reached the steps leading up to the riser, an intense feeling of doom engulfed him. The pounding in his chest now kept beat with the pounding in his head. He couldn't do it. He glanced back at the audience's grinning faces, CeCe's smile the biggest and brightest, but all he could envision was everyone's faces scowling as they prepared to stone him. He turned his focus forward, where Townsend was holding the award out toward him. It was as if a huge boulder were sitting on his chest, crushing his ribs. He placed his right foot on the first of the five short steps up to the stage and then paused. I can't do this.

When the option to flee entered his mind, he seriously considered acting on the impulse and damn the consequences. He should just walk out. CeCe was the one who had orchestrated this event in spite of his objections. If he escaped, then she would have to accept the damn award.

Instead, he stepped onto the stage, shook Townsend's hand vigorously, and grabbed and kissed the award. He stood looking out at the audience, allowing himself to absorb their admiration. "I am humbled by your recognition of my work"—he gestured around the room with his free hand—"of our work at the Foundation for New Visions in Giving. We are Kingdom focused, accepting the challenge to change the world for the glory of God. Everybody working for the foundation, staff, donors, and nonprofits have the same dream, the same mission. And we—*you*—are making a tremendous difference in the world. *In the world!*" he shouted, holding the crystal award high.

***

The following morning, Cuddy resumed his usual routine. He slipped on his dog-walking clothes—the T-shirt and sweatpants laid out on the chair next to the bed—and then grabbed his socks and sneakers. Without waking CeCe, he quietly left the room.

When he opened the bedroom door, Potter, his little white terrier was in the hallway waiting for him. CeCe had locked him out of the room again. Cuddy knelt and greeted the pup with a full face nuzzle.

"Hey, little buddy. Ready for your walk?"

Cuddy tiptoed down the stairs with Potter following close behind, tiny paws clicking at his heels. The award from last night had been placed in the center of the kitchen table. He barely glanced at it as he hurried into the laundry room, where he stopped to clip on Potter's leash and pull on a jacket. After checking the pocket to make sure he had waste bags, they headed out into the crisp morning air.

Cuddy cherished the solitude and peace of these twice-daily walks in the woods, the chance to think. His one-on-one time with God could be found when walking Potter along the train tracks behind his home. When his mother was living, she went to mass every morning and was so proud when he would join her several times a month. He had always been a good Catholic boy, eager to make up for his mamma's disappointment that he had not joined the priesthood. Now, these woods near the Westover Bird Sanctuary were his spiritual shelter.

When Potter stopped to sniff the roots of an oak tree, Cuddy paused to appreciate the beauty of the wooded surroundings. The well-worn dirt path beneath his feet led to his deepest connection with God.

Only the scheduled horn blast of the Paoli-Thorndale Line train pierced the tranquility of the woods. As soon as the Regional Rail rounded the bend of track behind their house, the sweet peace of birds whistling and small beasts scurrying returned. And, of course, Potter's playful barking. When they reached the small clearing behind the high school, he unleashed Potter, threw a stick, and smiled as the pup bounded through the tall grass after it. He returned with one end dragging on the ground. Cuddy snapped off a third, making it easier for the little dog to handle, and threw it again. Once again, Potter chased after it. It was on a morning like this when he'd first had his vision to change the world for the glory of God. He had been a drug counselor and had also been asked to raise funds for the rehab clinic where he worked. That success had led him to help other nonprofits find funding, and from there, he had created the Foundation for New Visions in Giving. It seemed so pure, so right. And now he had lost sight of the vision. For the last week or so, he had been reciting Psalm 42 in his head as he walked along the train tracks.

Why are you in despair, O my soul? And why have you become disturbed within me? Hope in God, for I shall again praise Him for the help of His presence.

As he recited the passage to himself, he immediately felt calmer. He looked up beyond the leafy treetops and said out loud, "Everything I do, I do for Your glory."

***

By the time he and Potter had returned to the house, CeCe was awake and up. He could see her through the sliding glass door in the atrium, reading the paper. Her face was glowing with excitement. He tried to ease into the kitchen through the back door, but she bounced into the room as soon as she heard him.

"Good morning, sunshine. The paper's in there," she said, motioning toward the adjoining, sun-filled room. "There's a huge picture of you with me in the background on the front of section B and another smaller one with the Townsends and us on the 'Cause and Celebration' social page."

He turned his head in the direction of the next room but didn't move.

She picked up the coffeepot with one hand and reached into the cabinet above with her other. "Did you want anything else with your coffee?" She handed him a mug. "Juice, some eggs, or toast?"

He stared into the black liquid.

"Cuddy?"

"No, thank you. Just coffee." He raised the cup to his lips.

When he didn't budge, she walked toward the threshold to the adjoining room and beckoned to him. "Come on and look." She pointed to the Metro section of the thick Sunday edition spread out on the table. The rest of the paper did not appear to have been touched. He stepped past her and stood over the paper. Staring back at him were their photogenic faces. He was in his rented tuxedo—he had refused to purchase one of his own—and CeCe in her ridiculously expensive designer gown. He perched himself on the edge of one of the sunroom's wicker chairs and, after Potter leaped up and settled onto his lap, began to read the article.

Cuddy Mullins Honored by Philadelphia Philanthropic Society
By Kitty Oliphant, Inquirer Staff Writer

The text and photos continued onto the next page. As he read, CeCe sat next to him, and began combing her fingers through his hair and rubbing the raised scar on the back of his head. After reading several paragraphs, he folded the paper in half, tucking the image of him and CeCe away from view.

"What are you doing?" said CeCe, her voice suddenly sharp. She flipped the paper open again. "It's a great photo of us. There's a full-length shot on the other page."

He arched a brow and shook his head. "We should have never agreed to accept the award, and we definitely should not have granted that interview."

"Don't be so damn modest," she said. She looked at him with disappointment in her eyes.

Here it comes, Cuddy thought. He knew she wouldn't be able to hold back for too long.

"They should have recognized you long before this. How many times did I tell you that you needed to embrace the love of your followers?"

"Followers? You always make it sound like I'm some kind of cult figure." He looked at her with sad eyes. "It's not about me. It's about the work. It's about—"

"Stop lecturing me." CeCe scooched her chair away from the table, startling Potter, who began to yap in response to her sudden movement. "I won't be criticized by you either," she shouted at the dog.

"Don't yell at him." Cuddy stroked Potter's fur.

She grabbed the article with both hands and held it inches from his face. "This city and every charitable organization and nonprofit in it owe you for the work you've done for poor people, addicts, the disability community, the arts..." Before he could respond, she pleaded, "Aren't you even going to read what it says?"

"I don't need to." He swatted the newspaper away from his face and brushed his left palm against Potter's shaggy, white fur, the terrier jumping from the sudden movement. "I minister to people in need. The people in the room last night don't need anyone. We may need their money, but they're not the ones I'm here to serve."

"But there are some great quotes from influential people. Listen to the nice things Jon Hamilton said about you—"

He held up his hand to stop her from reading. "I'm sure he did."

"I'm sorry you didn't enjoy it as much as I did. It was magical—all of those rich people finally recognizing you for all you do for others."

She sat down next to him and proceeded to read highlights from the article out loud—highlights he didn't want to hear.

He shook his head. "But this isn't about me. It never was."

"You never change," she said. "Could you get down off that cross? We're gonna need the wood."

"That's not funny," he said. This was not the time for jokes.

"It's so hard for humble men like you to accept tribute. You did the same thing when you were listed in that forty-under-forty article in *Philadelphia Magazine* a few years back. God knows you do what you do in His name, for His glory."

His guilt expanded. CeCe assumed he was overwhelmed with modesty. The truth was he was well past believing his own press. "CeCe, that's not it at all. The Foundation for New Visions in Giving is exclusive, only for causes who meet our stringent requirements. We shouldn't be advertising what we're doing to the general public."

"So let me guess, you have a verse for this too?" she said.

He reached for the small Bible he always carried in his pocket. "Matthew 6:1," he said and flipped open the pocket-sized New Testament to locate and recite the passage. "'Beware of practicing your righteousness before men to be noticed by them; otherwise, you have no reward with your Father who is in Heaven. So when you give to the poor, do not sound a trumpet before you, as the hypocrites do in the synagogues and in the streets, so that they may be honored by men.'"

That's what he was—a hypocrite. But he couldn't tell her that.

"Well...I agree with you there. You don't need an awards ceremony or a story in the paper to know that you're doing God's work," she said. "But if they want to write about you, let 'em. You don't need to get caught up in any of that. You've helped so many people. Just keep on doing His work. Got it?"

"Absolutely." Cuddy sighed and nodded. "The first rule about God's work is you don't talk about God's work." He glanced again at the photo of him and CeCe at the ceremony. "You looked beautiful last night." He placed his hand on her neck to pull her toward him and kiss her cheek. "Absolutely stunning."

CeCe batted her eyelashes at him. "Not too bad for a girl from Swamp Poodle."

As soon as she left the room, he gathered up the newspaper, walked into the kitchen, and tossed it in the garbage can. CeCe was right. He was personally responsible for the success of a few hundred nonprofits and charities that had been unable to get the funding they needed to serve their clients. Now they had that funding. His intentions were pure. He was saving lives. He would just keep doing what he was doing.

Until the FBI came.

CHAPTER 2

The foundation's offices were located in a high-rise on JFK Boulevard. Parking in the city was expensive, so Cuddy occasionally ferreted Potter on the train in his carrying case among the standing-room-only rush-hour commuters. This had been one of those mornings that he didn't feel like driving into Center City. Although a number of his fellow passengers must have noticed he had brought his pet along for the ride, nobody complained. When they exited at Suburban Station, he let Potter out and they strolled side-by-side to their second home.

As Cuddy entered the office space, the young intern answering the phones was full of earnest enthusiasm. "Hello. You've reached the Foundation for New Visions in Giving. How may I direct your call?" She smiled and gave him a one finger wave as she worked. "Certainly, let me transfer you to our beneficiary department. Please hold."

Good morning, he mouthed to her and continued through the reception area into the main office. It had been several weeks since that glowing article about the foundation had appeared in the newspaper. The phones were still telethon-ringing off the hook from the publicity. Every nonprofit agency in the country that needed cash and every kindhearted person with some extra pennies to donate had been calling. He scanned the room quickly. It appeared as if every one of the twelve staff members was busy fielding calls. Potter squirmed to be put down, but he held on to the pup with both hands. Cuddy planned to go straight to his office and close the door.

"Oh good, you're here." Melinda came out of her office with a stack of prospectuses addressed and ready to be mailed. On paper, Melinda was his chief of staff, but she really served as the foundation's CEO. He rejected those fancy corporate titles though. She patted Potter's fluffy curls and scratched him under his chin. "And how are you today, Hairy Potter?"

Cuddy looked at the large envelopes she was hugging to her chest. "What are you doing? Get one of the kids to take care of that stuff."

"Kids? Mr. 'Philadelphia's Top Entrepreneurs Under 40.'" Melinda who was in her mid-fifties laughed and held out the envelopes as if to whack him over the head. "I want to make sure these go out today." Although almost old enough to be their mother, Melinda had the same excited, idealistic pitch to her voice as the younger staff members. "We're changing the world, and that can't wait."

"You are such a cheerleader," he said. He patted her shoulder and then started to walk away.

"Cuddy, once you get settled, please call that professor from Hunter Valley Christian College. He's already called this morning, and he left three messages for you yesterday."

"Didn't you tell him what I said?"

"I did, and he didn't take it well. He said it sounded like a threat."

"I wasn't threatening anyone. But if he doesn't believe his trustees made the right decision by participating in our matching-fund program, I'll be happy to return their money."

"Just call him back. Okay?" She used her head to motion to his office. "His information is on your desk."

Cuddy spoke briefly with his admin, Sarah Browning, before entering his office and shutting the door—his other sanctuary. He set Potter down on the carpeted floor and lowered himself into the soft leather chair behind his massive desk. Potter crawled under the desk and plopped onto the dog bed in the roomy well next to Cuddy's feet. He contemplated what he needed to do to slow down the inevitable as he softly drummed his fingers on the beveled edge of the rich mahogany surface. In the Sotheby's auction brochure, the desk had been described as "an executive two pedestal partners' desk circa 1765." CeCe had seen a similar one in the cover photo of a *Town & Country* feature about some young, rich mogul making waves in the tech business. She had insisted that Cuddy should have one for his office. She subscribed to all the luxury magazines—*Vanity Fair, Architectural Digest, Upscale Living Magazine, Dolce Vita*, and, of course, *Vogue*—but considered *Town & Country* her bible for fashion and lifestyle tips. CeCe was determined that they project prosperity in everything they did and in everything they touched. A photo of him at the desk was the background photo for the foundation's Facebook page, Instagram, and Twitter account. The photo embarrassed him greatly. He didn't want or need any of CeCe's fancy furnishings and trimmings.

He glared at the little, yellow sticky note affixed to his leather blotter. Professor Walden Burton from tiny Hunter Valley Christian College was getting on his nerves.

Cuddy took a deep breath and picked up the desk phone. He hoped Burton was teaching one of his accounting classes. Then he could leave a message and avoid the inquisition.

No such luck. The professor answered on the first ring.

Cuddy took in another deep breath before he spoke. "Professor Burton. Cuddy Mullins over at New Visions returning your call," he said with more enthusiasm than warranted for a conversation he had been trying to avoid.

"Thanks for getting back to me. Did you receive the list of questions I emailed you?"

"I did."

"Although I appreciate the call, I was anticipating a written response." Burton's voice faded away, as if he were turning his head away from the receiver, maybe looking for something. "Your responses to my concerns should be documented. Give me a second to open up my file so I can take some notes."

"Are the college's trustees aware of your email?"

"They know I have a few issues with the donation."

"And they've authorized—"

"Look, I just have a few questions—"

"You need to address your concerns and questions with your trustees."

"I don't understand." Cuddy could hear the frustration in Burton's voice. "I'm asking for basic accounting data."

"They have been fully briefed about New Visions."

"Can you at least send me your last audit?"

"The trustees have our financials."

"No, they don't," said Burton, the agitation in his voice rising sharply. "Nobody seems to have your financials."

"Professor Burton, I returned your call as a courtesy," Cuddy said in an authoritative tone. "To advise you that your communications are in violation of the matching program."

"In violation? And what exactly does that mean?"

"It means that my staff and I have already provided program details to the college's trustees."

"And if I keep asking questions?"

"It could result in the college losing the opportunity to continue to participate."

"Oh yes, there's that threat again."

"Do you want to transfer this call to the president of the college, or do you prefer that I dial his number as soon as we hang up?"

"Your refusal to answer even the simplest of accounting questions causes me grave concern. I've already sent her and the trustees a memo listing my concerns."

"And yet, they decided to continue participating. Please note that you contacting me this way is in total disregard of the agreement between New Visions in Giving and Hunter Valley College."

"About that *agreement*." The professor's sarcasm was palpable.

"Wally, I'm ending this call and will immediately advise my staff to return $500,000 to Hunter Valley, which will deny your institution the opportunity to receive matching donor funds."

"Yeah, about that." There was that sarcasm again. "Who exactly are your donors?"

"What did you just ask me?"

"I asked you who the anonymous donors are. I guess that's yet another violation of the agreement?"

"You know perfectly well that information is strictly confidential. I'll definitely be having a serious conversation with President…"

"President Fitzgerald. Do you have her number handy?"

"How dare you." He could feel his heart hammering in his chest. "You are seriously jeopardizing the college's chance to partici—"

"Mr. Mullins, I'm a CPA and what you're doing makes no sense."

"What we are doing here is groundbreaking in the field of fundraising, participatory giving. We consider ourselves philanthropic entrepreneurs and venture capitalists in charitable giving. Donors often express a desire to give to a favorite cause but never seem to get around to it because there's no inherent sense of urgency. What we did was create that urgency to make people want to get involved, to be a part of the movement."

"Matching funds are not new. The college encourages charitable giving by matching staff donations twice a year, but that's not what you're doing here. I read that propaganda piece you had placed in the paper this weekend. It sounds good, but—"

Cuddy cut him off. "It doesn't just sound good; it is good. We are doing good work. We're doing God's work."

"Sounds like you're reading me a line from your fancy brochure." Cuddy could hear the hesitancy in Burton's voice as he spoke his next words. "But, Mr. Mullins, I think I can prove that the Foundation of New Visions in Giving's matching program is a Ponzi scheme."

Cuddy released an audible gasp. "If you continue to make false and inflammatory accusations like that, I'll sue you."

"Now, that doesn't sound very charitable. I need just a bit more before I report you to the authorities. I'm almost there."

Before Cuddy could slam down the receiver, Professor Burton hung up first.

He stared at the phone. It was all falling apart at an alarming pace. But he reminded himself that he didn't need to be worried about the professor. The president of the college promised to fire Burton if he continued to rock the boat. Hunter Valley College had already doubled their money once. The foundation had already established that the matching program worked. Cuddy absentmindedly patted his thigh, and as if on cue, Potter hopped into his lap. He hugged him tight and kissed the top of his snowy white head. His pup was the only thing keeping him sane.

***

Cuddy did not want to have to speak with anyone else that morning. It was all getting to be too much.

He poked his head out his office door and said to Sarah, "Please make sure I'm not disturbed. Not even Melinda and definitely not CeCe. I have to jump on an emergency call with the anonymous donors."

Sarah's eyes widened. "Is something wrong?"

"Nothing to worry about." He waved her off, turned back into his office, and closed the door behind him. Sarah would make sure no one bothered him until he stuck his head out again and signaled that he was done. He was guaranteed at least an hour and a half without interruptions.

His calendar indicated that the next conference with the anonymous donors was actually scheduled to take place on Tuesday at noon in New York. Cuddy was planning to go up that day. He had already let Melinda know that one of the benefactors couldn't attend in person and needed to delay the start until his yacht was moored in order to get adequate cell reception. Cuddy thought it best to change up scenarios every now and then to keep things fresh. He opened his Bible and began to read.

After ninety minutes had passed, he opened his office door, signaling to staff that he was once again available. Melinda and two other foundation workers were waiting to talk to him, and Sarah was in the middle of answering his phone.

"I'll see if he's able to take your call. May I have your name so I may tell him who's calling?" Whatever the caller said caused Sarah to raise her eyebrows and point to the phone. "Oh, yes. Really?" A huge grin covered her face. "Please hold." She tapped the hold button, raising her hand as if she were flicking a magic wand.

"Who's that?" he asked. He lowered his hands in the universal "calm down" motion. Sometimes she was like a puppy, all giddy and bouncy.

"It's Katie Zuckerman from the mayor's office of civic engagement and volunteer service."

Melinda and the others leaned in to hear. Cuddy held up his hand to hold down Melinda's enthusiasm too.

"What does she want?"

Pointing to the phone, she beamed. "They want to sponsor a proclamation before city council naming a Cuddy Mullins Day or a New Visions Day. Isn't that cool?"

"Good Lord," said Melinda.

Cuddy grimaced. "No, it's not cool. I told CeCe that damn article would start bringing unnecessary attention." He let out an angry growl and made a tight fist.

Sarah pointed to the blinking hold button on the desk phone. "What do you want me to tell the mayor's office?

"Tell her someone will call her back."

"Who? CeCe?"

"Definitely not." His thoughts turned to his wife. The success of that damn *Inquirer* article had made her even more insistent to tout his good works. His eyes darted around the room. It all had to stop. Before it was too late. What the hell was CeCe up to now?

He ignored the surprised looks of everyone and turned to Sarah. "Get CeCe on the phone."

CHAPTER 3

CeCe looked down at her vibrating phone. She was standing before the most gorgeous display of designer handbags at Nordstrom in King of Prussia.

"Do you need to get that?" asked the salesgirl.

"No." CeCe slipped her phone back into her handbag. She didn't work for the foundation. They had all made it very clear that they didn't appreciate any of her observations or suggestions. "It's my husband's foundation. If it's important, they'll text me."

The saleswoman smiled and pointed a finger at CeCe. "I thought I recognized you."

CeCe gave her a puzzled look. She was sure she had never seen the woman before.

"You were in the *Inquirer* last week. On the 'Cause and Celebration' social page. You were wearing a gorgeous magenta ball gown."

CeCe smiled and nodded. "Wasn't it fabulous?"

The gown brought back happy memories now, but when Cuddy had discovered how much the dress had cost, it had caused another shouting match between them. She had argued that her off-the-rack gown was half the cost of what the other women would be wearing. Theirs would undoubtedly be custom made. He hadn't understood the importance of looking the part, but he hadn't made her return it. The dress had been the right choice. Even the Nordstrom salesperson remembered how fabulous she had looked in it.

"My name is Lisa. It's a pleasure to meet you."

"I'm Cecelia Mullins, but please call me CeCe."

"Well, CeCe," she said as they shook hands, "you have excellent taste." Lisa then gave CeCe's black, quilted Chanel bag an admiring touch. "That's gorgeous. A classic. I want to show you a few of the special bags we have in the back." She gave a conspiratorial wink and slipped through the door marked *Employees Only*.

Lisa returned from the storeroom with an armful of colorful, square boxes. "With your fashion sense, I thought you would appreciate the newest releases from our high-end designers," she said, opening the boxes to display one luxurious purse after another. CeCe stroked the soft leather and rich embellishments on the greenish-gray Fendi bag; she knew she should walk away, but her hands continued to caress the fine Italian workmanship. The last time she came home toting shopping bags full of designer outfits and shoes, Cuddy had looked like he was going to explode. He didn't understand that, in her role as his wife, she needed to represent, to show the wealthy donors and philanthropists who invited them to dinners and parties that they belonged. They may have thought it quaint that Cuddy continued to sport suits from Men's Wearhouse, but even a department store salesgirl recognized that she shouldn't be caught dead carrying around last year's Coach bag purchased from the outlets. How bogus, how wannabe she would appear to the people they were trying to impress.

"I love this one," said CeCe. She adjusted the shoulder strap and stared at herself in the mirror behind the counter.

"You're lucky. It just came in. Usually they send two per store, but we received only one of these."

"Really? So no else in the area will have this one?"

Lisa raised her eyebrows and leaned forward. "Just you."

CeCe admired the delicate hand stitching along the edges of the opulent leather bag. "In that case, I'll take it." She handed the salesclerk her American Express.

As Lisa the salesgirl slipped the bag back into its felt drawstring dustcover and then the designer box, CeCe tingled with the thrill of acquisition. But somewhere in the back of her mind, the niggling feeling remained. Moments like this would never make up for her life before she met Cuddy. It was painful how something she wanted so much to forget always popped into her mind whenever she least expected it—like now, when she so wanted to enjoy her new purchase.

"Did you want the receipt, or should I place it in the bag?"

"I'll take it." She scanned the little slip of paper and felt her face redden. She managed to maintain her pleasant expression in spite of seeing that she had just spent $3,909 on a handbag.

"You'll appreciate your purchase even more when I tell you that there's a similar Hermes Birkin bag being sold for around ten thousand dollars. This is a bargain." The salesgirl handed CeCe the purse. "Now, you should go directly to the shoe department to find a pair to match. That's a unique shade of green. I think it's more like a moss green or fern. I wouldn't try to match it later by memory."

CeCe smiled and tucked the package under her arm. Cuddy would be angry, but Lisa's advice was valid. Although people called him a saint, that was no reason for them to take a vow of poverty. Upon arriving in the shoe department, she spied several styles in colors that, if not exact matches, complemented the new bag. She glanced around the sales floor and caught the eye of another eager to please salesclerk. Holding up two different models, she smiled broadly and called out, "I need both of these in size eight and a half," and took a seat to wait for them to be brought to her.

As soon as she got home, she would hide them in her walk-in closet. She wouldn't have to deal with Cuddy until the bill came.

CHAPTER 4

Special agent Kari Wheeler escorted the professor into one of the small interview rooms off the reception area of the FBI's Philadelphia field office in Center City. When he had called to set up the appointment, his voice had been whiny and demanding, and she had expected him to be short, thin, white, and more than a little nerdy. But Walden Burton, professor at Hunter Valley Christian College, a small Midwestern school in Michigan, was taller, more fit than she had imagined, and Asian. He was sporting the standard-issue professorial glasses, and a brown, well-worn, leather backpack was slung over his left shoulder. She knew that whatever was inside the bag had already been placed through the magnetometer and scanned by the security before he would have been allowed to enter the building. He gave her a weak handshake, and when she sat in a chair near the door and motioned for him to sit on the opposite side, he seemed perplexed.

"How can I help you?"

"Is Special Agent Wheeler coming?"

"I'm Agent Wheeler." She patted her chest with both hands. "We spoke on the phone this morning."

"Oh." His eyes widen. A pink flush of embarrassment began creeping across his cheeks and neck. "When you answered you said, 'Kari Wheeler's office...' I thought—"

She laughed. "You thought I was the assistant for C-A-R-Y. As in

Cary Grant. I'm Kari with a K and an I." She laughed again, louder this time. "We answer our own phones around here."

"I'm sorry for the misunderstanding."

"No problem." She raised her hands. "It's just that that hasn't happened in a long time."

His eyes scanned her frame in what felt to be a nonsexual, but nonetheless probing, way. "I apologize again. It's just that you're not at all what I was expecting."

He wasn't what she had pictured either, but she decided against responding *ditto* and instead said, "I get it. You were expecting a guy. Not a black female. So, Mr. Burton—"

"Please, call me Wally."

"Thank you, Wally." She did not offer for him to call her *Kari*. She had learned it was best to first establish her authoritative position before relaxing protocols. "During your phone call, you mentioned that you were an accounting professor at a Christian college in Michigan."

"I'm a CPA and I also handle their books, their financials. It's a small college."

"What brings you to Philadelphia?"

"Business." He patted the backpack. "Your name came up when I asked for a referral."

"A referral? From whom?"

"It doesn't matter. I'm just glad you were able to see me on short notice."

"You have a fraudulent matter—a potential case—you think I should look into?"

"I was told that you are an expert in investigating frauds and scams."

"I've been working these types of cases for a number of years. They're important to pursue." She was about to launch into her spiel about white-collar crime being the barometer of morals and ethics in this country, but she stopped herself. "So, what can I help you with?"

He took a piece of paper out of one of the front pockets of his backpack, unfolded it, and handed it to her. It was a copy of a newspaper clipping. "Did you see this article in the Philly paper last week?"

She put on her reading glasses, held the sheet in both hands and, quickly scanned it. The headline read, "Cuddy Mullins Honored by Philadelphia Philanthropic Society, By Kitty Oliphant, *Inquirer* Staff Writer." It appeared to be a positive feature story about someone she had never heard of doing charitable work. After less than a minute of reading, Kari looked at Professor Burton and shrugged. "It makes him sound like one of the good guys. He's the person you think is running a scam?"

"All this flattering press makes me sick. Cuddy Mullins has everyone fooled. That article gives them credibility. And as we all know credibility is contagious." His tone turned sour. "I've been trying to get someone to listen to me."

Kari handed the article back to Burton. "I'm listening. What did the reporter get wrong?"

He placed his backpack on the conference table and took out a massive, white, vinyl binder packed full of documents and slid it across the table toward her. "It's all in here."

Kari tapped her fingers over the cover art embossed on the cover. The logo showed a man and a woman sowing seeds as beautiful flowers and plants sprung up behind them as they walked through a vacant lot. She opened the binder, which contained several thick, multicolored folders. She flipped through the pockets of the first folder and removed a fancy prospectus printed on fine linen paper.

"It's based here in Philadelphia. It's supposed to be a charitable foundation, but technically it's not. He's fooled a lot of accountants, but not me," said Burton.

"Who's 'he'?"

"The New Visions in Giving's president, Cuthbert 'Cuddy' Mullins, III."

"Cuthbert?"

He pushed up the tip of his nose with his right index finger, a mocking gesture. "His name makes it sound like he's from Mainline money, but my investigation has revealed that he grew up far away from the equestrian-and-champagne social set."

"Your investigation?"

"I've been gathering some preliminary facts." He patted the binder twice. "My research is all in here."

Kari gazed at the elaborately designed materials inserted under the initial offer tab in the binder. The offer was printed on high-quality paper, with embossed gold lettering. She reviewed the formal solicitation. It looked good but read like a chain letter.

"You collected all of this and put this binder together?"

"The slick marketing materials are from New Visions. I added my findings to the folders in the back section." He came around to her side of the table, stood behind her, and reached over her shoulder as he flipped the book to the last few folders, which resembled paperboard files from a local office supply store. "This is my stuff. Let me show you what I discovered."

Kari backed her chair into him. The tight confines of the small interview room made him too close for comfort. He was unaware that her fingers were just inches away from the panic alarm button installed under her side of the table. She pointed to the chair where he had been sitting. "Make yourself comfortable. You have my full attention."

Burton huffed, returned to his side of the table, and plunked the binder down. Everything about him seemed clenched. She waited silently as he pulled in a calming breath, took off his jacket, and hung it over the back of his chair.

When he seemed settled, she said, "Talk to me."

"These people are ripping off nonprofits and scamming donors, and nobody will do anything about it."

"Let me figure out what you have here and if it's something I can help you with." She folded her arms and leaned back in her chair. "Can you give me a moment to take a look at the materials and ask you some questions?"

They sat in silence for a beat. Kari watched as Burton took in yet another deep breath, let it out slowly, and nodded. He wasn't manic—he was full of nervous tension.

"What's going on? I can see that this means a lot to you, that you're frustrated." She pulled out the narrow metal drawer under the table, grabbed a notebook and pen, and laid them in front of her. "Can we dial things back a bit, so I can better understand what's going on here?"

"It's been difficult to get anyone to take me seriously. I'm afraid that more organizations will be harmed." He rested his elbows on the table, his chin on his cupped hands, and stared blankly at the papers laid out in front of them.

"Let's start with the basics." She gave him an encouraging smile. "What do I need to know?"

"What you need to know about the 'foundation,'" he said flatly, using air quotes, "is that they're doing an aggressive money grab. While other charitable foundations practice with what I would say is a quiet benevolence, New Visions in Giving is practically predatory."

"But this article says that they're exclusive and selective in who they let in."

"That's bull crap. New Visions is like the Publishers Clearing House of donations."

"So, why is your college participating? Did you tell them what you're telling me?"

"I've been sounding the warning bells for six months now. I wrote a letter to the board of trustees, and now my employer is threatening to take action against me." He poked himself with his thumb. "It's all smoke and mirrors."

"What's your connection to New Visions? Did you lose any personal funds to this alleged scam?"

"No, but I believe I have a fiduciary responsibility to advise the school administration and the trustees that New Visions is not legitimate."

"And why do you think that?"

"I discovered a five-hundred-thousand-dollar wire transfer that the college sent to New Visions earlier in the year. The money is supposed to be matched and—"

She held out her hand to interrupt him. "Let me play devil's advocate for a minute. Matching funds are a legitimate tool for incentivizing charitable giving. I get notifications from my favorite cause, Smile Train, several times a year pledging to double and even triple my support," said Kari.

"But you're not making a donation to yourself, and you're not being asked to first funnel your donation through a third party."

"I'm not following you."

"When I asked about that wire transfer, I was told that the money was being held in escrow, and after six months, New Visions would match the funds and return one million dollars to Hunter."

"Who's supposed to be providing the matching funds?"

Burton paused, seemingly for dramatic effect, before answering, "Nine anonymous donors."

"What?" Kari scrunched up her face. "Anonymous donors? Let me guess, six months passed and the college never received back the money and matching funds?"

"No, they did. Sort of. But only for one week. Despite my protests, Cuddy Mullins convinced them to reinvest the whole thing for another six-month matching term."

"They're now expecting two million dollars to be coming to them?"

"That's right." Burton pulled a tax return from one of the folders, turned it around so that she could read it. He pointed to a line at the bottom of the form. "This is the foundation's 2017 tax return. And here's the major red flag I detected. See?"

Kari stared at the entry listed under *non-taxable investment interest*. "What am I looking at?"

"The New Vision financials indicate that the foundation's operating budget comes directly from interest generated by funds being held in escrow by the foundation."

Kari stroked her chin with her thumb and forefinger as she tried to follow his point.

"It's all right here," he said. "If New Visions took in eighty million dollars in funds to be matched, they should have earned at least a couple million in interest. Yet their return shows they only earned $63,000."

"New Visions was holding $80 million?"

"And this is just last year's records. They've been operating for four or five years." Surprised, she raised her eyebrows. A huge grin split his face. "I think I just piqued your curiosity."

"If that number's correct, if we're talking about millions in potential losses, I'm absolutely interested."

Burton showed her once again how the dollar amounts didn't make sense.

"And this tax return reflects the escrow account where the matching funds are being held?" she asked.

Burton smiled and slowly nodded his head. "This is the right account. But it appears the money isn't in the account long enough to earn any interest."

Now Kari was smiling too. "I see where you're going with this. New money is deposited, but it's immediately withdrawn."

Burton was grinning, and now his head was bobbing up and down. "You're a quick study."

"I've been doing this for a long time." She looked over her glasses. "I've seen a thing or two." Kari pressed the tips of her fingertips together and leaned forward. "Old investors are repaid from the funds of new investors. Just like a Ponzi scheme."

"Exactly." Excitement shone from his eyes. "The investor list is pretty impressive. Victims of the scheme include Christian colleges like mine, but also large institutions like the American Red Cross, the Salvation Army, United Way, Juvenile Diabetes Foundation, Free Library of Philadelphia, the orchestra—"

"What? How could they be victims and I haven't heard anything about this?" She shot Burton a look of skepticism.

"Because they don't know it yet." He handed her another document. "This investor list was submitted with New Vision's last tax return." He ran his finger down the page. "See? They're all here."

"Wow," said Kari. "This could be a huge fraud case."

"It's a relief to hear you say that and to know that you understand the scam being run by New Visions. If I leave this with you today, how soon do you think you'll take action?"

"I'll be able to open a case first thing tomorrow and to get a prosecutor on board to issue subpoenas immediately after that."

"And then to shut down the foundation? Two days, three days more?"

Kari knew that Burton wasn't going to like what she was about to tell him. "No. I'm sorry, but that's not how it works."

He gave her a puzzled look. "How much time do you need? Two weeks, a month?"

"If we gather the evidence to prove what you think is going on, it will take a few months, but probably less than a year."

"What do you mean?" He smacked the binder's cover with his palm. "I have everything you need right in here."

"What you have in that binder might be, and I repeat might be, enough for me to initiate an investigation, but I'll need much more than what you have there to recommend charges and pursue an indictment. The FBI can't shut down a business without presenting authenticated evidence."

She could see his visceral reaction to her words. His face was tight, his fists clenched, and as he stared back at her his eyes were piercing.

"I've been telling him for months now that I'm going to bring him down. It's no wonder he doesn't believe me—"

"You've been in contact with Mullins?"

"I spoke with him when that propaganda-filled article came out."

"Do me a favor—don't call him anymore."

"I had to. No one else is doing anything to stop him."

"That's not fair. You called me this morning, and I agreed to meet with you today, all without any notice." Kari pushed the air in a hands-off motion.

After several more minutes of heated discussion, she convinced him that she believed he was onto something, and then they spent another half hour reviewing the documents in the binder. He didn't want to hear anything about holding back and following procedures, but she remained steadfast. "There's no cutting corners on a case like this," she said.

When he caught her looking at the time on her cell phone screen, he became irritated again. She tried to assure him that she wasn't blowing him off, but she had another appointment, and they would schedule another meeting to go over everything he had gathered. He whined like an impetuous child, and she considered calling and canceling her counseling session. But she was doing so well in her recovery and was determined to stay on track.

"If you leave the binder here, I can get someone to make copies and return it to you before you leave. When are you heading home?"

"Tomorrow evening, but I already have plans for the morning."

"About this?" Kari said. She noticed his hesitation before answering.

"My first trip to Philadelphia. I thought I owed myself a couple of hours to do the tourist stuff. The binder has all the information you need to get started. I put together several. You can have this one. I have even more documents scanned as pdfs. I'll Dropbox the files to you when I get back to my hotel. Do you have a business card?"

She took one of her cards from her jacket pocket and handed it to him.

"Can I have three?" he asked.

She gave him two more, assuming he wanted to take them back to his bosses. "I'm happy to speak with a school administrator or trustee over the phone, but I'll probably request that an agent from the Ann Arbor resident agency come out to the college and conduct a more thorough, in-person interview later on."

He scanned the info on the card. "So your full name is Karolina?"

"I prefer Kari."

"Well… Agent Wheeler, I'm sure we'll be in touch soon."

"Absolutely. I plan on looking at everything you've given me over the next couple of days. Can I circle back with you at the end of the week?"

"I'm betting on it," he said with a sly smile.

"And thank you for understanding that these things take time. "

She thought she detected a flash of sarcasm when he said, "Yep, I get it."

CHAPTER 5

Kari settled into the comfy leather recliner and pushed back, so the chair would lift her feet. She looked forward to these counseling sessions because it was the only place she could speak her truth. The only place where, without fear of judgment and rejection, she could talk about her past and try to forgive herself for the things she had done. Dr. Nina Patel, a University of Pennsylvania Medical School–trained psychiatrist with a specialty in posttraumatic stress syndrome, was on retainer with the Department of Justice, and as part of the FBI's Employee Assistance Program, Kari had started seeing her immediately after the shootout. She knew the routine—Dr. Patel would sit in a chair beside her desk and wait until Kari began.

"I'm still having trouble sleeping."

"Kari, it's only been five months."

"Everett seems to have bounced back quickly. He seems to have been able to move on."

"We both know that you had other issues to deal with related to the shootout that he didn't have to work on."

"I guess."

"Have you given any more thought to talking to Kevin?"

"No. And I wish you would stop asking me about that."

No matter how much the guilt about keeping the truth from her husband was eating away at Kari, she knew revealing her secret would mean jeopardizing her marriage, her career, and the career of her former partner, Everett Hildebrand.

"Your inability to move forward is related one hundred percent to you keeping this from your husband. I'm not saying you should or shouldn't tell him, but I am telling you that you need to make peace with whatever you decide to do."

"I've made that decision. I think it would be selfish to share the burden of the truth with him." Kari lowered the foot rest and propelled herself from the chair. She began to pace the room. "He'd hate me. He would leave and take the kids with him."

"He'd never hate you as much as you hate yourself."

Kari paused for a beat and absorbed Nina's words before she spoke again. She buried her head in her hands, but there were no tears. She had stopped crying about what she had done and was now almost numb with the shame.

"You did what you did because you are punishing yourself— punishing yourself for your success. Success you feel you don't deserve."

"I should never have taken on that case. It dug up issues from my past that I had buried deep inside me a long time ago."

"The good thing is that you're here now, and you're dealing with them so you never have to worry about them again."

Kari returned to the recliner, lowered herself into it, and, remaining on its edge, placed her hands on her knees. "No. I'll never have to worry about cheating on Kevin ever again." She hesitated before she spoke again. "I killed those desires."

***

The calmness Kari had gotten from talking out her feelings at the counseling session floated away as soon as she arrived home. She was immediately overwhelmed by the needs of her family. Their twelve-year-old twins, Casey and Morgan, helped her remove her coat and then Kari placed her briefcase in the dining room, knowing that she might do some work later that evening if things settled down. They pestered her about what had happened at soccer practice that day, while her fourteen-year-old son complained that he was quite unhappy with what was planned for dinner that evening—meatloaf. Even their golden retriever, Auggie, bumped against her leg and nudged her hand with his nose, demanding her attention. Her husband was in the kitchen, putting together the last components of the meal.

"You guys haven't eaten yet?" said Kari as she came up behind him and nuzzled his neck. He acknowledged her greeting with an air kiss but remained focused and didn't look up from his task. "You didn't have to wait for me to come home from work."

"No problem. I've been waiting fifteen years for you to come home from work," said Kevin.

Kari didn't take the bait. She was doing the best she could to balance home and work responsibilities. Right after the shooting incident, she and Kevin had become closer than ever, but lately, things were a bit strained. He claimed that she was getting caught up in her work again. He had always thought she cared more about the FBI than she did her family. And the truth was she sometimes struggled to prove he was wrong.

She thought about mentioning she was opening an exciting new case but thought better of the idea. It was obvious that Kevin wasn't in the mood to pretend he was the slightest bit interested in what happened at her work.

"What do you need me to do?" she asked.

He pointed to the veggies laid out on the counter and put her to work making a quick salad to accompany the meal he was preparing. She washed her hands and commenced her culinary assignment. When everything was ready, they called the kids to the table for dinner. Kari smiled as she lovingly gazed at her happy family. Carter caught her looking at him.

"Mom. Why are you looking at me like that?" He slouched back in his chair and raised both hands. "I didn't do anything."

"Don't be so paranoid," she laughed. "Can't I just admire my three adorable kids and handsome husband?"

Carter's eyes rolled skyward, while the others grinned.

It was a typical evening at the Wheeler-Jackson household.

CHAPTER 6

A few days after he had sparred with Professor Wally Burton on the phone, Cuddy left his office and headed to the Dilworth Park to catch the subway/elevated Market-Frankford Line. As he stood on the underground platform at City Hall station, with the commuters checking their watches and rubbernecking down the track to see if the next train was coming, his mind raced with worry. Soon, Professor Burton would bring the foundation crashing down, but until that happened, Cuddy still had time to continue his work. He had decided to take care of his favorite charities first. When the train arrived, he squeezed past the crush of bodies off-loading from the train car and lowered himself onto one of the blue, plastic, molded seats. By the time the motorman had steered through the underground tunnel, stopping at several stations along the way, and out onto the elevated tracks heading east, Cuddy had switched concerns and was deep in thought about his and CeCe's troubled childhoods. Returning to Kensington always triggered sad memories of struggle and loss.

He took out his Bible and opened it to the dog-eared page where he had left off reading that morning. He had no way of knowing how many times he had read that little, vinyl, green book from cover to cover but was sure it was well past one hundred. All he had to do was close his eyes, and he could visualize every single page, every psalm and proverb. He owed his gift to the most harrowing event in his life, the incident where he had found his purpose. Since the attack, he had been aiding others in finding theirs by sharing the word of God. That's all he had wanted to do—help people by raising funds for important causes.

He disembarked at Somerset Station and took the stairs down to the street level where he encountered a man with a dog lying out in front of the station exit. He believed homelessness in the United States was a sign that something was terribly wrong with society. The disheveled man with matted, blond hair and sunken cheeks spoke in a rush, urgently begging for money. The homeless guy could have been Cuddy's brother, Patrick, or CeCe's mother, Sherry, desperately pleading for strangers to give them cash so they could buy drugs. He scanned the handwritten cardboard sign the propped against the wall. *Dog is hungry. So am I. Need money for food.*

Cuddy knelt and asked permission to pet the German shepherd mix who, in spite of the circumstances, looked well cared for. He suspected the pup was kept for protection on the mean streets of Kensington as well as to pry sympathy and pocket change from those who were more concerned for animals than humans.

"I got to run an errand. When I come back, if you're still here, I'll take you to get something to eat."

"Man, I need money now." The homeless guy stuck out his hand.

"I can't do that." Cuddy shook his head. "I'm headed to Salida del Sol, to the recovery center. I would be happy to escort you there. I know the guy who runs the clinic—"

The man scowled, threw up his hands, and turned away. "Shit. Man, I need money."

In this area, food was never the problem. When Cuddy had worked as a drug counselor at a clinic on the corner of Kensington and Cambria, there were plenty of groups that came around to feed the drug addicts who populated the area. That clinic had closed, but there were plenty of clinics and food banks in the area to serve the community. Salida del Sol was five blocks north of the el stop, conveniently located on East Indiana across from McPherson Square. Help was not the issue. It was available if and when those in the grip of their addiction were ready.

***

The receptionist spotted him as soon as he walked through the door and gave him an enthusiastic smile.

"Mr. Cuddy, we didn't expect you so soon," said the lovely young woman with a thick Spanish accent sitting at the front desk. "Please, if you could take a seat for a moment and I will let Reverend Tejada know you are here. He's in his office."

Instead of buzzing him on the phone, she sprang from her seat behind the counter and jogged to the back. Cuddy chuckled to himself. When the rehab clinic applied for additional funding, the staff had been advised about the possibility of New Visions' making an impromptu site visit. It appeared to him that a plan had been put in place for when he showed. While he waited for her to return and escort him to Reverend Tejada's office, he looked around at the improvements the rehab clinic had made with the initial funding they had received from the New Visions. They had certainly made good use of the money. The first thing he had noticed when he approached the center as he walked over from Somerset Station was the new entrance sign. The name Salida del Sol Recovery Center was highlighted by the painted image of a bright and beautiful sun. The interior improvements were dramatic too; what used to be mismatched and soiled furniture were now comfortable and colorful pieces in a welcoming reception area. He couldn't wait to hear all about the enhanced services to clients, so much more important than cosmetic fixes that the clients nevertheless also deserved.

As he strolled around the room, smiling and nodding at the young father waiting patiently with his infant son resting in his arms, Cuddy detected that news of his unannounced visit had quickly spread and created a stampede of activity—he could see across the partial dividing wall separating the front room from the rest of the office that employees were scurrying about, tidying their workspaces by moving files and clearing off desktops.

Soon, Reverend Tejada came barreling out from the back of the center with his hand extended. He grabbed Cuddy's right hand and began pumping it at the same time his other hand patted Cuddy on his shoulder.

"What a surprise. Oh my." The reverend continued to pump his hand and patted his back. "We are, of course, always ready for a site visit, but I assumed you would send out someone from your staff to visit us."

"So, show me around." Cuddy pointed to the area on the other side of the reception counter. "Let's see what you've done with the place."

"It will be my honor to show you how much we appreciate the funding we've received and the improvements that funding has allowed us to make."

As they toured the facility, Cuddy thought back to his first job at a similar drug recovery clinic. It was when that center had to close down due to lack of funding Cuddy had been inspired to begin working with nonprofits to train them how to fundraise and become less dependent on federal grants. His reputation as a skilled fundraiser grew once he was able to convince philanthropist Sir Middleton to personally finance his training sessions under the auspices of the Middleton Symposium. His classes on strategic planning and specialized training in managing operational budgets were invaluable to the do-gooders who wanted to help the community but who lacked the business expertise needed to run their grassroots organizations. He had provided this training as a paid consultant, and then, after convincing more donors to contribute, he had opened the Foundation for New Visions in Giving several years ago.

What he had grown was his life's work. His commitment to helping those in need was genuine. And now he couldn't believe that he was responsible for possibly destroying everything that he had so painstakingly built. He brushed away tears that were collecting in the corners of his eyes. Reverend Tejada and his staff, assuming that he was emotional due to their improvements, also shed tears, theirs tears of joy. Cuddy sat in on a group-therapy session and observed the reverend mentoring the young father he'd seen earlier. The father was getting advice on applying for his first on-the-books job. After a nearly two-hour visit, Cuddy let Reverend Tejada know it was time for him to go.

"What you've been able to do here is remarkable." Cuddy's eyes roamed across the room, stopping and connecting with individual staffers to show how much he appreciated the work they were doing. "As you know, my wife and I appreciate the remarkable work you're doing here in the Kensington and old Swamp Poodle areas. I hope this recovery center will be able to continue to do good work for years and years to come."

"And we appreciate the special attention, especially after learning of your personal connection."

"This area has always been plagued by drugs—first crack, then meth, now heroin. This community has continuously been hit pretty hard and has changed little over the years."

"Not for lack of trying. Did you see McPherson Square?"

"Yeah, I noticed that they had cleaned it up. Now at least kids can play without fear that they'll step on a used needle."

The reverend sighed. "Or a used condom."

"But, of course, that only means that the drug traffic moved somewhere else."

"Most of them are living under the bridge."

"Our work is never done." Cuddy and the Reverend both nodded in consensus.

"So true. Thank you. Let me walk you to your car," said Tejada.

"I rode the Market-Frankford Line up here."

"The subway? You?"

"You keep forgetting; I grew up in Kensington. I didn't get a car or learn how to drive a car until I graduated from Temple U. I didn't buy my first one until three years after that."

"Mr. Mullins, you are a remarkable man."

"No. I'm just Cuddy Mullins from Kensington. Every day, I make sure that I don't ever forget that."

"Many of our clients are Puerto Rican, but when you lived here, I guess this wasn't the case."

"Not as much, but this area has always been a melting pot of races and cultures brought together, unfortunately, by poverty and drug addiction—even when I was a kid."

"Well, I truly believe that Salida del Sol is making a difference here."

"And I do too. And that's why you are gonna get that second round of funding."

Reverend Tejada grabbed Cuddy with both hands and held him close. "Thank you, thank you so much. We won't let you down."

"I know you won't. But I want to sit down with you before the funding comes through to look over your operation and make sure that we do everything we can to invest in the future." Cuddy felt a connection to Reverend Tejada that he could never put into words. He and Tejada shared a strong spiritual connection to God.

"You're a good man, Cuddy Mullins."

Cuddy stared into his eyes and said, "No matter what happens, I hope you will always believe that." He shook Reverend Tejada's hand and left the clinic, strolling back in the direction of the entrance for subway/elevated line.

CHAPTER 7

As he got closer to the station, Cuddy peered through the filtered sun and shadows blanketing the street and sidewalk below the rails and could see that the man and dog he had encountered earlier were no longer there. He picked up his pace when he heard the rattling and vibration of track above signaling that the train was approaching. Cuddy mounted the stairs two at a time to the elevated platform at Somerset Station, tapped his transit card, and rushed through the turnstile onto the platform… just as the westbound train was pulling away. He slowed his gait. He wouldn't have long to wait, at that time of the day, the next one would come within eight minutes. A group of boisterous high schoolers was hanging out in front of the large *Southeastern Public Transportation Authority - SEPTA* sign painted on the platform wall. He checked his phone for messages and emails while he waited, casually glancing from side to side at the teens and other passengers standing along the platform.

It had been several years since he'd had his phone snatched out of his hands at that very station, but he was still cautious, safeguarding his cell by holding it close to his body and under his chin. He spotted a young, slightly built Hispanic woman out of the corner of his eye. She was wearing jeans and lime-green sneakers, pacing in a tight circle near the west end of the platform. She wasn't crying, but something about her body language—her stooped posture, the way she hugged and patted her shoulders, the way she shuffled her feet—caught his attention. She looked like she needed help. He watched her for a minute more and just as he decided he would walk over to offer his assistance, she turned and started walking toward where he was standing. He was caught off guard when she approached him and mumbled something.

"I'm sorry. What did you say?" He held his phone against his chest.

She pointed to it. Her eyes were red and swollen. It was obvious she had been crying.

"I need to use your phone," she said. It was more like a demand instead of a question.

He hesitated.

"Please, may I use your phone?" This time, the request was more cordial. "I ran out of the house without mine. I wouldn't ask, but it's an emergency." Tears welled up in her eyes. She was a pretty girl.

"Is there something I can help you with?"

"No. I just need to make a quick call."

Cuddy looked into her lovely, sad eyes and decided he could trust her. Whatever was bothering her was more important than his electronics. He held out his phone, and she took it and stepped a few feet away, with her back to him. Before long, she returned to his side and handed it back.

"No answer. I hope you don't mind, I left my boyfriend a voice message and sent him a text. If he calls back before the train comes, will you let me know?"

"Sure. And if he calls while we're on the train, I'll let you know that too."

"Thanks," she said and began to walk away. Her waifish body shuddered with each step and divulged that she was sobbing again.

"Wait," he called after her, stretching out his arms. "Can I give you a—" Before he finished his sentence, she turned back and stepped into his embrace. "It's gonna be all right. Whatever is wrong is gonna hurt for a while. But I promise you it's gonna be all right."

Through her sobs, he heard her squeak out a, "No, it won't. Not this time." She was so distraught and crying so hard she was gasping for air.

"Let's sit," he said and led her by her shoulders to a metal bench bolted to the back wall of the platform. "You can talk, and I'll listen, or I can talk, and you listen, but let me help you."

She sat next to him and leaned her head against his shoulder. Her body continued to quiver, but her sobs were less violent. After a little while, she spoke.

"I did something stupid. I can't blame anyone but me for what happened."

Cuddy didn't know what to say. Should he ask her what she did? Or just wait until she said something more?

"We all make mistakes," he finally said, pulling the New Testament from his jacket pocket. "Can I pray with you?"

She looked up and gave him a quizzical stare. "Are you a minister?" Tears glistened along her lower eyelids.

"No," he said, waving his little Bible in between them. "At one time, I thought I might want to be one. But I'm doing God's work in other ways." He smiled at the beautiful, young stranger, hoping to make her feel a tiny bit better. He flipped through the pages. He knew the perfect passage to ease her troubled spirits. "I think I might have something here that will help you."

She listened politely but stared off down the track.

"Here it is. Psalm 32." He read it to her. "'How blessed is he whose transgression is forgiven, Whose sin is covered! How blessed is the man to whom the Lord does not impute iniquity, And in whose spirit there is no deceit!'"

She turned and gave him a blank look. He could tell that the meaning of the verse had escaped her.

"It basically means if you're honest with yourself about your shortcomings and learn from your mistakes, God will not judge or punish you.

She placed her hand over his hand holding the Bible, blocking the page. "I'm not sure I even believe in God."

"Let me finish reading the passage, and we can talk about how it applies to your life. You don't have to believe in God to find comfort in the words."

"I don't know," she repeated, still looking toward the track.

"Let me take a photo of the passage and text it to you, so you can read it when you get home and find your phone." He hovered his phone over the page and snapped its image. "What's your number?" he asked. She took his phone, entered her number, and sent the text to herself.

At that moment, the passengers on the platform moved closer to the yellow tactile safety surface near the edge of the platform, indicating the eastbound train had come in to view further down the track. "Did you want to try and make that call again once we get on?"

"Is the train coming?" she asked, ignoring his question.

He nodded. "Yeah, it looks like it is.

She stood and stared down at him. Her face seemed calmer, almost serene. He was pleased that he had been able to give her some comfort. But then, in one quick movement, she bolted to the western end of the platform, where she had been previously pacing. From the progressively increasing sound of the engine, he could tell that the train was just about to enter the station. To his horror, she lunged forward, flinging herself down onto the tracks just as the train approached. She landed in a crouched position and had just enough time to stand up and catch Cuddy's eye before she folded her hands as though in prayer and closed her eyes.

The air filled with the sounds of steel on steel as the brakes ground the wheels of the six-car train, straining to reduce speed as it entered the station. Cuddy caught a glance through the cab's window of the horrified look on the face of the motorman as he spied her in the track area and registered what was happening. The screeching sound grew violently louder as the motorman attempted but failed to stop prior to the designated area at the end of the platform. In an instant, she was gone, as the train slammed into her and pulled her under its carriage. The train was not brought to a complete stop until it was three-quarters of the way into the station.

Cuddy scrambled over to the front of the train and knelt to peer onto the sliver of track between the car and the platform. He realized that he'd never asked her name. Regardless, he heard himself crying out for the nameless stranger.

"Oh my God. No, no, no."

"She was probably dragged back here."

Cuddy turned toward the voice and saw the motorman directing him to the middle of the train. The man dropped to all fours and crawled along the side of the train, looking for something to indicate the position of the jumper. Cuddy creeped beside him.

"Wait," said Cuddy. "I see her pants."

The train operator lay down and examined the underbelly of the train closer. "That's just her leg. I think the rest of her body is up ahead." He continued his search.

As what the man had said sunk in, Cuddy cupped his hand over his mouth; he felt as though he was about to get sick.

"She's here. I found her." The motorman dressed in blue work overalls laid flat on his belly, took a flashlight from his pocket and flashed it under the train. After a few seconds, he raised up to his knees and shouted to Cuddy, "What's her name?"

"What? I don't know her name. I don't know her."

The subway operator scrutinized him with a quizzical frown. "When I got off the train, the other passengers pointed you out and said you two were together?"

"I was talking to her for a few minutes before the train arrived. Before she jumped." Cuddy began to cry. "She never told me her name."

"That's okay, buddy." The operator pulled a bright-orange rag from his pocket and wiped his hands on the cloth. "I believe you. It's always a horrible thing to watch. It's hard for everyone who witnesses a jumper."

His words jerked Cuddy out of his singularly focused mind, and he began to hear and see the crowd that had gathered behind them. He heard someone ask if 911 had been called. The motorman told them he had called the control center and that police and rescue were on the way. As he tried to calm the crowd, Cuddy could hear the sirens. Moments later, police and firemen flooded into the station, directing onlookers to move back and clear the platform area.

As Cuddy started to walk away, he felt a strong hand on his shoulder.

The hand belonged to a burly transit police officer. "Not you, sir. We need you to stick around until the medical examiner arrives."

Cuddy was just about to ask why when he saw several people in the crowd pointing at him. He didn't correct the misunderstanding but instead returned to the bench where, just moments earlier, he'd been sitting with the girl. He watched as the EMTs, Philadelphia Police Department's Accident Investigative Division, and transit police and safety workers extricated the mangled body from under the train.

Cuddy closed his eyes and bowed his head, using the time to say a prayer for the young woman. He prayed for forgiveness for her and whoever had caused her such pain that she preferred death to living. He prayed for her soul to be quickly delivered to God in Heaven. He had no idea how much time had passed as he watched a small group of men climb down between the subway cars with a gurney. He quickly averted his gaze when one of the workers handed up what appeared to be the white, shattered bone and bloody, jagged flesh of the young woman's severed leg, the lime-green shoe still on. The limb was placed in a red, plastic biohazard bag.

One of the workers on-site, a short, black male with a pleasant smile and a jacket with the SEPTA logo on the left side chest pocket, walked over to Cuddy. He started to stand.

"No. Stay where you are." The man took a seat on the bench next to him. "Burnett Jones. Burnie." he said, extending his hand. "SEPTA System Safety."

They shook hands.

"I understand you were a friend or relative of the young lady. Could you tell us what happened?"

"That's not correct. I didn't know her. I told the other guy, the one that found her." He pointed out the operator, who was leaning against the first door of the train car talking with a Philadelphia police officer. "I was just talking to her before the train came. She asked if she could use my phone."

"Was she upset about something?" asked Jones.

He nodded. "I think she might have had an argument with her boyfriend."

"And what's his name?"

Cuddy gave him a confused look. "I have no idea. I told you already, I didn't know her. I don't know who her boyfriend is." He felt a vibration in his hands and realized that he was still clutching his phone, which was now buzzing with an incoming call.

"Do you mind holding off on answering that until after we finish talking here?"

"It's a number I don't recognize. It could be him, her boyfriend."

Cuddy could see that Jones was now the confused one. "She used my phone. She said she left a message and texted him. I think this might be him."

"Well, if that's the case, I guess you should answer it."

Cuddy tapped the receive button and held the phone up to his ear. "Hello?"

"Put Tracy on the phone," the voice on the other end demanded.

He placed the phone on his chest. "It's him." His chest tightened as he scrambled to find the right words.

"Tracy? Is that the name of the girl who used my phone to call you?"

"Yeah. Waiting for the el at Somerset." He paused for a beat and then with an exasperated sigh asked, "So, is she there?"

Cuddy stared ahead at the emergency personnel working to free Tracy's body. His voice was full of emotion as he informed the young man on the phone of the tragic news. "I hate to inform you, but there was an accident."

"What are you talking about, man? Who the hell are you? Where's Tracy?"

Cuddy closed his eyes as he told her boyfriend, "She jumped in front of the train."

"What?"

"She died. She's dead."

Burnie Jones rose up from the bench, shook his head, and waved his hands about dramatically. "No. No," he said in an exaggerated, but whispered outcry. "She's not dead. Not yet anyway."

A bewildered Cuddy rubbed his head with his free hand. How could she have survived being run over by a train? He had seen her severed leg. Nothing was making any sense. "Wait. Let me put you on speaker."

"What the hell did you just say?" The boyfriend's voice boomed loud into the station. "Tracy's dead?"

The transit manager leaned closer to the phone Cuddy held in his direction. "Hello. This is Burnie Jones from SEPTA's safety department. Who am I speaking with?"

"Ken Hayes." His tone was gruff and demanding. "Will somebody tell me what the fuck is going on with Tracy?"

"She has suffered blunt-force trauma to the head and torso from two impact points—first when she was struck by the train and second when her body made contact with the ground surface."

Cuddy recoiled from the matter-of-fact recitation of her injuries. Jones obviously had been handling scenes like this for many years.

"She's... dead?" the boyfriend haltingly asked.

Cuddy could hear the anguish in the boyfriend's voice. Cuddy gulped for air.

"No, she's not dead." Jones patted Cuddy's shoulder. "That was a misunderstanding."

Cuddy bit his lip and laced his fingers together. He felt awful about his premature pronouncement.

"Ken, the EMTs are trying to stabilize her now. But she's lost a lot of blood."

"I'm leaving work now. I can get there in ten minutes on the train."

"The Market-Frankford Line's gonna be suspended for a while. Meet the ambulance at the Temple Trauma Center. You know where the hospital is?"

"Yeah."

"Before you go, I need to get some basics from you. What's Tracy's last name?" Jones took a small spiral notebook out of his jacket pocket. "How old is she? And her address?"

"Tracy Cordoza. She's seventeen." The boyfriend let out a long tension-filled whistle. "She said she was going to do it, but I… Are you sure she's alive? She didn't kill herself, right?"

Cuddy and Jones stayed on the line for a few moments more, gathering info as first responders loaded Tracy onto a stretcher. After a quick exchange of silent acknowledgment with the EMTs, the return of a simple nod of the head as they transported her from the scene, Jones reassured Kenneth of her current status. He hung up, after letting them know he said he would contact Tracy's mother on his way to the hospital.

"Good Lord," said Jones. "If she was set on suicide by train, she should have chosen Regional Rail. That's the way to do it."

"Suicide by train?" Cuddy stared sadly at the immobile train.

"Unfortunately, we get a jumper every month or so. To take a dive in front of a subway train, you got an eighty percent chance of dying. But if you don't…" Jones scrunched up his face and grimaced. "Victim can end up breaking nearly every bone in their body and slicing off a few limbs but living anyway. Just like our girl here."

"Once a month?"

"Just about." Jones pointed to the suicide-prevention sign on the wall near where they were sitting. Cuddy had not noticed it before.

He made a note of the phone number on the sign. A nonprofit dedicated to suicide prevention? With his family history, this was a group he certainly would want the foundation to support. "Who runs this program?" He tapped his finger on the suicide prevention sign.

Jones shrugged. "SEPTA Operations prints and installs the signs. Who knows how many people change their minds after reading one?"

"Is there one at every station?"

"Yep. Market-Frankford Line, Broad Street Line, trolleys, and definitely Regional Rail. Getting hit by a train on the commuter line going about sixty-five miles an hour? Now, that's a whole different story. A body will explode like it was hit by an IED at that speed. Kapow!" Jones made an explosive gesture, bringing his hands together and fanning them outward dramatically. "If you gotta do it, if you're serious about ending your life, SEPTA Regional Rail is the way to go or, even better, Amtrak. Their trains travel at 110 miles per hour in some spots. There's no surviving that."

Cuddy wondered how anyone could hate themselves, their life, so much that they would contemplate doing something like throwing themselves in front of a train. And then he remembered that CeCe had been in such a state several times early in their relationship. None worse than when her mother had died from an overdose, and he had ended up in intensive care after having been struck in the back of the head with a lead pipe and left for dead when he had tried to find and rescue Sherry.

"Do you have a business card? I'd like to talk with you some more about suicide prevention." Jones took out his card and handed it to Cuddy, who added, "I work with nonprofits that provide hope and health…" He gently placed his hands over his heart as he said, "Mind, body, and soul, to people in need all over the world."

"I don't know much about these suicide prevention folks, other than the signs, but I'd be interested in helping them too. I'm a deacon at my church. Maybe our outreach auxiliary can get involved too."

"Let's keep in touch." Cuddy reached into his jacket pocket and handed him a card. "Here's mine. There's a reason I'm here, at this moment. Synchronicity. Something God wants me to learn, to take away from this experience."

Cuddy began to organize his thoughts. He couldn't help Tracy, but maybe he could help the next person. He would have to hide his involvement from CeCe—suicide was something they could never talk about. Perhaps that's why he felt so strongly about helping. If they were a local group and he had never heard about them, they needed his help in raising their profile. When he got back to the office, he would see if they had a website and were using social media to spread their message. In addition to working with them on their digital presence, he would offer them a grant to fund the enhancements. Perhaps he could convince one of his donors to become a member of their board and provide the group additional exposure.

And then reality tumbled back onto him.

Soon, the Foundation for New Visions in Giving would no longer exist.

Soon, he wouldn't be able to help any new causes, any needy souls. Not even himself.

CHAPTER 8

Cuddy arrived at work the next day with renewed determination. Yesterday at Somerset Station he had been overcome with desperation, but during a sleepless night, he had decided that his fate was in God's hands and that he needed to continue helping organizations to raise funds through New Visions until the very end. His methods would be criticized, but no one could deny his intentions were good. He immediately went to see Melinda to share his latest plans.

"What happened to you yesterday?" Melinda asked as soon as Cuddy entered her office.

"I got held up at a horrible incident on the Market-Frankford Line after I left Salida del Sol."

"What incident?"

"A young woman jumped in front of the train as it was pulling into the Somerset."

"You saw her do it?" Melinda placed a hand over her mouth.

"Unfortunately, yes. Actually, she used my phone, and I had a chance to pray with her. I wish I could have done more."

"Don't take on that blame. You had no idea what she was planning."

"I was talking to the transit system safety manager about the suicide-prevention signs installed in all their stations, and this morning, I called the twenty-four-seven hotline number."

"Yeah…"

"I scheduled a meeting with Calvin Mackie from the Montgomery County Suicide Prevention Group for this morning at eleven."

"What about CeCe?" Melinda shot him a surprised look. "I thought you said—"

"I'm not going to tell her. After seeing what happened with that young lady who jumped in front of the train, I thought an outreach involving suicide prevention is something that we need to do."

"What else is going on, Cuddy?" Melinda spoke with a caring tone.

"Nothing else. I woke up at three a.m., and God spoke to me."

"But you and I already talked, and we agreed to slow things down, to be super selective about the nonprofits we're bringing into the program. And now you've taken it upon yourself to invite another recipient."

Cuddy made an apologetic face and raised his hand and raised two fingers.

"You invited two new recipients?" She stared into his eyes. "Wait a minute. What were you doing at Salida del Sol? We decided not to let the drug center apply for additional funding."

"I made a surprise site visit. They're doing good stuff over there. I want to give them a chance to secure solid footing."

She shook her finger at him. "Who are you and what did you do to Cuddy 'no more new recipients' Mullins? I thought we agreed to tighten things up around here."

"But they're doing such good work."

"You said that already."

"Because it's true."

"We can't save everyone. Aren't you the one who's always telling me that?"

"That area will turn into a wasteland again if we don't help them anchor the ship." He started moving toward his office. "Is it a crime that I want to help as many good programs as possible?"

"Are the anonymous donors aware of your plans to expand? Are they all on board?"

He waved her off as if it were nothing. "I'll discuss it with them at our next meeting. I'm sure I can convince them it's the right thing to do." Over his shoulder, as he walked toward her office door, he said with authority, "Please prepare a welcome package for our meeting with Mr. Mackie."

"Wait. You didn't finish telling me about the girl who committed suicide."

"She didn't commit suicide. She tried."

"She lived?"

"Lost a leg."

Melinda grimaced and shuddered.

"I am going to visit her in the hospital."

"Cuddy. Slow down. We can't save everyone." She absentmindedly shuffled file folders on her desk. "We've got to stick to the new system we just put in place. We've got to keep a strategic look at the money coming in from the donors and the money going out. The foundation has gotten too big. We're overextended as it is." Melinda waited for his response.

He stood in the doorway, content to allow the silence to linger between them. He wished his staff could understand how important it was for them to help as many people and groups as possible—before it was too late.

Finally, he said, "I just want to serve the Lord the best I can."

"I know," she said. "I know you do."

CHAPTER 9

The following morning, a chirping sound nudged Cuddy awake at 5:42 a.m. He grabbed his cell phone from the nightstand and scanned the Google alert. He had been waiting for the article to be posted. The reporter, Sam Shiffler, had left a voice message on his phone the evening before requesting a statement. Cuddy had not returned the call. Even before he read the headline, he knew this article was not going to be another puff piece.

It was worse than he had imagined.

Is the Foundation for New Visions in Giving a Ponzi Scheme?
By Sam Shiffler, Inquirer Staff Writer

He reacted with a soft, "Damn it." He turned to look at CeCe, who was asleep in the bed next to him. Good. He continued reading and when he got to the part where Shiffler wrote "Cuddy Mullins will be measured on the Bernie Madoff-meter," Cuddy sat up and swung his legs to the floor. Panic rose up from his gut like a burning gas bubble, and he reacted with a loudly expelled, "Jesus Christ."

"Huh?" CeCe stirred next to him and placed her hand on his bare back.

He pivoted to look at her and motioned for her to stay in bed. "There's an article about New Visions in the paper."

CeCe brushed her blond hair away from her face and a smile spread across her face. "Another one?"

He nodded but then shook his head. "This one's not good."

He continued to read the article. It contained a quote from Professor Wally Burton. Of all the reporters in Philadelphia, Wally Burton had managed to find the city's best investigative reporter, the one who was always writing gotcha stories about corrupt officials. But this time, Cuddy was his target.

"CeCe," he said, staring into the puzzled eyes of his wife, "we need to talk."

***

The foundation's staff was already at work and anxiously waiting for him by the time Cuddy arrived. CeCe, who had no real connection to the business, had nonetheless insisted on accompanying him. Someone had printed multiple copies of the *Inquirer* article, and as soon as they stepped into reception, Melinda approached them, waving her copy.

"How come you didn't answer my calls? Have you seen this?"

Cuddy nodded. CeCe scowled.

"The phones have been ringing off the hook and emails are flooding in." Melinda's eyes searched his for answers. "We need to figure out what to tell everyone. Especially the staff."

"Okay. We'll work it out," Cuddy held out both hands to signal that he wasn't concerned and then gestured for Melinda to follow him through the reception area into the main office, where the rest of the foundation's employees were milling about. He scanned the room, making eye contact with each member of his staff. They looked pale and anemic, as if they were in shock. He lifted his hand high in a kind of presidential wave, giving them all a weak smile.

"This is all a big misunderstanding," he said. "A misunderstanding created by a misinformed applicant not accepted into New Visions' challenge grant program." He continued to walk toward his office.

"Wait. What do you want us to tell the clients?" asked Melinda.

"Don't say anything to anyone yet. I'm going to go into my office and get on the phone with our attorneys. By tomorrow morning, there will be a retraction in the *Inquirer*, and everything will return to normal."

Nobody moved. They stood frozen, staring at him.

He snatched the article from Melinda's hands. "Does anyone here think this crap is true?" His eyes swept the room. "Anyone?"

At first, they appeared to be numb with confusion. No one spoke, but the half a dozen devoted millennials finally began to shake their heads vigorously, and this active show of support seemed to awaken their circulations and return color to their cheeks. Only then did Cuddy realize how worried they had been, waiting with bated breath for his assurances until they felt safe enough to take in air again.

"This is fake news. It's all a big misunderstanding," Cuddy repeated for a third time as he strode through the spacious room with his chin held high and his shoulders pushed back. Before anyone could ask another question, he slipped into his office and closed the door behind him making it clear to all that he did not want to be disturbed.

Once inside, he slumped against the paneled door. With his eyes closed, he softly banged the back of his head against it for a beat, before turning the lock and moving to the tufted leather couch facing his desk. He parked himself on the middle cushion and stared at all the pictures of him with elected officials, prominent citizens, and even a few movie and music stars. He let the left side of his body slide down the soft leather back of the sofa into an awkward, semi-supine position, and stared at the ceiling. He regretted his earlier decision to leave Potter at home. He and CeCe had come in on the early rush-hour train and, even in his carry case, the hustle and bustle of the commuters made Potter anxious, so he'd left the dog at home. Cuddy knew driving in from Devon, crawling along the Schuylkill Expressway would have made him nervous, and he needed to stay sharp and keep his wits about him today. Maybe if things quieted down, he would send that new Temple marketing intern out to the house to pick up the pup.

Cuddy glanced down at his right hand and discovered that he was still holding the printout of the *Inquirer* article he had grabbed from Melinda. He laid it flat on the coffee table in front of the sofa, smoothed out the wrinkles he'd made when he clutched the paper in his fist, and attempted, for the fourth time, to read it all the way through. As he read, he could feel his blood pressure rising and his heart rate quickening.

He didn't want to read the things that had been written about him. He couldn't do it.

Instead, he folded the article into quarters, placed it in his breast pocket, and patted it gently. He took out his Bible and began to read and pray until he regained his composure. His heart rhythm soon returned to a steady, even beat. In the sanctuary of his office, peace and sanity were restored. He didn't know how long he had been reading, but he jumped when there was a knock on his door.

"Cuddy, it's me. Why is the door locked?" He could hear Melinda whispering to someone, "Is he okay?" And then, with urgency, she banged on the door and said loudly, "Cuddy, are you okay? Cuddy, open the door."

What do they think I'm in here doing, trying to slit my wrists? He had been prepared for it all to crash and burn. He knew it was just a matter of time before the whole thing blew up in his face.

"Don't break down the door. I'm not doing anything crazy in here." Cuddy stretched and got ready for the Inquisition. "I'm coming, I'm coming."

He walked over and unlocked the door. He was surprised to see not just Melinda and CeCe, but also Jillian Stevens, the foundation's attorney, and one of her associates.

"Who called you guys?" he asked.

"No one," said Jillian, her eyes peering over her glasses.

"I thought that's what you were supposed to be doing in there," said Melinda, stepping farther into his office and looking around.

"We saw this morning's paper," said Jillian. "Someone should have called me."

"This is no big deal." Cuddy hiked his shoulders up to signal that he was unconcerned. "I decided to call the anonymous donors first. You guys were next."

"I wouldn't say that an eviscerating article about New Visions on the front page of the *Philadelphia Inquirer* is no big deal." Jillian tapped his chest with a rolled-up copy of the paper. "What did they say?"

"What did who say?"

"The donors. You said you spoke to the donors." Jillian gave him a quizzical stare.

"Oh, yes. I explained to them that the sole source for the article was some professor from Hunter Valley Christian College who doesn't understand the concept of participatory donations and who's been trying to cause trouble for us."

"It looks like he succeeded," said Melinda. "He's quoted in the article."

Cuddy spent the rest of the morning with his attorneys, denying that New Visions was a Ponzi scheme. And based on his assurances alone, the employees, donors, and all of the recipients whose calls were returned seemed to believe he had done nothing wrong. However, the financial institutions where he had massive outstanding loans were not as confident, and his investment broker called to advise Cuddy they were calling in his margins. After that news, everything quickly turned uglier. By lunchtime, the attorneys were pressuring him to declare bankruptcy.

Cuddy blamed his lack of business sense as a reason for the mess things were in. He'd been too busy with juggling the donor's and recipients' requests. He had no time to deal with the financial end. He was an ideas guy, a creative problem solver. He depended on Tony McCullough, a former SEC insider who had once served in the securities enforcement practice group, to serve as his CFO.

"I can't make this kind of decision without talking to Tony first. He has all the bank records and audits."

Jillian looked through the door into the office. "He should be part of this meeting. I definitely need to speak with him too. Can you call him in here?"

Melinda spoke up quickly. "He's at an off-site location."

"Where?"

"He works out of his home office in Bethlehem."

Jillian's eyes clouded over with confusion. "Your accounts total several hundred million, and your CFO works remotely from the little town of Bethlehem seventy miles away from Philadelphia?"

"We weren't always this big, and as a matter of fact, he wasn't always living in Bethlehem. But when his parents needed eldercare, he wanted to move closer to them," said Cuddy. "I'm loyal to those who are loyal to me. He's doing a great job. That's what's important, right?"

Jillian leaned in close and stated almost apologetically, "I didn't mean to insinuate anything was wrong. But the article claims that you've never received undesignated funds and that the anonymous donors do not exist. I think the first two things we need to do are: one, sit down with McCullough"—she held up one finger and then another—"and two, get a list of the anonymous donors' names, contact information, everything you have."

Cuddy studied his hands as he thought about how to respond. He took in a deep breath and finally said, "Jillian, we've talked about this many times—that list is confidential."

"Are you saying you still won't share it with your attorneys?"

"I know all about attorney privilege." He gave her a woeful look to signal he was sincerely sorry. "I just need to give the anonymous donors a heads-up first. I'll share the list with you by the end of the day." He hesitated for a moment. "First thing tomorrow morning at the latest."

***

He used his extra cell phone, the one he told everyone he used to communicate with the anonymous donors, to search for a cyber service that would meet him after hours to wipe clean his computer hard drive. The first two he called said that they could do it but couldn't come that evening. The third person he spoke with had suggested an easier fix and started to walk Cuddy through how to remove the hard drive and install a new one. He hadn't even thought about that. That's what he would do. He told the guy on the phone he would stop by his store later that day to purchase a brand-new hard drive and return to the office that night and make the switch, but he might need to call back and have him explain everything again once he had the drive. Cuddy didn't know much about computers, but it sounded easy enough to do.

CHAPTER 10

Kari walked into the pantry, gathered items for the kids' breakfast, and set the boxes and packages in the middle of the kitchen table. She wanted to get into the office as soon as possible to finish preparing her opening communication for the New Visions case. She had spent the day after her meeting with Professor Burton verifying the information he had provided, and from her initial analysis, it looked like he was right on the money—big money. The case could prove to be the biggest Ponzi scheme that the Philadelphia economic fraud squad had ever worked.

Her kids—the twins, Morgan and Casey, and her son, Carter—strolled into the kitchen at the same time. "How are all my favorite little people doing this morning?"

Carter grunted a greeting, followed by, "I'm hungry."

"Your selections for this morning are English muffin or a bowl of cereal."

"Those are the choices every school-day morning." Casey slung her heavy book bag on her chair, practically tipping it over.

"Yeah, we only get eggs and pancakes on the weekend," said Morgan, laying her bag on the floor next to her chair.

"Well, if you to want to get up twenty minutes early to help me cook said eggs and pancakes and then clean up the cooking utensils used to make said eggs and pancakes, I'll be happy to be at your service."

"What if you make it the night before?" said Carter. "And then all you would have to do is warm it up."

"Same thing goes. Help me cook said big breakfast tonight, do the cleanup, and tomorrow, a feast will be yours." Kari looked around and didn't see his book bag. She cocked her head and gave him a questioning look.

"What?" he said.

"Where're your books?"

"I don't know." He hiked his shoulders up. "I might've left them on the bus or at school."

"I recall asking you last night if you did your homework, and you said yes."

"I'll do it when I find my books."

Casey gave a disapproving look and said, "If you find your books."

"Why don't you mind your own business?" said Carter.

Kevin walked into the room at that moment and placed his hand on Carter's shoulder. "Don't start fighting, you two. Carter, I expect to see a book bag full of books this afternoon, or you're grounded for the weekend. You've got to be more responsible."

Casey began to speak. "I told—"

Before she got all the words out, Kevin held a finger up to his lips. "Not another word, young lady. This has nothing to do with you."

Kari walked over to her husband and kissed his cheek. "Coach and referee. You establish the game rules so the fight is over before it even begins. I love having you on my team."

"Well, teammate, I see that new case you were telling me about made the paper."

"Which case?"

"The accounting professor, charity fraud, Ponzi scheme one."

"What? It's in the paper?"

He pointed to the counter.

Kari walked over to where the morning paper lay. The front-page headline announced to the world that she had lost control of the investigation before she had even officially opened the case. She pulled out a stool and sat to read the latest article.

Serious Questions raised about the Foundation for New Visions in Giving Tax Returns Indicate Matching Grants Program may be a Ponzi Scheme

By Sam Shiffler

Many of the nation's nonprofits, hurt by the economic downturn that affected government funding, view Cuddy Mullins as a pilot on a disaster-relief mission, flying in to toss care packages overboard to help the needy. But Walden Burton, a professor at Hunter Valley Christian College, a small college in Ann Arbor, Michigan, is telling everyone who will listen that Mullins and his Foundation for New Visions in Giving (FNVG) is a fraud—and that those care packages are actually time-sensitive grenades set to detonate at any moment.

Burton said he did not doubt the existence of a ticking bomb after reviewing the FNVG's tax returns. One of the first things he determined was that FNVG is not a true foundation: there is no perpetual endowment. Instead, FNVG promises health clinics, churches, museums, religious colleges, and a variety of nonprofits to double their money through a matching program supported by wealthy, anonymous donors. But first, the institutions must allow FNVG to hold the funds to be matched for at least six months. FNVG claimed that the interest earned would be used to offset administrative expenses. When Burton discovered the foundation's last few years of tax returns reported that only $47,023 in interest was earned on $450 million in contributions, he surmised that money coming into the FNVG accounts was being quickly withdrawn, before significant interest had accrued. To Wally Burton, the solicitation sounded like a typical Ponzi scheme. This reporter was able to verify that Burton *has referred his misgivings to federal authorities, but no action has been taken against FNVG as of yet.*

Burton believes he is fulfilling his fiduciary duties as a certified public accountant in advising the public of his concerns, while the more cautious criminal investigators pursue and augment the evidence he has already gathered against FNVG. "I chose to come forward, despite admonitions to keep quiet about what I've learned, in order to help the nonprofits, charities and donors currently being victimized by this scheme. I can no longer wait until federal authorities deem it appropriate to issue warnings and charges," said Burton.

As is the case in all Ponzi schemes, the pyramid topples when new investors can no longer be enticed to contribute to the fraud. It appears that after operating for nearly five years, New Visions may be running out of "contributors."

That is, unless there really are wealthy anonymous donors who will be parachuting in to assist with the mission.

When she got to the part where Wally Burton complained about taking the information to the authorities only to be encouraged to keep quiet, she whispered, "Damn it, Wally."

***

It took Kari forty-five minutes in rush-hour traffic to reach the FBI's Philadelphia offices in Center City. She entered the squad area and set her bag down on the carpeted floor next to her cubicle. She immediately noticed a clipping of the newspaper article faceup on her desk. There were notations in her supervisor's handwriting on the right side of the blank paper it had been stapled to.

That's also when she noticed the handwritten note on a yellow sticky that had been placed on her desk alongside it: *See me.* She looked over at her supervisor's office. Harrison "Harry" Bilder was standing in his doorway talking to another one of her squad mates. Harry was a pleasant man, who, for the most part, stayed out the way of the agents assigned to his squad. He was a 180-degree change from her previous supervisor, Juanita Negron, who was suspicious about anyone who worked for her, constantly assuming they were up to something that would eventually ruin her meteoric rise through the bureau. Harry, in comparison, went out of his way to make sure the agents had everything they needed to be successful. He was content with keeping his current status for three more years, when he could retire. Kari diverted her gaze, so as not to catch his eye and be called over before she had time to formulate an explanation.

Her plan had been to get into the office this morning and read through the preliminary search reports, the National Crime Information Center also known as NCIC records, the FBI's indices Sentinel files, and, of course, Google results she had requested the day before to discover what she could gather about New Visions and Cuddy Mullins in addition to what Professor Burton had told her.

The article contained several quotes from others confirming the information Shiffler had received from Burton. Kari wondered if Burton also arranged to meet with the reporter while he was in town? Perhaps he had gone to meet Shiffler right after he had left her at the federal building? How else did he have the time in a day and a half to write such a comprehensive article? The *Inquirer* office was only two blocks away from the federal building. How convenient. Why hadn't she rescheduled her counseling appointment and continued her meeting with Burton? "Damn it, Kari," she said out loud to herself.

She heard the admonishment again: "Damn it, Kari." She looked around the squad area. Her supervisor was motioning and pointing with his index finger for her to come into his office and to bring the article with her. She took her time, and when she entered his boxlike office, he was already behind his desk, rocking back and forth in his swivel chair.

"Did you read it yet?" Harry pointed at the article in her hand.
"Yes, and—"

"I'm assigning the case to you. A potentially $450-million fraud. Can you imagine that?" He laced his fingers together on top of his head and continued to rock on his chair, a technique he used to stimulate his thinking, or at least that's what he claimed the perpetual motion accomplished. "You'll need to jump in on this right away. From the article, it's apparent that some other agency gave the source the brush off. We need to open a 196-new immediately and then call over to the United States Attorney's Office to establish the FBI as lead. I know you like to work with Whitmore. Tell him if the IRS or the SEC calls, to let them know we already have a case opened on this."

"Yeah, um…" Kari shifted from one foot to the other. "I think the federal agency he was referring to was the FBI, not the IRS, not the SEC."

"No. I would know if an opening memo about a Ponzi scheme came across my desk."

"Not if the initiating interview was conducted the day before yesterday and the interviewing agent was in the process of preparing an opening memo."

Harry's hands flopped from the top of his head onto the surface of his desk with a thud. "Am I to assume that the interviewing agent was you?"

Kari nodded.

"Sit." He pointed to one of the two hunter-green leather chairs parked in front of his desk. He caught her mid-sitting when he added, "Close that door first."

After explaining what had happened with Burton and that she would immediately jump on the investigation, she was dismissed from her supervisor's office. Kari returned to her desk to place a call to her preferred federal prosecutor, AUSA Mitch Whitmore.

"Mitch, I got a good one for you. Did you see this morning's Inky?"

"Shiffler's piece about the possible Ponzi scheme? New Givings something? You got that ticket?"

"That's the plan."

"I'll let Pete know to jacket the case to me. I have a trial coming up, but I'll be available for subpoenas or whatever you need in the meantime."

"I need more than that. I think we got to move quickly to shut down the foundation."

"You mean you want to freeze their accounts? You got enough evidence to support that kind of action?"

"Tell me what I need, and I'll get it."

"You're going to have to ask Pete for help with that. I'm swamped right now. If I'm lucky, I might be able to convince the defense attorney on the case I'm on to accept the plea deal on the table, and then I'll be freed up sooner."

"I'll call Pete in the interim."

"The article says that the accountant already reached out to the feds—"

"That was me. I met with him on Monday for the first time but had to cut the meeting short for my weekly"—even though Whitmore couldn't see her she pointed to her temple—"tune-up."

"You still dealing with issues from the shooting?"

"No. I'm good with that for the most part, but if Uncle Sam is paying…"

"That's smart."

"Well, it appears that Mr. Wally Burton was upset that I had to leave. I'm thinking that he left here and ran right over to Shiffler. He's back in Michigan. I'm calling him as soon as I hang up with you."

"I feel sorry for him. I know you're pissed that he went to the media. But don't forget we'll need his cooperation. He's a good witness."

"I'll be nice. But I'm going to let him know that he might have done irrevocable harm to the scope of the investigation. The foundation's staff could be shredding documents as we speak, and I don't have enough yet to stop them."

She didn't like anyone interfering with the integrity of her investigations. That had happened to her once before, and she'd vowed never to let it happen again.

Whitmore called back a few hours later. He had just learned that the SEC had filed a complaint, shut down the offices of the Foundation for New Visions in Giving, and changed the locks. New Visions' attorneys responded by filing for bankruptcy.

"No rush on the search warrant," he said. "That evidence isn't going anywhere."

CHAPTER 11

Kari's cell phone buzzed. She had called Professor Burton and left a message but it wasn't him. Although she didn't recognize the number she answered it anyway.

"Hello?"

"Hey, Kari. It's Sam Shiffler from the *Inquirer*."

"Shiffler." She hadn't spoken to him since the office made her talk to him for an exposé about the shootout. "Why are you calling me directly? You know you're supposed to clear all media calls with the media rep."

"And hello to you too."

"The only reason I haven't hung up on you already is it won't erase the digital record that you called me."

"Nice to hear from you too."

"Is this your cell?"

"I get it. You don't want to be like that colleague of yours who had to admit in open court that he had tipped off one of our reporters about a search."

"Exactly. Call Klinger for a sound bite."

"Agent Klinger doesn't know anything about the case I want to ask you about."

"And how do you know that?"

"Because you haven't officially opened it yet."

She paused and waited for him to say more.

"You read my article, didn't you? I know he met with you the other day. I have one of the business cards you gave him."

Kari didn't answer.

"I'm asking because I'm getting a little pushback from my editor on my story. We ran a story a few weeks back trumpeting how great this Cuddy Mullins guy is, and the paper is getting some heat about now running a story with the opposite message." Shiffler paused for a beat, then continued when she didn't respond. "So, I guess you can see my dilemma. I need confirmation of the FBI's involvement before the paper can print my follow-up piece. It'd be greatly appreciated."

She didn't respond.

"Did I just hear you give me a sly nod and a wink?"

She let out an impatient breath. "No."

"An encouraging cough?"

She didn't respond.

"Your refusal to cooperate is interfering with my ability to post my second story."

"Well, your reporting keeps interfering with my investigations."

"Was that a confirmation?"

"I'm hanging up, Sam."

"Wait. I just want to hear you say it."

"Not happening."

"Please?"

"Bye."

"Wait. You can't give me a simple 'I can neither confirm nor deny'?"

"Call Klinger. That's his catchphrase." She tapped the end call button. She liked Shiffler and thought his reporting was top-notch. Under different circumstances, they might have even been friends. But agents weren't authorized to speak to reporters, and the last thing she needed was to be accused of leaking information to the media.

She punched in Wally Burton's number again. It went straight to voice mail. He was probably already back in Ann Arbor. She wondered if he would lose his job for defying the trustees and the president of the college and publicly accusing their funding source of fraud; she hoped he had tenure. She left another voice mail and a text message for him to call her as soon as possible. She needed to know how much he had told Shiffler and who else he had spoken to. She wanted to blast him for going to the media but she would instead explain that if he was under the impression that she wasn't interested in what he had to say, she absolutely was. Getting the evidence was the priority, not settling personal grievances.

***

This time when she dialed Burton's number, he picked up.

"Professor Burton, this is Kari Wheeler. We spoke the other day."

"Yes, Agent Wheeler, how are you?"

"Not happy. I read the article in today's *Inquirer*, and I'm… disappointed that you chose to make your complaints public before I had a chance to open an investigation into the issues we discussed."

"You're disappointed?" Burton raised his voice. He sounded incredulous.

"Yes. And I'm pissed."

"Well, you had made it clear to me that you weren't going to take immediate action to protect potential new victims. That was something I could not let happen."

"Do you realize that by talking to newspapers, the people operating New Visions could be destroying evidence as we speak?"

"Looks like you better get moving then," said Burton. "It sounds like you should be at the foundation's offices trying to stop them, instead of complaining to me about what I did or didn't do."

"Professor, I understand how you feel, but if you really want to help me investigate this case, then you have to let me do it my way."

"I did what I felt I needed to do: let people know that Mr. Cuddy Mullins is not who he says he is or doing what he says he does. Now that I've done that, I promise I won't get in your way again, but I had to get the ball rolling."

Kari snorted. "Careful," she warned. "I wouldn't want that ball to knock you over."

CHAPTER 12

Cuddy couldn't concentrate. He had been trying to read the new Dennis Lehane novel, but his mind kept wandering. He had his own problems to worry about, but for some reason, he couldn't stop thinking about Tracy Cordoza, the young woman who had tried to kill herself. The image of her bolting onto the track and the screech of steel against steel as the motorman futilely attempted to stop the train before it ran over her body played out in his mind again and again.

CeCe must have noticed his eyes focusing off into space and not on the page of his book. She said, "I hope you're not worrying yourself sick over that stupid article in the paper. Nobody cares about that."

"I care," he said. "I'll be working with the legal team tomorrow to get in front of the story and make sure our donors and recipients have the real facts." He snapped the book closed with one hand, removed his reading glasses, and rubbed the bridge of his nose with his forefinger and thumb. "But I got this. Thanks for coming to the office today, but you have enough to do around here. Let me take care of foundation business. You take care of everything around here."

She smiled while she scanned the beautifully appointed media room and then went back to watching one of those *Real Housewives* shows on TV. She never missed an episode of the *Real Housewives* series. She had told him she thought she was gaining valuable insights on how the rich and famous live. Little did she know that the wealthy philanthropists who contributed to New Visions' causes would not be caught dead associating with the vulgar women portrayed on those shows.

He preferred that she thought he was thinking about that newspaper article. He wasn't. He had placed all of that in God's hands. He, however, knew better than to tell her about what had happened at Somerset Station earlier in the week. He had not and would not share with her anything about the attempted suicide he had witnessed. Even after all these years, the topic of suicide was still too sensitive and too painful for CeCe.

He took a sideways glance at her and realized why he felt such a powerful connection to what had happened at Somerset station. In addition to witnessing the tragic attempt, CeCe's past had unconsciously ignited his desire to help the suicide prevention folks. For the first time since the incident, he considered if there was a spiritual message he was to learn from his encounter with Tracy Cordoza. He put aside his novel and leaned forward to pick up the Bible resting on the coffee table. God works in such mysterious ways.

As he prayed, he recalled the first time he saw CeCe. They were both on the number three bus. She had been crying and was distraught, just like Tracy Cordoza was the other day. He was on his way home from Temple, where he was majoring in pre-med. He couldn't remember where she had been coming from. He walked back to where she was sitting and asked if she needed help. He asked if he could call someone for her and quickly learned that there was no one she could reach out to. That's why she was crying—she felt so alone. For nearly five days, she hadn't known where her mother was. She had left the house to make some quick cash, and CeCe hadn't seen her since. Until the moment when she'd seen her mother leaning into the window of a gray SUV. CeCe had told him she wanted to jump off the bus and run after her, but she knew that by the time the bus had pulled over at the next stop, her mom would have completed negotiations and hopped inside the SUV to find a place to park and perform her part of the transaction.

When they got to CeCe's stop, he got off the bus with her. They went to her house, where they ended up having sex in her bedroom, the only clean area of the deplorable home. It wasn't something he had wanted, but he figured it all out later—she wanted to thank him for his kindness, and this was the only way she knew how. A few months later, her mother was dead from an overdose, and he was in the hospital, healing from emergency brain surgery after his failed attempt to free CeCe's mother from the streets. During the first months of their relationship, CeCe had been suicidal, either distraught about her mother or distraught about him. Cuddy had been the only reason she had not actually taken drastic measures to end her pain. Even from his hospital bed, he did everything he could to keep her happy, to ward off the depression and bad thoughts. Those times seemed like such a long time ago, but her sad memories could quickly rush back to the forefront.

It was a miracle that he was able to finish school, considering the migraines and short-term memory loss he suffered. His grades showed it, and his plans to attend medical school were thwarted. But that really was okay by him. More than anything, he wanted to help the community, to fight the heroin and opioid epidemic that had taken over his old neighborhood.

After they got married, he and CeCe lived in Fishtown for a while, in a funky loft apartment just two subway stops away from where they had spent most of their childhoods. But CeCe, claiming that her nightmares would lessen if they could get farther away from the mean streets of Kensington, convinced him they needed to move to the suburbs. They couldn't afford their new home. And, years later, the beach house was yet another decision he regretted as soon as the purchase had gone through. But she had always dreamed of a second home at the Jersey shore.

He glanced over at her now. She was stretched out on the couch, totally absorbed by the antics of the rich housewives bitching and moaning about their overblown problems. Was she strong enough to handle what was coming? He feared that her dark thoughts would return. He loved his wife, but she really did live in a fantasy world, one full of wants and desires. No one from her new life knew that her mother was a drug addict for most of CeCe's childhood and that she paid for her drugs by giving blow jobs to strangers in backseats and alleys.

He could see why she found money such a comfort, but material wealth was never what he was about. He always thought he would be of service, a physician or, when he was younger, even a priest. And although it may have been in an unconventional way, New Visions was all about helping the unfortunate and poor all over the world. His little foundation was doing that. He was doing that.

CHAPTER 13

Later that evening after he fell asleep, he had the nightmare again. An unknown person walks up behind him and cracks him over the head with a steel pipe. And just before consciousness slips away, he sees a woman's face. It's usually CeCe and he wants to save her. But this time, instead of CeCe, the woman was Tracy Cordoza. Her face reflected peace and serenity, just as it had before she'd jumped on the tracks. She looked as though she had finally found a way to escape her misery and pain.

He woke up abruptly with a feeling of dread, and for the rest of the morning, he found himself thinking about Tracy. He wondered if she was still alive. He wondered what made her so desperate to want to kill herself. He wondered whether she regretted her decision to end her life or if she would try again. His curiosity nagged him, refusing to leave him alone. He needed to find out what had happened to her as if it were a prophecy of CeCe's fate. He searched through the recent calls on his phone to see if her boyfriend's number was still logged in. When was it that he had made that site visit to the rehab clinic in Kensington? It seemed impossible that it had only been a week.

He found a number from that day that he didn't recognize and tapped the call button. When the boyfriend picked up, Cuddy realized he hadn't thought about what he was going to say.

"Who's this?" said a gruff voice.

It was early. He must have woken him. "You probably don't remember me," he said with a rush. "I'm calling to find out how Tracy's doing."

"Who wants to know?" It was definitely the right number and the right person, but Cuddy detected the irritation in his tone. He should have waited until midmorning to make the call.

"Cuddy Mullins. I was there that day. I'm the person who told you about her... accident."

"Oh yeah, you the one who told me Tracy was dead." He laughed out loud.

Cuddy was taken aback. Why would he laugh about such a terrible mistake? There was nothing funny about that.

"Yes, I'm so sorry about that... What was your name again?" Cuddy said.

"Ken. Kenny Hayes."

"Ken, I'm calling to check up on her, to see how she's doing."

"Man, how would I know?"

"She's your girlfriend, right?"

"She's my ex."

"But, I thought... Are you still in touch with Tracy?"

"She jumped because I dumped her. And I don't regret it. She showed everyone how crazy she is." He chuckled again. "Nah, she's definitely not still my girlfriend, especially now that she's got one leg. Man, I went over to the hospital after the accident and saw that and I was like... damn."

Cuddy cringed. That poor girl. "I'd like to call or maybe visit her. Do you have a number for her?"

"Sure." He looked up the number, which Cuddy was surprised was still in his phone. Kenny recited it for Cuddy to jot down. "If you talk to her, tell her I said what's up."

"Of course—"

"Second thought, don't do that. I don't need her to start stalking me again. Heh heh."

Cuddy hung up quickly, without saying goodbye. He suddenly felt weak and lethargic, and laid his head down on his desk. He felt worse than he had before he called. People without compassion for those in need hurt his heart.

***

Cuddy called the number Kenny had given him, and when she answered, he explained who he was. Tracy started crying as soon as she understood it was him.

"I'm sorry," she said. Her voice sounded brittle and small. "I was out of my mind that day. But I'm grateful for what you did for me." When he offered to visit, she told him she had been transferred from the hospital to Magee Rehab Center. She immediately said yes, she wanted her mother to meet him.

He arrived at the facility at Race and Broad Street less than thirty minutes later. When he was asked to show his driver's license and sign in, he wasn't sure what to write under the "relationship to patient" column. Feeling a bit presumptuous, he wrote down friend, pinned on his visitor's pass, and took the elevator to the fifth floor. It wasn't until he was walking down the hall toward her room that he wondered if Tracy and her mom had read the story in the paper about him and New Visions. If they had, he would have to explain that it was all a big misunderstanding.

The door was ajar, so he knocked softly and peeked inside. She was sitting in a wheelchair next to the bed. His eyes unconsciously traveled to the bandaged stub of her left leg and then to her face. She looked much younger than he recalled.

"Come in," she said and beckoned him inside with an enthusiastic wave of her hand. "Momma, this is Reverend Cuddy. Remember I told you he prayed with me before I…"

Tracy's mom, a thin Latina woman with dark, puffy rings underneath her eyes held him in a full-body embrace and wept tears of gratitude. "Thank you, Reverend Cuddy, thank you. Your prayers for Tracy went straight to God, who saved her life because of you. I truly believe that. I truly do," she said, her words heavily accented.

He stayed and sat with them for almost an hour, correcting Tracy and her mother when they continued to call him Reverend Cuddy.

"God has anointed you to carry his message." Mrs. Cordoza patted his arm. "You are his special servant. Tracy said you read a special passage to her. Do you remember which one it was? Can you read it again?"

He pulled his Bible from his pocket but didn't open it to find the page the scripture was on. Instead, he placed the tiny tome between his palms, bowed his head in prayer, and recited the verse from memory. "'How blessed is he whose transgression is forgiven, Whose sin is covered! How blessed is the man to whom the Lord does not impute iniquity, And in whose spirit there is no deceit!'" He raised his head and opened his eyes. "Psalm 32," he said and opened to the correct page for them to read it for themselves.

"How do you do that?" asked Tracy. "Did you memorize the Bible?"

He shook his head. "I suffered a traumatic brain injury, and just like your mother is here by your side, my mother sat reading the Bible to me the entire time I was in a coma. When I woke up, I could recite every scripture, psalm, and passage in the Bible." He pointed to the ceiling. "There is only one explanation for it."

"Your mom must be very proud of you."

"She was. She died of lung cancer a couple of years ago. But she was a devout Catholic who went to mass every day until she couldn't get out of bed anymore. She was so proud of my gift that having me at her bedside reciting scripture was the next best thing to receiving the holy sacraments from a real priest." He smiled at the thought.

"We're Catholic too," said Mrs. Cordoza. "Which parish do you attend?"

"I don't go to mass anymore. I'm a sinner. When I was a child, I remember my mother telling me I was saving the souls of pagan babies with each penny I donated at Sunday school. Now, I continue to do that work, God's work, by being of service to others."

Tracy and her mother nodded.

"God has something special planned for you. I doubt my Tracy is the only one blessed to have met you." Tears appeared in Mrs. Cordoza's now-bright eyes.

"Thank you. I believe that He has special plans for all of us."

CHAPTER 14

The conference room in the United States Attorney's' Office was filled to capacity. In addition to Special Agent Kari Wheeler and her co-case agent, Becca Benner; AUSA Mitch Whitmore; two attorneys from the Security Exchange Commission and one from the Bankruptcy Trustee's office sat across from Cuddy Mullins; his chief of staff, Melinda Tribble; his personal attorney, Jillian Stevens; and two more defense attorneys who represented the Foundation for New Visions in Giving. Cuddy also held his little, white terrier in his arms.

"What's your dog's name?" Kari asked, resisting the urge to ask if she could pet the adorable canine. She loved dogs.

"Potter," said Cuddy. "He's a service animal and authorized to go with me wherever I go."

His attorney added, "As you can imagine, Mr. Mullins has been under intense stress since that newspaper article was published."

"I understand." AUSA Whitmore tapped his pen on the table. "Taking that into consideration, I must ask, for the purposes of this proffer meeting, if Mr. Mullins is under the influence of any drugs, prescription or otherwise."

Attorney Jillian Stevens answered for Mullins. "He is under a doctor's care. As I explained, this ordeal has been devastating for him. But his physician believes that animal therapy is an effective treatment for now."

"I imagine a lot of people are under extreme stress due to the collapse of the foundation. We have been fielding lots of questions from the victims." Whitmore patted a thick pile of paper on the table in front of him as if to indicate it was a collection of victim statements. Kari wasn't sure what the documents were, but she knew they were still negotiating with the SEC and the bankruptcy court for access to the foundation's files.

"Victims?" Melinda Tribble's tone indicated indignation. "We've only heard from donors and grant recipients who are concerned about the drastic actions that were undertaken by the SEC and the bankruptcy court." Her voice quavered, and a nervous tick was happening near her left eye. One of the foundation's attorneys reached out and touched her arm to calm her.

Mitch turned to Cuddy. "And you understand, Mr. Mullins, that what you say in this room can be used against you if you lie to us?"

The older attorney with the white hair answered this time. "Mr. Mullins understands."

Kari turned to Melinda Tribble, who was there without an attorney of her own to look out for her best interests. "Ms. Tribble, we weren't aware that you would be attending this meeting. Do you understand that the proffer agreement doesn't extend to you?"

Mitch nodded and added, "Ms. Tribble, the proffer agreement is officially between my office and Mr. Mullins. You're welcome to stay and contribute if you like, but I want to be perfectly clear that you have no assurances and that whatever you say can be used against you. I take it the attorneys here, the foundation's attorneys, have explained all of that to you?"

"Yes, they have. I was told that you would probably want to speak to the staff at some point. I thought if I came here today with Cuddy, we could resolve this whole situation before it got too far and did permanent damage to the work we're doing and, in turn, to the organizations we're funding… that we're helping."

"And Mrs. Mullins? Why isn't she here? What role does she play in the business?" asked Kari.

Before any of the attorneys could answer, Cuddy said, "My wife, CeCe, Cecelia, doesn't know anything about the inner workings of the foundation. She's more like a cultural ambassador. She has no knowledge of how we do things around here."

Kari thought she noticed Melinda Tribble give Cuddy a look out of the corner of her eye.

When Cuddy added, "Melinda will be much more helpful in providing information about those administrative issues than I can be. That's why she's here and not CeCe."

There it was again, a subtle side glance from Melinda Tribble to Cuddy Mullins. Kari wondered if Becca had caught it too.

"I get that," said Kari. "As the second in charge of the foundation, Ms. Tribble is someone I was planning to contact and set up an interview with." Kari addressed Tribble directly. "I'm curious as to why you wanted to accompany Mr. Mullins and his attorneys here today."

Melinda looked down at her hands as if to contemplate that for the first time. "I'm aware that the allegations are very serious. But complaints that New Visions is a Ponzi scheme are absolutely, positively ludicrous."

"You sound sure of that." Kari noted Tribble's confident stance.

"Those allegations are coming from one person," said Melinda her voice a few octaves higher.

"Is that what you've been told?" asked Kari. She noticed Tribble shifted in her chair as if she was suddenly uncomfortable.

"I read the newspaper article. That professor is the one who's causing all of this chaos."

"We thank you for your willingness to cooperate, but if you don't mind, I'm going to address my initial inquiries directly to Mr. Mullins." Kari smiled, nodded in his attorneys' direction, and then looked directly at Cuddy. "Mr. Mullins, the main allegation is that there are no anonymous donors. What can you tell us about them?"

All eyes turned to Cuddy Mullins. He seemed sad and shaken.

Kari said, "Did you bring that list of anonymous donors with you today?"

"Mr. Mullins is prepared to provide that information to you." Jillian Stevens said and gave him a reassuring look. "However, what we would like to do is first give you a full explanation as to how the program works."

"The way the program has been explained to me is that you take other people's money, tell them that an anonymous donor is gonna double it, and then six to nine months later, they get twice that amount back. Except now that the program is suspended, we seem to be short of the large sums that are supposed to be in escrow."

"That's not how it works," said Cuddy.

Kari clasped her hands in front of her. "What part did I get wrong?"

"We've established a strict guideline for recipients. The reason we need to hold on to the funds is to make sure they aren't taking it for their operations budget. An influx of cash to temporarily hold up a failing program is not what we're about. The nonprofits need to demonstrate to us that the money being matched has been raised for capital improvements to enhance the overall value of what they already have in place."

"Okay." Kari patted her hands together once to indicate she understood. "But then why do you need to hold the benefactors' funds as well?"

"We've been able to take a somewhat complicated concept and break it down into a systematic process. I'm sure Melinda can help me explain everything to you. That's why we're here, isn't it?"

Kari turned to the credenza behind her, picked up the binder she had received from Burton, and placed it on the table in front of Mullins. "Fair enough. Do you mind walking me through this binder and explaining to me exactly how the Foundation for New Visions in Giving program works?"

Jillian, who was sitting next to Cuddy Mullins, flipped through the binder. "Mr. Mullins is a pragmatist. He knows that he needs to answer all your questions."

"About the fraud?" said Becca who, until now, had remained silent.

A look of frustration and hurt crossed Cuddy's face. "I plan to cooperate fully but let me be clear that New Visions is not and never was a fraud. The good we have done has been well documented."

"Exactly," said Jillian. "Monies may have been inadvertently mismanaged, but there is nothing to indicate that Mullins intentionally misappropriated funds."

"So, where shall we start?" Kari placed her hands flat on the table. "I think we all need a basic understanding of how the matching program worked and how New Visions took in $450 million and ended up in bankruptcy. Can someone explain that to me?"

"That is exactly what we would like to do." Tribble scooted her chair closer to the table and laid her hands on the table, her fingers laced together. "I believe you've been given a totally inaccurate picture of who Cuddy Mullins is and what New Visions in Giving is all about. He's an innovator in the fundraising field and the concept of participatory giving."

"Participatory giving?" said Kari. She had directed her question to Cuddy, but when Melinda Tribble began to speak, Kari raised her index finger to signal that she should stay quiet. "Before we go over what that means exactly, am I to assume that you plan to do most of the talking during this meeting?"

As if he had suddenly awoken from a nap, Mullins finally spoke up. "I asked Melinda to accompany me here. Although I am the visionary of the foundation, she understands the daily workings of the various programs much better than I do. Management was never my talent; administration was never my expertise."

"Well, if that's the case," Kari said to Melinda Tribble, "let me get a better understanding of what role you play in the foundation. Okay?"

The woman nodded.

Kari took down basic identifying information about Melinda Tribble and then asked her first investigative question of the woman. "Ms. Tribble, do you know the identities of the anonymous donors?"

Kari wasn't surprised when Tribble shook her head. She once again turned to face Mullins. "Are we going to get the list of the anonymous donors today? The most important thing you can do to prove your intention to cooperate is to tell us who these anonymous donors are."

"Of course, but I'll have to send it to you later."

Kari made a writing gesture. "Just tell us. I have pen and paper here. I'll write it down. How many are there? Eight? Nine? Ten?"

"Over the years, different donors have gotten on and off the list. I want to give you accurate information. I know accuracy is important."

"The truth is what's important to us, and it should be important to you too. It doesn't matter whether they used to be on the list or are on the list now. We need to know the names of everyone ever designated as an anonymous donor. Every single person."

Cuddy's blank gaze was focused at the wall behind her as he said, "I'll send you the full list. It's on my computer in a password-protected file only I can access."

Kari raised her hands wide in disbelief.

His attorney tapped him on the forearm. "Just tell them. Why won't you just give us the names?"

"So, Jillian, he hasn't yet told you their names either. That's telling us everything we need to know about the existence of these so-called anonymous donors."

Jillian opened her mouth to refute the accusation, but Kari held up her hand to stop her.

"Jillian, your client is full of crap."

***

An hour later, as the last lawyer representing the foundation left the room muttering apologies, Kari turned to Becca, Mitch, and the other government attorneys and said, "That was one huge waste of time. Can you believe that they waltzed him in here and they didn't even know he didn't have the list of anonymous donors with him?"

"Sorry about that, folks. If I had known they were going to play games with us, I would have postponed the proffer," said Whitmore.

"You know what I think we need to do next? I think we need to start going through all the files and records left behind at the foundation's offices.

Kari turned to the SEC attorneys. "I take it you've already begun to prepare an accounting, laying out the irregularities in the way the foundation was collecting and withdrawing funds. Mitch, can't we use that for an affidavit for a search warrant to access those documents?"

"Yeah. I agree with you. This guy is full of it. I'm not waiting one second longer. Go get that list of anonymous donors."

Kari smirked. "If it exists... and that's a big if."

CHAPTER 15

Kari sat in the plush office of one of Philadelphia's most successful entrepreneurs and couldn't believe what she was hearing.

"He is a savior," said Alan Fillmore. "When the recession hit nonprofits like a stiff headwind, knocking them off their support systems, Cuddy Mullins was there to stabilize them with an infusion of cash."

After an awkward pause, Kari said, "You're still a believer? Despite the allegations that have been made?"

Fillmore waved his hands in the air, as if swatting away Kari's words. "That article? Yeah, I read it. I wish that reporter had called me for a comment. If I were Cuddy, I would demand a retraction. I'm thinking about writing a letter to the editor. And the Inky better print it."

During the interview, Kari, accompanied by Becca Benner, listened as Fillmore continued to defend Cuddy and the Foundation for New Visions in Giving. He was the city's most famous businessman, with car dealerships and fast-food emporiums sprinkled throughout the Delaware Valley area of Philadelphia, South Jersey, and Delaware. He gave millions away, and he made sure everybody knew it. The high rise where the meeting was taking place bore his name in massive letters on its exterior, and there were at least twenty more buildings, hospital wings, and conference centers that attested to his generosity.

Fillmore had been one of the first to have his donations matched by

New Vision's anonymous donors. And once his donations were doubled and sent off to the charities of his choice, Fillmore became a de facto publicist for the foundation, hawking the authenticity and benefits of the matching program to all of his rich buddies. Kari realized he had to continue to believe. To do otherwise would mean accepting that he had been duped and, even worse, had cajoled his friends and colleagues into giving money to New Visions so they could be scammed too. She wondered if he still believed in the Easter bunny. Fortunately, it wasn't her job to convince him that he was a victim of potentially the largest charity Ponzi scheme ever. She just needed him to tell her his story, so that was what she asked him to do.

"I've known Cuddy for years."

"How many exactly?" she interrupted.

He shrugged. "I don't know. I guess it's been seven or eight. I first met him when he was raising funds for drug rehab centers in Kensington. I admired his work. I'm a self-made man, born and raised in North Philadelphia. For the grace of God, there go I." Fillmore rose from his chair and moved to the window behind his desk. His back was to her, but his reflection caught him dabbing at his eyes with a handkerchief. After a beat, he turned to face them. "I love that guy. He has a special gift, you know."

"A gift? For raising money?"

"Yes, but that wasn't what I meant. He has the uncanny ability to know what's in someone's heart. If you're troubled, he can tell you what God wants you to hear. When I first met him, my wife was dying of cervical cancer. I kept dragging her from doctor to doctor, trying to find a miracle, and they all told me the same thing—it was incurable. But even when she begged me to allow her to spend that time with the kids and grandkids, I couldn't stop. I said nothing to Cuddy about it, but one day, he showed up and gave me this." Fillmore walked back over to his desk, retrieved something from his top drawer, and handed Kari a Post-it note sealed in plastic.

She read it silently.

And I set my mind to know wisdom and to know madness and folly; I realized that this also is striving after wind. Because in much wisdom there is much grief, and increasing knowledge results in increasing pain.

She looked up at him.

"Cuddy knew. Somehow, he knew and with that verse told me how fruitless and silly I was being. I wasn't helping my wife. I was hurting her with my selfish refusal to accept the..." Fillmore's eyes again filled with tears. "How am I supposed to doubt someone who was there when I needed him? Is that what you're asking me to do?"

Kari wondered how strong his confidence in Cuddy Mullins really was. Was this a crack in his resolute trust? A small fissure perhaps? "No. I'm here to ask a few questions," she said. "It's up to you to determine what you want to believe."

Fillmore explained that when he was first approached by Cuddy with the new charitable concept, there were only five anonymous donors. Cuddy said they all had asked him not to divulge their names. "That was three years ago," he said. "The foundation helped me make a wise decision about where to invest my money. I'm constantly courted by professional fundraisers. Why wouldn't I take advantage of Cuddy's expertise in identifying the smaller, needier organizations who needed my help?"

"Mr. Fillmore, I've been reading about your success, your wealth, for years. Aren't you even a little bit intrigued by the anonymous donors? I mean, who's richer than you?" She hoped flattery would encourage him to tell them all he knew about these unidentified philanthropists.

"I barely make the Forbes list. Believe me, there are people all over the world who have more than I do." He surprised them with a full-bellied laugh.

"You never wondered? Never asked Cuddy Mullins about who the anonymous donors were?"

"No. He said they wanted to remain anonymous, and I respected their wishes. I have, however, wished that I could let them know how much their support of my charities means to me." He paused for a beat and looked out the window at the sweeping view of the city below. "Cuddy told me not to worry, that they knew. And I believed him."

Kari surmised that he might think fairies, goblins, and leprechauns existed too. Alan Fillmore was one believing man. She continued to push. "There's not a lot of information about them in the brochure—"

"All I can tell you is that they're mostly from old money, people who have inherited their wealth. And through the Foundation for New Visions in Giving, they are using old money to create and encourage a new way of giving."

"Participatory giving."

"Exactly."

"When this case goes to court—"

"If this goes to court. Nobody's been charged with anything. You're quite presumptuous."

"I hear you," she said humoring him. "If this matter goes to court, the judge will, in all likelihood, institute the clawback provision."

"Clawback? What the hell is that?"

"You haven't come across the term before in your business dealings?" He shook his head. "It's a legal recourse where the money that has already been disbursed has to be returned, is taken back." Kari watched as a look of despair crossed his face. "You might want to check with your attorneys about it."

Fillmore removed a sheet of paper from his desk and scribbled a reminder note to himself.

"Just in case," she added.

***

Lennie Adams pointed to the words of wisdom framed and hanging on the wall above the mantel of the great room's stone fireplace and read them out loud. "With Great Wealth Comes Great Responsibility."

Kari recognized the quote. "Bill Gates, right?" she asks.

Lennie nodded and then glanced woefully over the shoulders of Kari and Becca Benner to his wife, Tanya, who stood directly behind them. "He and Melinda Gates are our role models. But it was my father who first drilled the importance of community and giving back into my brain. We believed in Cuddy Mullins and the Foundation for New Visions in Giving. We thought we were doing the right thing."

"We're trying to get a handle on what actually happened. Everyone says that we should speak with you two," she said with a sober tone and a simple nod. Inwardly, she was thrilled, in spite of the difficult circumstances, that she had been invited inside the mansion and was in the presence of one of her favorite Philadelphia Eagles. Lennie Adams was a six-foot-three-inch, 253-pound true believer, known for his Christian-based ethics and the good works he had been doing in the community before and since his retirement from the NFL last year.

Kari was a true fangirl, but she managed to maintain her composure. She decided she would wait until after the interview to let him know how much she admired him on and off the field. She wondered if he regretted leaving the team and missing out on playing in the Eagles' recent, successful Super Bowl appearance. Even if she was bold enough to ask it, that question would have to wait until all of her inquiries about New Visions and its president had been addressed.

"My father was a great man, a rock-solid provider, and a passionate, God-fearing servant, who instilled a commitment to community in us kids," he said. "Tanya and I honor his legacy through our philanthropy. All of our donations are in his name."

His wife walked over and stood next to her husband. "We're blessed," she added. "My husband's playing in the NFL for all those years means we can make sure others less fortunate than us can share in our blessings." Tanya's mouth formed a tight line of concentration. "We met Cuddy years ago and immediately felt connected to his passion, his energy. We've read the articles, but we're trying to keep an open mind. We're glad you asked to meet with us."

As in the case of Alan Fillmore, Kari could tell that Lennie and Tanya Adams were clinging to hope that this was all a misunderstanding. During her twelve years working on the economic fraud and corruption squad, she had witnessed most victims of Ponzi schemes accept without much resistance that they had been involved in a scam; the implausibility of the source of their newfound prosperity had been needling at them from the very start. But a charity-based Ponzi scheme? Kari was discovering charity-minded victims were different. They desperately needed to believe their con man deserved their trust. Who would take from those whose only goal was to help others?

"Please, come sit. Can I offer you tea or coffee?" Lennie directed them to one of the many seating areas in a huge library off the great room.

"Maybe just a glass of water?" Kari sat down next to Becca on the upholstered couch. "I wouldn't want you to go to any trouble for us."

"It wouldn't be any trouble," Tanya said almost apologetically. "We have… help."

Of course, they do. Before coming out to their home today, Kari had conducted a quick internet search. Tanya had parlayed their fortune into building her own educational toy empire, frequently demonstrating and selling the toys on QVC, the home shopping network. Together, Tanya and Lennie had amassed impressive wealth. "A cup of coffee would be good. Thank you."

Tanya turned to Becca. "Tea, please," she said.

Lennie stepped out of the room and returned a few moments later. "A tray will be brought out. Did you want to start going over your questions while we wait?"

"Sure," said Kari, reaching into her bag and pulling out a notebook and pen. "The first time you met Cuddy is a good place to start."

"Seven years ago, when I was drafted by the Eagles and we moved to Philadelphia, I was stoked. There's a real need here in the inner city, true poverty and deprivation." Kari contrasted the image Lennie's remarks conjure up, as she interviewed him in his multimillion-dollar home in Wynnewood. It seemed a bit ironic. "We give generously to support two Philly charter schools for low-income students. 'Education is the most powerful weapon which you can use to change the world.'"

"I know that quote too." Kari smiled. "Nelson Mandela."

Lennie and Tanya Adams both bobbed their heads. "One of my father's favorites," said Lennie. "At Washington State, I majored in business with a minor in comparative ethnic studies. My education gave me a basic understanding of racial inequality worldwide but attending Cuddy's seminars at the Middleton Institute is what really gave us the tools to become agents of change."

Kari looked up from her notebook. "What's the Middleton Institute?"

"Cuddy has someone else running that now, but it's an innovative, two-prong program to teach benefactors how to make wise decisions about donating and to teach nonprofits how to make wise decisions about spending and budgeting." Tanya Adams smiled broadly. "We're alumni of Leadership Philadelphia, so we know the needs of our adopted city. We wanted to help those who were struggling, but we didn't want to just throw money at a problem."

"Cuddy taught us what it meant to be a change agent and a Christian. We miss our weekly breakfast Bible study sessions with him," said Lennie. "This has been extra difficult for us, because until recently we've been used to going to him for spiritual guidance.'

"Has he tried to reach out to you?"

"No. But our attorneys believe we shouldn't speak with him until everything gets cleared up."

Kari sneaked a look at Becca, who raised her eyebrows in disbelief. Until everything gets cleared up?

"About three and a half years ago, he told us about the anonymous donors. Initially, we made a conservative contribution of $15,000, to check it out." As Tanya spoke, Lennie laid his hand over his wife's. She paused and brought his hand up to her face and kissed it. Tears collected in her eyes. "The money was matched six months later as promised," she continued. "And every time after that as well. Eventually, we started encouraging everyone we knew who had money to participate."

Lennie pulled a box of tissue from the sofa table behind where he and his wife sat and handed her one so that she could wipe her eyes.

Tanya looked pleadingly at Kari and Becca. "What can you tell us about the allegations? Do you really believe the foundation is a Ponzi scheme and that Cuddy knew?"

"Our investigation is at the early stages," said Kari. "I can't tell you any more than that."

After the coffee and tea were carried in by a member of their staff, Kari and Becca continued to question the Adamses about their relationship with Cuddy. Each time Tanya reached for her cup, her hands were visibly shaking. Even though they had no real loss—any money that might have been misspent as part of the fraud was money they were giving away anyway—Kari could feel their despair. They thought they had created a lasting legacy to aid future generations, and now look what Cuddy Mullins and his Foundation for New Visions in Giving had done. Kari left the Adams' home without mentioning the Eagles or the Super Bowl. She realized that today was not the time to talk about football. This couple was in the midst of true grief.

Cuddy Mullins had murdered their dreams of establishing a forever-replenishing endowment for area charter schools. They were victims of economic homicide.

CHAPTER 16

Kari waved to the receptionist and badged her way into the inner sanctum of the United States Attorney's Office. She was headed to Mitch Whitmore's office. Her case against Cuddy Mullins and his Foundation for New Visions in Giving had been active for less than a month. She had emailed him her FD-302s, reports of interviews, with the victim-donors, but this was Kari's first opportunity to speak directly with him about what she was learning from the so-called victims of the Ponzi scheme. She knocked on the partially open door and proceeded inside, only to stop halfway across the threshold. Her smile immediately disappeared.

Sitting in Whitmore's office was IRS criminal investigative agent Bryant Duffy. She would have recognized that bald head and bushy upper lip anywhere. It was as if all of the hair follicles had refused to reside on top of his big head and had migrated down below his nose. The last time she had seen him, he had unjustly accused her of trying to cheat his agency. Kari did not like him or trust him.

"I'm sorry. Looks like I'm a little early for our eleven o'clock." She absentmindedly looked down at her wrist, even though she never wore a watch. "We were going to bang out the affidavits for the Cuddy Mullin's search warrants." She remained standing in the office doorway. "I'll wait out here while you guys finish up. We need to wait for Becca anyway. She'll be here soon."

"No, come in. Come in." Whitmore waved his hands in a welcoming motion. He wore a huge grin.

"How are you, Kari?" Duffy gave her a too-big-to-be-genuine smile and nodded. She wished she could smack the smugness off his face.

"Oh good. You already know each other." Whitmore directed his attention to Becca, who had come up behind Kari. He motioned them in farther. "And have you also met Becca Benner?"

"No. I don't think I have." Duffy stood and reached out to shake Becca's hand. Kari noticed the way he quickly scanned Becca's athletic frame and short hair. "Bryant Duffy, IRS CID. Nice to meet you, Becca." He did not attempt to shake Kari's hand. He knew better.

Before Becca had a chance to respond, Kari poked her in the side. Becca received her message and said simply, "Okay."

Agent Duffy looked over the top of his glasses at Kari and laughed. "When did you have a chance to tell her about me?"

"I didn't say a thing. Perhaps she can read my thoughts," Kari said with raised eyebrows.

Whitmore turned to Duffy. "You didn't mention that you and Kari had worked together."

"It must have slipped my mind."

Becca said, "How can you forget about having worked with Kari Wheeler? She's been all over the news. A shootout with a man who had already shot two people. Recipient of two medals of bravery. Did that slip your mind too?"

"Nope, I heard all about that." He formed both his hands into imaginary guns and pretended to fire off a blaze of bullets. "I'm breathing the same air as a true American hero."

"Kari saved the lives of everyone outside that hotel. She absolutely is a hero," said Becca. "How dare you joke about that."

His eyes swung back and forth between Kari and Becca. "You've got a real fangirl here," he smirked. "How long have you two been partnered up?"

Before Kari could respond, Whitmore spoke. "I'm glad we can all get together today." He looked around the room at the agents and pretended the unpleasant exchange had not just occurred. "If we're lucky, there's still a good chance that we will be able to find the money."

"Whoa, what's with the 'we'? Duffy is not on this case." Kari placed her hands on her hips and made no attempt to hide the pissed-off look she knew was on her face.

Whitmore used his index finger to draw a circle in the air that indicated everyone in the room. "From the initial interviews that Kari and Becca have conducted, it appears that we could have one of the biggest financial scandals in the history of American charities here. That's why Duffy asked to be put on the case."

"There are significant tax fraud implications here," said Duffy. "Kari, I think we're both mature enough to put the past behind us and start this new case together with a clean slate." He gave her a lopsided smile.

"Sure, as long as you can guarantee that you won't scream at me in an open conference room full of our superiors and accuse me of trying to cheat the IRS out of their share of case forfeiture funds."

Whitmore rose from his chair and took a seat on the edge of his desk between Kari and Duffy. "I wasn't aware that you had a history together."

"Why is he here?" Kari stared at Whitmore while she waited for an answer.

"I told you. He volunteered." Whitmore nodded as if she should agree that this was a good thing. "Initial reports indicate that New Visions took in contributions valued at approximately $500 million. As you are aware, the initial allegation included a fraudulent tax return. I thought we needed a CPA—"

"The FBI has lots of agents who are CPAs," Becca offered, indicating her alliance to Kari.

Whitmore raised his hands. "I agree with Duffy that an investigator from the IRS is needed."

"Mitch, I brought this case to you. I invited you to work on it with me." Kari jabbed her thumb into her chest. "You should have asked me before inviting someone else to join my case."

"I forgot that the FBI doesn't play well with others. How was I supposed to know that the FBI can't get along with the IRS either?" said Whitmore.

Kari bristled at the overused cliché and glared at Whitmore and Duffy. "Spare me that fabricated TV show BS. This isn't an agency thing. It's about professional respect between people."

"I apologized for my previous behavior," said Duffy. "I think we can put this all behind us."

"Like you had a choice. Even your bosses were embarrassed by the way you verbally attacked me," said Kari.

"We moved on and worked well together for the rest of the case, didn't we?"

Kari hiked a shoulder. "We were civil."

"I think we can be adults about this. At least I can," said Duffy. "This is a great case, and I want to be a part of it. I'm sorry for how I acted the last time. I promise it won't happen again."

"So we're good then?" Whitmore looked at Kari.

Kari hesitated for several moments before answering. "I'm not fully committed to the idea yet, but I'm willing to give it a chance for the sake of the investigation." She pointed her finger at Duffy. "But I'm not putting up with any BS this time."

"Understood and agreed." He bowed his head.

Whitmore let out an exaggerated sigh and said, "Great. Let's get to work."

***

Kari did her best to be civil to Duffy as she described what she had discovered so far in the investigation. "Cuddy Mullins has been able to get people to donate their money to the foundation because he takes advantage of the donors' desire to impress others with their generosity.

They have a need to be seen as benevolent benefactors. As for Cuddy, he's like a mad scientist who discovered the perfect formula—the point where greed and giving collide."

"So, basically, it's a scam, but a scam with a twist," said Whitmore.

"It seems to me that the case can easily be divided into three areas: the nonprofits, the donors—real and anonymous—and the money." Duffy shot Kari a sideways glance. "So we don't get in each other's way, maybe we should divvy up the workload," he said.

"Exactly what do you have in mind?" Kari was willing to do almost anything not to have to deal directly with him.

"Why don't you and Becca"—he hesitated a bit before continuing—"partner up on the bulk of the work, interviewing the donors and nonprofits, and I'll handle the financial matters and begin tracking the money?"

"Absolutely not," Kari said with real defiance as she glared at Duffy. "Don't start that again. No one tried to steal your agency's share of forfeiture funds, and I'm getting sick and tired of you accusing me —
."

"Don't be so paranoid. I'm a CPA. I just thought it would be easier for me to take a crack at the financial side of this. I already took a look at the tax records. This thing isn't even a foundation. There's no permanent endowment, no investment income."

"Look, Kari, can we try this and see if we can make it work?" asked Whitmore.

"From what I can tell, there will be some tax-related charges." Duffy pointed to papers laid out on the desk. "This matching-funds thing could prove to be problematic for some of the donors. I'm thinking that some of them may not have been real honest on their taxes. Some contributors probably took the doubled deduction. Those victims won't be getting off so easy."

"Let's have Duffy handle financial interviews with the brokerage firm and accountants. You and Becca can handle donors and organizations that don't require his expertise. We don't need to designate who does what on everything, but that's a start. You're all case agents on this with equal responsibilities."

The room grew awkwardly silent while Kari and the others considered Whitmore's solution.

They made a tentative agreement to work the case together. Kari would be the affiant on the warrant to search the foundation's offices and the Mullin's residence. Duffy would be the affiant on warrants related to offshore accounts, if any were located. After talking for another thirty minutes, Duffy left for another meeting. As he headed out the door, he paused in front of Becca. "Do you have a business card?"

Becca pulled one out of the breast pocket of her jacket and handed it to him.

"I'm all out," said Duffy. "But I'll give you one of mine the next time we meet."

"That's okay," said Becca. "I think Kari has your number."

***

After Duffy departed the office, Kari turned to Mitch Whitmore and shook her head.

Whitmore shrugged. "How was I supposed to know—"

"I've been working scams and frauds for twelve years. I can read a spreadsheet, and I know how to use a calculator." Kari drew in a deep breath and released it slowly before continuing. "Why would you invite someone to be a part of this case without asking me first?"

"We're all adults here and without a doubt, down the road, there will be tax charges. We need someone from the IRS to work on this."

"You know what? I agree… but why did it have to be him?"

CHAPTER 17

At the conclusion of their initial meeting with the SEC and the bankruptcy trustee, it had been agreed that the Bureau would need to obtain a separate search warrant to access the New Visions files and records already under the other agencies' control. Using the evidence she had gathered from her interviews with Professor Burton, Alan Fillmore, and Lennie and Tanya Adams and the documents they had provided, Kari had prepared an affidavit indicating she had reason to believe that instrumentalities of a crime were being housed at the Foundation for New Visions in Giving's JFK Boulevard office suite. She had no problem getting the magistrate judge to sign off on the warrant. This was their second meeting with the agencies to advise them that the FBI would conduct their search the following morning.

Kari addressed the group. "The first thing the FBI will need to do once we get inside is to go through all the records and see what's there."

"You know we've already inventoried many of the items in here," said the representative from the bankruptcy court.

"Yes, I'm aware." Kari chose her words carefully. "However, your inventory includes physical properties of value, such as the paintings, chairs, cabinets, and conference tables. Our interests lie primarily in the documents. We're going to be looking to verify deceptions and falsehoods, anything that would indicate that what Cuddy Mullins and his staff told investors, donors, and recipients was not based on actual truths. Our plan is not to disturb anything. We want to first see what we find before determining what documents we need to pursue criminal charges." Kari emphasized the word criminal.

The SEC attorney sat a little higher in her chair and leaned forward. "Was it your intention to take those documents with you to another location?"

Kari nodded, but before she could speak the attorney interrupted her.

"The reason I ask is that I have a proposition I hope you'll consider. Perhaps the answer is for both of our agencies to leave everything in place and conduct our investigations, our civil and your criminal, from this office space."

Kari looked over at Mitch Whitmore, who tilted his head right, then left as he considered the proposal. "That certainly is a possibility," he said.

The SEC attorney was obviously pleased to hear that the United States Attorneys' office was on board. He turned back to Kari. "What do you think?"

"I'm willing to work something out," she said.

"Good. Let's draw up a memorandum of understanding."

***

Kari led her team through the doors of the Foundation of New Visions in Giving at approximately seven o'clock the following morning. At the same time, out in the suburbs of Devon, Pennsylvania, a smaller search team lead by Becca was knocking on the front door of the Mullins' personal residence. Kari, the affiant for both search warrants, had laid out the purpose of the searches in the affidavit, the summary of the investigation to date, the scheme, and victim statements.

Because the foundation's offices had been shuttered and Cuddy and staff had been locked out ever since the SEC filed a temporary restraining order and the Bankruptcy court seized all physical assets, the search team did not have to actually pack evidence into boxes to be carted away. They could do their work right in the building. Kari and several members of the squad entered the space to conduct a thorough inventory of evidence, they would also speak with the SEC and bankruptcy representatives to authenticate that the items had not been removed or altered. At the Mullins' house, Becca's team would be conducting a more traditional search, packing up any documents and records associated with New Visions that they found. Once both searches were underway, Whitmore had placed a courtesy call to the foundation's attorney to advise them.

There were offices, file cabinets, and storage shelves full of documents, and they would need to review and log in each and every one of them. After squad mate Scott Brickland drew up a site map of all the rooms and labeled them accordingly, teams of two were assigned to begin cataloging everything. Kari's plan was to locate bank statements, wire transfer reports, and account summaries. She needed to take a look at anything that would allow her and Duffy to accurately calculate every single penny Cuddy had acquired in the scheme. And if there were hidden bank accounts, she needed the paperwork that would take them directly to them. She had been working steadily for about an hour when Tommy Tanzola, one of her squad mates, approached her.

"There's someone outside you might be interested in speaking to," he said.

"Who is it?"

"Don't you want to be surprised?"

"Not really."

With a flourish of his hand, he bowed in front of her. "Your subject awaits. Cuddy Mullins is outside asking for you."

Cuddy Mullins? Here? She hoped he had his attorneys with him.

She found him waiting in the hall near the elevator. He looked more haggard and beat up since the first time they had met at the proffer. He had his little dog with him again.

"Mr. Mullins." She shook his hand as she greeted him. "How can I help you?"

"You people move fast."

"Just doing our job."

"I guess this means that you've decided to pursue a criminal case, that I'm being investigated? Melinda Tribble and I hoped we had convinced you that a criminal investigation was unwarranted. There may be some unintentional financial issues that need to be cleaned up but certainly nothing that the FBI would be interested in."

"We're here conducting a search of the premises. You'll need to discuss what that means with your legal team." She stood with her hands in her pockets, waiting for him to tell her why he was there, and when he didn't, she added, "We'll take a look-see at what we have and then make a determination of where we need to go from here."

Still, he said nothing.

"Are you aware that my partner, Becca Benner, is executing a search warrant over at your residence?"

Finally, he responded. "Yes. I was out walking Potter when they came." He bent over and rubbed the patient pup's head.

"You seem to be really attached to him. How does a dog become a therapy dog?"

"I have no idea," Cuddy winked. "I just tell people that so I can take him everywhere with me. I sometimes feel guilty about the intentional deception, but no one's ever asked me to show anything. I'm sure I could get my doctor to write up something if I ever really needed proof."

Kari arched her eyebrows. "Technically, that's fraud." They both chuckled at the veiled reference to his current situation.

Cuddy picked up Potter. "I'm grateful to have him in my life. He was given to me by a donor because he no longer fit in her purse. Can you believe that? She had been indignant, complaining that she had been told he was a teacup terrier and would never grow larger than her designer tote bags. When I admired him, she handed him to me and declared that I could have him."

"So, I guess that makes him a rescue dog," Kari laughed and petted the pup.

"I'm not sure who rescued who." He nuzzled the top of his head. "I thought all of those strange people trampling through the house would be confusing for him. So we stayed away."

"I would have thought you would want to be there."

"No way. My wife is probably having a conniption. She doesn't like strangers touching her things."

Kari noticed that he said her things and not our things.

"She's a true Philly girl, from Little Flower Catholic High. They have a bit of an edge, you know. I feel sorry for your partner. CeCe's probably watching them like a hawk. I was hoping we could have avoided all of this."

What did he want her to say? You're right? Never mind?

"I'm a good guy, you know."

"I know you believe that. But just because you say it, that doesn't make it so." The hint of rebuke visibly shook him. She watched as his already-pale face turned bloodless. She didn't care. She was growing impatient with the strange conversation. She pointed at the entrance to the foundation's offices. "Why are you here? I can't let you take anything from the premises."

He recovered quickly and waved his hand. "No. That's not why I'm here. I came to see you."

"Me?" She narrowed her gaze and gave him a quizzical look.

"I've been thinking about you since we met at the US Attorney's office last week. Agent Wheeler, are you a Christian?"

She flinched. "I'm don't think that's an appropriate question for you to ask me."

"Fair enough." He reached into his jacket pocket and pulled out a small book.

"Is that a Bible?"

"Yes. I hope you don't mind, but I've been told I have a gift for finding the most apropos verse for most occasions." He quickly flipped through the little book and stopped to scan one of the pages. "Yes, indeed, this works well. May I read it to you?"

Kari looked back at the entrance, where the search was underway. She was growing more uncomfortable with the conversation, but her curiosity caused her to nod in agreement. "This isn't one of those party tricks, is it?" she asked. "You distract me and then pull a quarter from behind my ear?"

He gave her a sober smile. "No, nothing like that. Romans 2:12. 'For all who have sinned without the law will also perish without the law, and all who have sinned under the law will be judged by the law. For it is not the hearers of the law who are righteous before God, but the doers of the law who will be justified—'"

She cut him off before he could finish. "Mr. Mullins, I have no idea why you're reading that to me, but I'm going back inside." She turned around and left Cuddy and his little dog in the hallway.

She hadn't heard much of what he was saying after the beginning line. For all those who have sinned. Was he calling her a sinner? What could he possibly know about her past? An uneasy feeling overtook her, but she brushed it off. She had felt his goodness, but how could that be? He was the subject of her criminal investigation. The evidence against him was mounting and she had little doubt about his guilt. Cuddy Mullins knew nothing about her. It was simply her guilt reaction to a coincidental choice of a Bible passage he gave to her. That's what it was—a coincidence.

CHAPTER 18

When CeCe heard someone pounding on the front door, she thought it might have been that damn professor who had told all those lies to the newspaper. She had instinctively grabbed her cell phone to call 911. She stopped when she heard someone shouting, "FBI. Open the door. We have a warrant to search the premises."

She had cautiously approached the front window and was shocked to see five FBI agents in their blue FBI raid jackets standing on her front step. Some were carrying flattened corrugated boxes. Concerned about what the neighbors might think, she flung open the door and quickly ushered them all inside the foyer, peeking up and down the cul-de-sac before she stepped inside. Before she shut the door, CeCe ran her hands across the beautiful wooden door with an inlaid glass design she had imported from the Andalusian coast. She scrutinized the female agent standing closest to her who was holding a pointy leather portfolio. CeCe scolded her, "I hope you weren't banging on my antique door with that," she said after inspecting the exterior, and closing the door. "You're lucky you didn't chip or scratch the finish. It would cost a fortune to have it redone. It was recovered from an ancient Moorish mosque."

The agent ignored the reproach and displayed her credentials. "I'm Special Agent Becca Benner with the FBI. Are you Mrs. Mullins? Cecelia Mullins?" She didn't wait for an answer and handed CeCe several sheets of paper stapled together. "We have a warrant to search the premises."

CeCe backed up and stood before the group of two women and three men holding boxes as well as packing supplies, and she raised her hands in front of her to stop them from stepping past the foyer. "Wait here," she said. "I need to call my husband."

The agent glanced down at her Apple watch. "The assistant U.S. attorney working with us on this matter is calling the foundation's lawyers right now." She turned to speak to one of her team members. "Donnelly, go ahead and start taking photos." Agent Benner moved passed CeCe into the living room. "Is there anyone else in the house?"

"No. What do you possibly think you're going to find here at our home?"

"The items are all listed in the addendum." The agent pointed to the document. "We've got people at New Visions searching the office too."

The agent addressed another team member, a short man wearing a black suit under his FBI jacket. "Murphy, do me a favor, take a quick lap through the house, draw up a floor plan, and designate who's going to take care of each room."

"Yes, Ma'am." He laughed slightly and saluted her. She smiled back.

"This isn't funny," said CeCe. "I am not giving you permission to touch anything until I talk to my husband or our attorneys."

"That's not the way this works." The female agent signaled to everyone to move into the house. "We don't need your attorneys' permission. We have the court's permission."

"Please, let me talk to my attorney first."

"Call your attorney. But let them know our search has started and we won't end until we've gone through every nook and cranny in this house. Don't forget to tell them I identified myself, Special Agent Becca Benner, and gave you a copy of the warrant."

CeCe felt panic rising inside her. Her palms were sweaty, and anxiety pulsed through her veins. She grabbed Agent Benner by the arm. "Don't touch my things!"

Agent Benner removed CeCe's hand. "I need you to calm down. We'll leave a list of everything we take." Before she could say another word, Benner walked over to the other female agent on the search team and said loud enough for her to hear, "Kathy, keep an eye on Mrs. Mullins."

As FBI agents walked through the house, CeCe stood in the middle of the room with her fists balled tightly. Her mouth twitched, and she cringed each time an agent poked the base of a lamp, rummaged through a drawer, or looked behind one of the gilded picture frames. These FBI agents were manhandling her treasures as if they were rummaging through a thrift store bin. She and Cuddy had worked hard to attain their lifestyle, and the fact that strangers were in her house manipulating everything they owned signaled to her for the first time that she could lose all of it.

CeCe called Cuddy's cell phone. No answer. She left a hurried message. "Cuddy. Get home now. The FBI is here at the house. They're going through all our stuff." CeCe ended the call and turned to see an agent picking up the hand-painted porcelain vase she had purchased during their trip to Italy. She rushed over to him.

"You're going to break it." She gently reached for it, cradling the vase he had tried to stick his big, fat hand inside. She tilted it so he could see inside. "There's nothing in here."

Agent Benner was suddenly at her side. She removed the vase from her hands, handing it back to the male agent. "Hey, Sid, be careful with that, okay? Hold that with two hands."

"Thank you. They need to be gentler with these things." She found herself grimacing again, as yet another agent left on the coffee table several photo frames he had pulled apart and failed to put back together. "May I fix that?" She pointed to the disassembled pieces.

"No. He left it like that so everyone will know it has been checked. We'll put it back together before we leave, I promise."

"What could you possibly be looking for behind a family photo?"

"You have the search warrant." Agent Benner pointed to the paper

CeCe still held in her hand. She had forgotten she had it. "We're mainly looking for anything that could identify the anonymous donors." The agent hiked her shoulders. "If you know where we can find that information, this search will move much faster."

"You have to talk to my husband about that. I'm not involved in the business. He'll be home any minute now. He's just out walking the dog."

"He came back already." The agent named Kathy interrupted their conversation. "Agent Murphy just told me Mr. Mullins said he needed to go somewhere, gave us his consent to search his car, and as soon as Murph checked it out, he took off. With the dog."

CeCe was confused. Why would he leave her here alone, especially without telling her? "I'm sure he'll be right back. You can ask him your questions but I don't think the foundation's lawyers want either of us talking to you."

"I didn't ask a question, just made an observation provided for your benefit."

"My benefit?" CeCe gave her a puzzled look.

"It's obvious you don't like us being here, looking through your things. You don't have to tell me anything, and let's be clear that I'm not asking you to. But we wouldn't have to do this if we had the donor list. That's all I'm saying." CeCe watched as Agent Benner turned her back to her and began removing the $200 Cliveden Square chinoiserie pillows from the couch and placing them on the rug. CeCe was horrified. While Benner crouched down to feel around the couch's fabric and the wooden frame, CeCe picked up the loose cushions from the floor, fluffed the braided trim, and stacked them neatly on a nearby chair. She would rather cut out her tongue than tell this disrespectful young agent anything.

She stepped into the atrium and scowled as she considered the actions of the search team. The one named Kathy had gone upstairs and was probably in CeCe's bedroom going through her most intimate belongings. She thought it best for her to remain downstairs. She feared that she would lose it if she caught her mishandling her clothes and accessories. Her possessions meant the world to her; they were proof that someone like her could get to where she was today. When she was growing up, CeCe could never have dreamed that one day she would live in a home like this, surrounded by all of these beautiful things. She owed it all to Cuddy Mullins. She had known he was the one the first time he sat next to her on the number three bus.

Since she was eight years old, she had known how her mother had earned money to feed her two kids and her habit. CeCe was told to stay in her room, but sometimes she would crack her door open and take a peek at her mother's "friends," who were always stopping by to say hello. Later, as her mother's addiction worsened, she simply handled her transactions out on the street. The neighborhood kids, and sometimes their parents, would say nasty, hurtful things to her about her mother, but CeCe learned to ignore them all. She spent her days watching TV shows and movies about living the good life—and Cuddy had made it all a reality.

Cuddy was her savior. So many times, he had helped her walk through the streets of Kensington to find her mother and bring her home. Having lived in the area all their lives, they had thought themselves invincible. The ugly scar on his scalp hidden under his thick hair was the ultimate proof of his unconditional love for her, his willingness to risk his life for her. She would never forget when he had gone looking and discovered her mother's body under the bridge. She knew the day would come, but the pain of her mom's death was more than CeCe thought she could bear. She had threatened and even attempted suicide several times during the following months, but Cuddy had been there for her. He said he had found his calling because of her. It was his work as a drug counselor that had introduced him to bigger and better opportunities—and to eventually establish the Foundation for New Visions in Giving.

She glowered from the corner as she watched the FBI rummage through her beautiful, precious treasures. How dare they? When she was a child wondering if her mother would come home she would never have imagined she would be living in this house among these lovely things. She wasn't about to give this up. She was willing to do just about anything to protect it.

***

CeCe Mullins was giving her the evil eye, but Becca refused to acknowledge her. Instead, with the search in good hands downstairs, Becca ventured upstairs to see how things were progressing. She stuck her head inside what appeared to be the Mullins' master suite.

"How's everything going in here?" asked Becca. Kathy was going through the dresser drawers. She had placed the clothes on the bed, removed the drawers and flipped them over.

"Okay. I haven't come across anything of interest other than what's back there." Kathy raised her eyebrows and pointed to double doors at the back of the bedroom.

"What's back there?" said Becca as she strolled over and entered the most exquisite walk-in closet she had ever seen. It was a mini boutique. Rows of shoes and handbags arranged by color lined the shelves along the interior wall. Cedar hangers exhibited rows of similarly arranged dresses, blouses, and pants. Becca had only seen photos of closets like this in celebrity magazines and designer show homes. She poked her head out into the bedroom and exclaimed, "Could this be heaven?"

"I told you," said Kathy, joining her. "If you and Kari are trying to find where all the Ponzi scheme funds are hidden, there you have it." Kathy laughed and sized up the room as she spun in a slow circle. "It's here, hiding in plain sight."

Becca combed through the racks of clothes, checking pockets and lifting and feeling for hidden objects or documents. Normally such a detailed search would be a tedious job, but the assignment allowed her to handle the amazing designer-labels outfits, many of which still displayed price tags way beyond what she could afford to buy on her government salary. "Oh my God, Kathy, you weren't kidding. Look at all this." She fingered the label affixed to a beautiful, midnight-blue, silk blouse. It read $680.

Kathy opened a small cabinet on the left side of the room. "Hey Becca, take a look at this." Inside were several rows of different lengths and styles of blond hair extensions—curly, wavy and super straight. "Now that's when you know you've got money to burn, when you have a mini-closet just for your hair."

There was a hatbox on the hair closet's upper shelf. Becca opened it and discovered a short orange-red wig pinned to a Styrofoam head. The color of the hair reminded Becca of one of the trainers at the gym she and Kari attended.

Becca peeked out into the bedroom to make sure CeCe Mullins wasn't around. With the coast clear, she unpinned the red wig, tucked her brown hair up, and placed it on her head.

"What are you doing?" said Kathy.

Becca held a finger to her lips, took out her personal phone, and sent a selfie to Kari. The accompanying text said, Who do I remind you of? She quickly removed the wig and had it back in the box and on the shelf before her phone started buzzing. Kari was calling her.

"Did you see my text?" Becca asked.

"That thing on your head? That's not one of Cece Mullins's wigs, is it?" asked Kari.

"I found it in her special hair closet," Becca chuckled. "I was channeling Tara from the gym."

"That's probably not a good idea. I deleted the photo. I suggest you do the same."

"You're right. You always are, Betty Bureau. But I have to tell you that it's a crime that you're not here to see her walk-in closet in person."

"I'll look at the pre-search photos. You did take photos of everything in its place before you started the search, right? Whitmore just called me and said Cece Mullins was complaining to the Foundation's attorneys that the FBI is destroying her home.

"Yikes. Can you imagine what she would have done if she caught me wearing her fake hair?"

"Is she giving you guys a hard time?"

"Not anymore. She's more upset with her husband. He was here but left without saying anything or telling her where he was going."

"I know where he went."

"Where?" asked Becca.

"Over here, at the foundation's offices. He paid me a courtesy visit. Apparently, he drove all the way from Devon to center city Philadelphia to read me a Bible verse."

"What?"

"Don't ask me what he said. I wasn't listening. Hold on for a minute, Becca." Becca could hear Kari speaking to someone. When she came back to the phone she said, "Scott just handed me a handwritten note from Cuddy Mullins."

"What does it say?" Becca waited while Kari read it.

"Apparently," said Kari, "it's the Bible verse he recited to me." Kari read a sentence out loud to Becca. "'They show that the work of the law is written on their hearts, while their conscience also bears witness, and their conflicting thoughts accuse or even excuse them.'"

"What's that supposed to mean? Why would he give that to you?"

"I have no idea," said Kari.

But Becca detected something in Kari's tone that made her wonder if Kari did understand the scripture's meaning. Or at least what it meant to her.

CHAPTER 19

"I executed a search yesterday, and afterward, the subject handed me a Bible quote."

Kari paused for a beat, waiting for Dr. Patel to react. But, as always, Nina Patel didn't prod her to continue. Her psychiatrist utilized the same interviewing techniques that the FBI used—do not respond and your subject would fill in the silence soon enough.

Thinking about the passage had kept her awake for three hours after she had gone to bed last night, and she was anxious to hear what Dr. Patel thought it meant. "I've been trying to decipher it, but I'm not sure what it means or why he gave it to me."

Even though by now she had read it so many times that she could recite it from memory, Kari reached into her pocket for the slip of paper Cuddy had given her and handed it to Dr. Patel, who quickly scanned it and then read part of it out loud. "'They show that the work of the law is written on their hearts, while their conscience also bears witness, and their conflicting thoughts accuse or even excuse them.'"

"So what do you think it means?"

"What do you think it means?"

Kari chuckled. "You're going to make me figure this out."

"Isn't that why you're here?"

"I guess it's about judgment and who has the right to pass judgment on another person." Kari let out an uneasy laugh. "That living in a glass house thing."

Dr. Patel simply nodded.

Kari took back the slip of paper and studied it some more. "The guy who gave it to me is supposed to be able to intuitively find the perfect spiritual messages for those who need to hear them," Kari said. "I don't know why he gave this one to me."

"Don't you?"

"Are you serious? You believe he chose this quote specifically for me?"

"I don't know if this guy has unique skills of observation. I'm not saying that. But the message does bring value to what you're going through and what we're doing here." Dr. Patel clasped her hands in her lap. "You've said many times that you're suffering from impostor syndrome, like someone's going to discover that you're a not-so-special special agent."

"Um, kind of freaky when you look at it that way." Kari stared at the piece of paper. "Accuse or excuse? You think this is referring to the shooting? I was cleared. They said it was justified."

"But you're still carrying around a tremendous amount of guilt about keeping the truth from the ones who care about you."

"And how would Cuddy Mullins know anything about that?"

Dr. Patel shrugged. "I think your reaction to the passage is an indication that, until you're honest with yourself and with your husband about what really happened, your recovery will continue to be delayed." She pointed to the slip of paper in Kari's hand. "I think that's what the Bible verse is saying, don't you?"

***

Kari entered the house from the side door, nearer to the driveway, and bumped into Kevin as he was about to take Auggie out for a walk.

"Surprise!" She gave the golden retriever a pat on the head and kissed her husband on the lips.

"Wow," said Kevin. "You're home early. The kids are over at the Myers', playing basketball in the backyard."

"I scheduled an appointment with Dr. Patel this afternoon and came home instead of going back to work. I figured, by the time I got there, it would be time to leave."

"I thought you saw Dr. Patel every other Thursday."

"I usually do, but I had something I wanted to talk to her about, and I didn't want to wait until next week." She dropped her purse on the kitchen counter, knelt next to Auggie, and scratched his big, hairy chest. "You guys heading out? I'll go with, check on the kids."

It was a beautiful late afternoon. The skies were that calming bluish-gray tint of the day just before dusk. Kari and Kevin strolled through their development of upper-middle-class homes of mostly manicured lawns and landscaped flower beds, stopping to chat with neighbors and remarking about who was and who was not keeping up with their yard work and chores. She knew she was the envy of most of her female neighbors because she had the amazingly fit, leading-man handsome, and rock-solid husband they wished they had. She was the lucky one—in so many ways.

"What did you need to talk to her about?" said Kevin.

"Huh?" She was perplexed. He was obviously continuing a conversation she had forgotten they were having.

"What was it you wanted to talk to your shrink about? The shootout or something new?"

"Something new, not a big deal."

"What was it?" He stopped and let the leash fall slack as Auggie inspected a section of grass. He stared at her as if to probe her innermost thoughts. "Do you talk about us during your sessions?"

"Sometimes, but not really. We're not having any problems." This time, she looked at Kevin. "Are we?"

"I think I'd be the last to know. There's so much about you that I feel I don't understand. Who really knows what you're talking about with your Dr. Patel?"

"What's that supposed to mean?" She spoke loudly and looked him in the eyes. Instantly, guilt caused her to lower her voice. "I tell you everything we discuss," she said softly.

"Do you? Really?"

"I wanted to talk to her about this." Kari took the Bible passage out and handed it to Kevin.

"I don't have my glasses on me."

"I don't have mine with me either." She took back the slip of paper and returned it to her pocket, hoping he would forget about it by the time they got home. "Just something the subject of my new case gave me. It's a verse from the Bible. I was hoping Dr. Patel could help me decipher its hidden meaning."

"It's from the Bible. How bad can it be? I hope she advised you not to let this guy mess with your head." He shook his head. "Every case you work seems to change you a little bit. You know how I feel about the FBI. I'm afraid one day you're going to walk through that door, and I won't recognize you anymore."

"Please don't. Not tonight."

"Okay, okay." He pointed at her pocket. "But that thing is bullshit. Why are you giving it a second thought?"

CHAPTER 20

Kari was fully aware that many of her FBI colleagues would rather stick needles in their eyes than have to go through file cabinets and bankers' boxes full of paper evidence. She chuckled when she thought about the dangerous aspects of being a white-collar crime agent—no bullet wounds or knife punctures here, but she did have to be extra careful of paper cuts.

This case was different from her other fraud and corruption assignments. First of all, she didn't have to go into the office every day. She liked the ease and autonomy of working the case out of the foundation's own office space. All the potential evidence had been left behind exactly where it had been the day the bankruptcy court closed the doors. Kari sat behind Cuddy Mullins's desk, in his chair, going through his personal files and belongings. She had been working for a couple of hours, and the most substantial information she had learned was that Cuddy Mullins really loved his little dog. In addition to toting him around to stress-producing proffers and searches, a little dog bed, water bowl, and chew toys were under the large mahogany desk, indicating that Cuddy also brought him to work on a frequent basis. That was only one of the things that was making her almost sympathetic to him. He was like no other con man she had encountered during her many years with the FBI. His victims were reluctant to be called victims, and his good deeds almost outweighed his bad. Almost.

Lennie and Tanya Adams had been among his first victims. All of the computerized records were with CART, the office computer analysis response team. Kari would have to wait until they had a chance to look at the hard drives that had been removed from Mullins and Tribble's CPU. But at the time, she was elbow deep in the paper files from desk drawers and file cabinets. One item she discovered, a burgundy Moleskine calendar marked with the dates Mullins had allegedly met with the anonymous donors, would perhaps play a significant evidentiary role in the investigation.

Kari's estimate was that the foundation had taken in approximately $450 million dollars and had distributed a good portion of that to nonprofits. How much of the money had been diverted to Cuddy's personal use was yet to be determined. Bryant Duffy had estimated that he would have an initial calculation prepared by the end of the week. She was relieved that the IRS agent had something to occupy his time and that she didn't have to deal with him directly.

Kari recalled how Mullins tried to convince her that he was a good guy and that this was all a misunderstanding. Yes, there were some troubling irregularities, but the old hard copy files were stuffed with documented tales of his good work, which bolstered his good-guy claims. She had to repeatedly remind herself that, in a Ponzi scheme, the earlier participants always made out well. It was those at the bottom of the pyramid who got squashed by the crushing weight of the scam.

She had taken all of the photos of Mullins with refugee children and the homeless, teaching the fundraising course, and being feted by the families of gun violence victims and the drug addicts he had counseled and had packed them away in a box and placed it in a storage closet. But she still had to deal with the framed awards on the walls and the beautiful letters of gratitude tucked within all of the files and records. When the investigation was complete, and the inevitable indictment made public, thousands of people would be shocked and forced to admit that Cuddy Mullins was no saint. All of the good had been financed by other people's money, and hundreds of nonprofits waiting for their funds to be matched were going to be left holding an empty bag. Cuddy still wasn't talking and nothing she had seen validated the existence of any anonymous donors. Kari looked up at a photo of Mullins receiving an award from former First Lady Michelle Obama, one of Kari's favorite people, and spoke. "Michelle, why don't you charm him into telling you why he did this? Why he created this charity charade?"

Kari drew in a deep breath and let it out in a heavy sigh. She got up, walked over to the photo, lifted it from the hook on the wall, and carried it to the storage closet, where she stuffed it into the box with all the other distracting, pro–Cuddy Mullins paraphernalia.

CHAPTER 21

Kari walked into the office of her former partner, Everett Hildebrand. Last year at this time, he had been suspended for unauthorized use of a Bureau laptop and for having an inappropriate relationship with an informant. Now, he was a member of the computer analysis recovery team. It's remarkable how, once you demonstrate your willingness to take a bullet for the Bureau, the title hero is thrust upon you and you can do no wrong. He had been in the shootout with Kari but had only fired his weapon once and his shot had not hit its target. She, on the other hand, had emptied her weapon into the subject but had steadfastly refused to wrap herself in the hero cloak of bravery and courage, even as Everett strutted around in his cape.

He looked up at her as she entered the room. "Good, you got my message." He walked over to a nearby table and, with his cotton-gloved hands, picked up a hard drive. "I hate to tell you this, but nothing's on it."

"What?" Kari pointed at the flat, metal box Everett was holding. "That's from the New Visions in Giving search?"

"Yeah. This came out of the office of the head guy." Everett picked up the evidence tag and read it. "This was taken out of Cuddy Mullins's CPU."

"This guy is killing me. Did someone wipe the drive clean or just swap out the one with the good stuff with a blank one?"

"The latter."

"We have another proffer scheduled with him and his attorneys tomorrow. He's still claiming it's all a big mismanagement issue," she smirked.

"Well, it looks like he could be guilty of manipulating evidence."

"Is it too late to send it down to the lab for fingerprints? If Whitmore wants to add an evidence tampering count, we'll need to eliminate other suspects and prove Cuddy was the only New Visions employee who accessed the hard drive."

"Yeah. I'd try it. It's not like the process is going to ruin it. Nothing's on it to muck up."

"Sign off on the chain of custody. I'll FedEx it down to HQ today." After Everett signed the form to release the evidence, she signed the hard drive back into her custody.

"Here." Everett handed her another chain-of-custody form to sign. "This is the data downloaded from…" he read the name listed on the inventory before handing her a USB flash drive sealed in a clear evidence envelope. "From the CPU in the office of Melinda Tribble. This is the CART original, and this"—he placed another flash drive in her palm—"is a virus scanned copy you can peruse. Let me know if you find what you're looking for."

Kari tossed the tiny, black device from one hand to the other and hoped that the anonymous donor list was on it. It was frustrating to have to investigate the legitimacy of a list she had yet to view.

"How's the case otherwise? It's getting a lot of press. Four hundred and fifty million dollars—that's a lot of gullible people."

"The subject, Cuddy Mullins, is a charismatic guy. You would probably like him if you met him before the whole thing came tumbling down."

"Why do you say that?"

"He's a spiritual savant."

"A what?"

"He has this thing he does where he can look at a person and find the perfect Bible verse that fits their life situation." Kari wondered for moment if calling him a savant was a stretch. But he claimed to have a gift, and, in her case, he had indeed selected for her a scripture that had meaning.

"Sounds like a routine perfect for America's Got Talent. They should book him on it."

"It's not like that."

"Really? How do you know?"

Kari slipped her fingers behind the leather cover of her credentials, pulled out the piece of paper, and handed it to Everett. "He gave me one. I thought about showing it to you right away, but, you know, we agreed never to talk about it."

An uneasiness crossed Everett's face. He hesitated before accepting the passage. "What does this have to do with—"

"Just read it."

Everett read it to himself and then read it out loud quietly, almost in a whisper. "'They show that the work of the law is written on their hearts, while their conscience also bears witness, and their conflicting thoughts accuse or even excuse them.'" Recognition grew in Everett's eyes.

"Does it mean something to you?"

"It's from Romans 2. God's Righteous Judgment and the Law." He moved over to his computer, where he typed something into the Google search box. "My ward leader directed me to several passages after the shootout." He held up the sticky note from Cuddy. "This was one of them."

Kari stood behind Everett and looked over his shoulder at the computer screen. A website called Bible Gateway was on the screen. He entered the words Romans 2 into the site's search bar and clicked the mouse.

Kari read the passage out loud. "'Therefore you are inexcusable, O man, whoever you are who judge, for in whatever you judge another you condemn yourself; for you who judge practice the same things.'"

He walked over to his office door and closed it. "Kari, I don't think we should be talking about this."

"Can we go somewhere away from the building so we can try and figure this out?"

"No," he snapped and then immediately said, in a softer tone, "we had an agreement."

He was right. He had already done so much for her. He had had her back. Kari nodded and picked up the piece of paper and tucked it back in her pants pocket.

Everett stared at her apologetically for a beat, turned away to pick up the evidence envelope containing the hard drive, and handed it to her. Then, he reached past her to open the door. "Good luck with the fingerprints. I hope you get a positive hit."

As she scooted past him through the doorway, he said, "My life is really good now. I wish you the same."

She nodded and walked away without looking back at him. She wished she could have the peace he had. She would keep going to counseling until, one day, maybe she would be able to live with her guilt. The shooting review team had deemed it a good shooting, clearly self-defense. She and Everett had done what needed to be done to protect themselves and to save the lives of everyone who had been caught in the crossfire.

So why wasn't she able to move on?

CHAPTER 22

Kari couldn't contain her curiosity. As soon as she returned to her squad area, she inserted the flash drive Everett had provided into her CPU and began to scan the files. The 32 GBs of data captured four years of correspondence, presentations, forms, and general financial records for the Foundation for New Visions in Giving, starting from its inception to the day the doors were shuttered.

Kari began her alphabetical review in the A section and wasn't surprised when she didn't find a file for anonymous donors listed. She chuckled to herself. Maybe when she got to the S's, she would find it under super-secret anonymous donor list. Hunched over her computer screen, she continued her review and after a couple of hours somewhere during the L files, her back had begun to ache. With her eyes still on her monitor, she did a series of shoulder rolls and stretched her neck from side to side. Her gaze settled on a file simply labeled List. Kari skipped the other L folders above it and clicked.

"Oh shit." Kari's hands flew to her opened mouth. Neatly typed and underlined at the top of the page were the words Anonymous Donor List. The list contained 9 names, the only name on the list that she recognized was Sir Alistair Middleton.

She may have allowed Cuddy Mullins to get inside her head, but now she would finally have the full picture about his so-called anonymous donors and would be able to dissect his lies. She straightened up and sat back in her chair. She thought: *Now we're getting somewhere.*

CHAPTER 23

Roger LaMott used his right thumb and forefinger to mimic the shape of a gun and placed it next to his right temple. "Even if you took out your gun and held it to my head, you couldn't make me say that the anonymous donors are not real. Why is it so hard to believe that a wealthy philanthropist would be willing to give away substantial gifts without wanting the whole world to know about it?"

Kari, a little unnerved by his gesture, waved her hand in a downward motion, and he removed the imaginary weapon from his head. "Let me be clear," she said, "I'm not trying to make you say anything you don't believe."

"I was just making a point," said LaMott. "That's how much I believe in the Foundation for New Visions in Giving and Cuddy Mullins. I would bet my life on him."

"I will note your adamant declaration of confidence and support for Mr. Mullins," she said with a touch of sarcasm.

"Cuddy Mullins is a good man doing God's—"

"God's work. I've heard that. Have you been reading the *Inquirer*?"

"About the bankruptcy? Of course they're bankrupt. With all the negative media, who's going to contribute? All of this has destroyed their cause."

"All this? New Visions would have collapsed even if the FBI had never heard of them. All Ponzi schemes eventually die—there's not enough money in the universe to keep them going."

"New Visions is not a Ponzi scheme."

"The bankruptcy filings show that New Visions was nearly two hundred million in debt before the investigation began," said Becca.

"I'm sure there's an explanation…" he trailed off.

"What has he told you?"

"I haven't been able to reach him."

Kari gave a sympathetic shrug and genuinely felt sorry for LaMott. He was a member of the board of trustees for the Pennsylvania Library of Fine Arts and was one of the many pillars of the community who had introduced Mullins to a number of Philadelphia-area nonprofits— he was as gullible as all the other victims. He supported Mullins 100 percent.

"You do understand that when the average person reads about this case in the newspaper, they immediately see something that's too good to be true. And you know what they say about things that are too good to be true."

"But those people don't know Cuddy. Did you know he wanted to be a priest? He's so good at what he does. He knows and understands the word of God better than any ordained minister. It's a shame he didn't get the opportunity to bring spiritual and religious strength to a congregation."

Becca nodded. "We heard he held weekly Bible study breakfasts."

"He did indeed." LaMott smiled enthusiastically. "He's an evangelist for the Lord, providing healing for the world."

"Let me ask you this question," said Kari as she slid a list of names across to his side of the table. "Take a look. As you can see, your name appears on a document allegedly prepared by Cuddy Mullins titled 'Anonymous donor list' with the subtitle 'Confidential, anonymous participatory philanthropist.'"

LaMott slowly picked up the document and stared at it. He said nothing, but his brow furrowed with concern and his face turned bloodless.

"Did you ever provide New Visions with undesignated and unrestricted donations for them to use as matching funds?"

"No, never," he said. He looked pleadingly from Kari to Becca. "Where did you get this?"

"Did Cuddy Mullins or any member of his staff request that you make a monetary gift to be used by the foundation anyway they saw fit?"

"No. Where did you say you got this list? There must be an explanation for my name being listed here."

"That's why we're here." Kari smiled. "Cuddy Mullins and his Foundation for New Visions in Giving represented to philanthropists and charitable organizations that anonymous donors were providing money to be matched dollar for dollar with funds raised by those charitable organizations. The best way to establish that this was not a Ponzi scheme is to prove that the anonymous donors exist."

"Did you ask Cuddy?" His voice cracked, and distress was clearly visible in his trembling jaw and moist eyes. "Did he give you this list?"

Kari shook her head and pointed to the paper LaMott was holding. "That list of names was found during the search of New Visions' offices. Do you have any idea how or why your name appears on it?"

"No. But there must be a simple explanation." He removed his glasses and used the knuckle of his forefinger to wipe away a tear.

"Again, that's why we're here. To find that explanation."

"I recognize a few of the names on this list." He took a pen from the inside pocket of his blazer. "Can I write on this?"

"Yes, please."

"Sir Alistair Middleton, of course, is an anonymous donor," he said and placed a check mark next to his name.

"Why do you say 'of course.' Why are you so sure of that?"

"Several of us have spoken to Sir Middleton's personal assistant. She confirmed to us that he was one of the anonymous donors."

"What's her name?"

"I don't remember, but if I remember it, I'll be sure to get back to you."

Kari tapped her finger on the list of names on the table in front of them. "Let's go over the rest of the folks on this list. As far as you know, are all of the people here anonymous donors?"

"Cuddy never said it straight out, but I always believed that Thaddeus Baker and Morrison Mindermann were anonymous donors too." He let out a soft whistle. "And these guys too," he said.

Kari watched as he soberly checked off the names of Vivian Periwinkle and Thomas Hightower. He looked as if he had been let in on a secret. "You understand of course," she said, "if your name appears on this list and you're not one of the anonymous donors, it is more likely than not that the other people whose names appear on this list are not anonymous donors either."

Kari watched as LaMott contemplated her statement. A sickening awareness seemed to envelop him as he leaned over and clutched his stomach. He sat back in his chair and let the pen roll from his fingers onto the table.

"I delivered so many people to the foundation. I told them to trust him and his matching-funds concept. And it wasn't a trick. It wasn't all smoke and mirrors. We had the previous successes to rely on. To build on."

Becca nodded. "Credibility is contagious. It's easy to understand why everyone wanted to believe."

"If you don't mind, we'd like to ask you some detailed questions about your interactions with Mr. Mullins and New Visions." Kari took out her pen and notepad. She pulled a document from her leather tote bag. "I want to go through this victim questionnaire but feel free to expand on anything I ask."

"I can't. Not right now. If the anonymous donors don't exist"— overcome with emotion he croaked out the words in a halting voice— "I need to hear it straight from Cuddy Mullins's lips."

Kari and Becca sat silently as Roger LaMott struggled and failed to calm himself. He looked at them with tears running down his face. He covered his mouth with his fist and shook his head. He began to sob and was so distraught that he barely acknowledged when they gathered up their belongings. They informed him that they would reschedule their interview for a time when he was able to compose himself. Kari was sure he would see things differently the next time they met.

At the elevator, Kari looked back in the direction of Roger LaMott's office. "I'm afraid to just leave him in there like that. Remember, he told us he would bet his life on Cuddy Mullins's innocence and the existence of the anonymous donors."

Becca formed her fingers into an imaginary gun just as LaMott had done at the beginning of the interview. "I seriously hope he doesn't own a real one of these."

CHAPTER 24

Olivia Flemings, the PR guru that Cuddy's attorney had insisted they retain, was a strikingly beautiful former news reporter who marketed herself as a "scandal whisperer" similar to the Olivia Pope character on *Scandal*, a TV show CeCe still loved to watch on demand.

"Cuddy, CeCe, let me introduce to you Olivia Flemings." Jillian grinned and paused as if she expected them to applaud. "She is an expert in crisis management and brand perception management. She's here to help us formulate a strategy."

CeCe, who was sitting next to Cuddy on the love seat in their living room, was grinning and obviously impressed with Olivia Flemings's beautifully packaged image before she had said a word. Cuddy knew Olivia's designer outfit and accessories, coiffed hair, and flawless makeup, represented exactly who CeCe wanted to be. He wondered if Olivia was really her first name or her personal gimmick to capitalize on the free advertising the reference to the show *Scandal* provided.

"Thank you for inviting me to your lovely home," said Olivia. She placed a laptop on the coffee table and angled it so they could see the first slide of her presentation. "Let's get right to it, shall we? The first thing I did was look at the Foundation for New Visions in Giving's Facebook page and Twitter. Posting on these platforms will allow us an opportunity to reach out to your followers, the people who believed in you and the wonderful work you were doing. We'll address them directly." She moved the cursor on her laptop, and stepped back so they could view a split screen of the foundation's social media pages. "The first thing that we must have you do is a Facebook Live video explaining what's happening from our point of view. No more having our thoughts filtered through the negative news media."

"Why live?" asked Cuddy. Just thinking about all of the things that could go wrong made him start to sweat. "Couldn't we just record a video and post it?"

"Your friends and followers haven't heard anything from you in the past few months. It will be more engaging and appear like you're being honest and transparent if we do it live."

"Why did you say *appear like* I'm being honest?" said Cuddy. "If you want me to go on to lie, I'm not interested in doing that. I've already hurt them enough."

Jillian interrupted, taking over the explanation of the live session. "That's not what we want. No lies, but during the session you may not be able to answer all of their questions. We'll help you prepare your responses to their comments," she said.

"Their comments?" Cuddy gave her a quizzical look.

"Yes. With Facebook Live, viewers will be able to submit comments in real time," said Jillian. "We will get through this. It will also be our chance to assess what potential witnesses will say if this goes to trial."

Although he immediately connected to her use of we and our, indicating that she truly was on his side, Cuddy wasn't sold on the idea. He ran his fingers through his hair and let out a loud breath. "I'm not confessing on Facebook."

"Of course not." Jillian addressed Olivia. "Why don't you continue. Explain that's not your plan."

"Not at all. But they haven't yet heard directly from you, Cuddy." She clicked to the next slide showing numerous newspaper headlines. "That's the other side's version. We're going to give them your version of what happened."

"Okay, what is my version?" asked Cuddy. "Jillian believes the feds are going to charge me with money laundering, mail and wire fraud, and tax evasion. How can you make that look good?"

"What the people don't know is why. People care much more about why you did something than they do about what it was you did. If you explain it well enough, then they will forgive you."

"I want their forgiveness, but I also seek forgiveness from God."

Olivia clapped her hands loudly and shrieked, "Yes," startling everyone in the room. "That's our message." She beamed and nodded as if they were all in agreement, but Cuddy had no idea what she was talking about.

"The reason you created the Foundation for New Visions in Giving was your commitment to God. And the reason that the concept of participatory giving was… mismanaged was because of your commitment to God." She moved to where Cuddy was sitting and leaned in close enough for him to smell her lightly applied perfume. She spoke deliberately and convincingly. "Your desire to help others in need, to do God's work, consumed you to the point of recklessness. To the point of delusion."

Cuddy looked around the room at the other attorneys, who were nodding their heads in agreement.

Jillian Stevens slowly began to nod. "I think that could work. We could tell them how you carry around the Bible and do that reciting-scripture thing."

Olivia noticed that Cuddy was holding a Bible. She knelt down in front of him and drummed her fingers on the cover and, after a beat, clapped again. "This is just too good," she said. "I didn't even know about this prop. We could say you're a Christian with unchecked religious fervor. How can anyone fault you for your devotion to God?"

Jillian rose from her seat and placed her hands on Olivia's shoulders. "Brilliant. Yes, a religious zealot. It's even a highly plausible defense."

"Whoa. Whoa." Cuddy stomped a foot and folded his arms. "Reading Bible verses is not a party trick. And I'm not a religious zealot." Cuddy held his Bible in his hand and placed it over his heart.

"I'm not going to make a joke out of my connection to God."

Olivia started to explain, but Jillian held up her hand. "I apologize, Cuddy. We mean no disrespect." She perched on the edge of her chair and leaned forward to pat him on his leg. "All we're really planning to do is have you share your truth, in your own words, with our help."

"You mean like a sermon?"

"Exactly," said Olivia. "It will be exactly like you're giving a sermon to your flock."

"I've missed putting together my weekly breakfast Bible study messages. Maybe I could start doing that on Facebook Live." He cast his eyes around the room but didn't get the response he hoped for.

"Let's not get ahead of ourselves. Let's first see how our initial message is received," said Jillian.

"Cuddy, I think we should get you a psychological evaluation. It would be helpful to have an expert testify in court on your behalf." Jillian turned to her legal assistant. "Jonathan, I'm assigning that task to you. Find us the best expert witness on religious zealots."

"I think we have a solid plan," said Olivia. "Don't you?"

CeCe laid her hand on his sleeve and nodded enthusiastically for them both.

"I apologize for the cavalier way we presented this defense. But you yourself just said that all of this to you was God's work. We understand your religious commitment, and we will present this defense in a reverential way. We'll need to get to work making sure the general public and the potential jury pool and witnesses know that too. That's all we're saying here. Okay?"

Cuddy took in a deep breath. "Okay."

"Perfect." Jillian reached over and patted the Bible. "We're going to make sure everyone knows about your heart, what motivates and inspires you, and how absolutely heartbroken you are that things didn't turn out the way you hoped they would."

Cuddy once again took in a deep breath. He exhaled slowly, feeling a calm take over. He felt like they understood him, that for the first time since things had crumbled beneath his feet, someone was helping him find stability. He struggled to hold back tears of relief.

"We've got your back, Cuddy. We're gonna do our very best for you." Jillian opened her binder and clicked her pen. "Okay, Olivia. I guess the first thing we need to do before we create a script for our Facebook Live campaign is to talk about our goals. What we want your supporters—"

"My former supporters," said Cuddy.

His new PR guru patted him on the shoulder. "We're going to want them to see the real you, we'll film you sitting in your favorite chair or perhaps at the kitchen table."

"How about in the atrium?" said Cuddy.

"Yes, that's a great idea. And when it's appropriate," Olivia continued, "I'm going to need you to flash that big, beautiful smile of yours. It invites trust."

On cue, he grinned at the compliment.

Jillian nodded. "There you go. Let's get started."

***

Kari motioned to Becca to look at her computer screen. "Right there. See what I mean? Doesn't it seem like he's blaming the Foundation for New Visions in Giving staff? You can't expect anyone to be okay with you ripping off $450 million. What is wrong with that guy?"

"Weren't you listening?" said Becca. "He's a religious zealot, crazy with a burning desire to do God's work."

Kari and Becca had missed the actual live performance a few hours earlier but heard from several victims that the Facebook Live video had been posted and was available for replay. They had watched it three times in a row.

"Jesus Christ," said Becca. "Look at the number of likes, hearts, and shares the video has already generated."

"Nearly three hundred in less than an afternoon? You've got to be kidding?" Kari moved the cursor to the comments. "Let's see who isn't buying his BS. Maybe we can discover a few witnesses willing to say something negative about him."

She scanned the posts listed under the real-time comments.

Becca groaned. "Ugh. Look at all those people weighing in."

"Let's get an analyst assigned to review the comments and see if there's anything relevant to our case among them. You never know."

"Good idea." Kari scrolled through a few more comments and then stopped. "You want to watch the video again?"

"Sure. I can't get enough of it."

Kari hit the play button, and Cuddy Mullins's mug appeared on the screen again. In his lap was his little, white terrier. During the video, he stroked the puppy's fur with a steady and loving touch.

"I accept full responsibility for what has happened. I was the engineer in the lead car when this train derailed and jumped the track. And for that, I am truly sorry."

"Great metaphor," said Kari. "That damn train wreck just about killed and maimed every person and nonprofit on board with him."

"I appreciate the kind words of encouragement that many of you have sent me. I wish I could return all of your calls and emails, but my attorneys have advised me to instead reach out to you through this medium. So I'm here with my little buddy Hairy Potter to answer your questions and hopefully relieve some of your concerns."

"I have to admit, the dog was a good idea," said Becca. "Who doesn't trust a man who loves his little doggie?" The video continued playing.

"The first thing that I must say to you all is that I never meant to hurt you. From the very beginning, my vision was to change the world for the glory of God. I believed creating the Foundation for New Visions in Giving as a vehicle for increasing charitable donations was my life's calling. I know you've already read and heard the foundation has ceased operations, but I thought it was important that you hear directly from me. The concept of participatory philanthropy was my greatest contribution to the world of charitable giving. Unfortunately, I took that idea but did not develop a platform strong enough to propel it forward. I guess you could say I'm an

idea guy not skilled in administration, not educated in management. I depended on others to develop those mechanisms, and in my doing so, I failed you."

Even though Cuddy's speech continued for at least four more minutes, Kari hit the pause button. Cuddy and Potter remained frozen on the screen. "I've changed my mind," she said. "I don't want to listen to him again. There's no mention of the non-existing anonymous donors or that his foundation was a big, fat fraud."

Becca leaned back into her chair and nodded in agreement.

Kari pointed at the monitor. "That wasn't a confession. It was a commercial."

CHAPTER 25

Kari escorted Nicholas McCullough, the Foundation for New Visions in Giving's accountant, into the small interview room where Special Agent Bryant Duffy was already waiting with his financial files stacked neatly on the table to his left and a notepad and pen directly in front of his clasped hands. He rose to greet them.

"I'm Special Agent Bryant Duffy. Thank you for coming in today." He shook hands with the witness and directed him to take a seat on the opposite side of the table. "I'm with the IRS." Duffy held out his credentials in order for McCullough to get a good look.

"Oh." Lines of apprehension creased McCullough's forehead. Kari had not mentioned that the IRS would also be present when she'd called to schedule the interview. Her pre-interview research had revealed that McCullough was a former SEC insider who had once served in the securities enforcement practice group. No wonder he seemed nervous. Even if he was unaware of the fraud statutes he knew the financial tax rules, and the consequences of breaking them.

"Thank you for traveling to Philadelphia to speak with us, Mr. McCullough," Kari said as she took a seat next to Duffy and across from McCullough. "We appreciate you making the trip, but we were more than willing to drive to Bethlehem to meet with you."

"I'm here a couple of times a month. My ex and our kids live in Northeast Philly." McCullough's eyes darted around the room.

"What took you out to Bethlehem?" She wanted to make him feel more at ease before they began the actual interview and hoped a few minutes of small talk would help.

"I grew up in Philly, but my parents were originally from out that way. They moved back after I left for college. Anyway, I had always dreamed of owning a farm and horse ranch. After I started working full-time for New Visions, Cuddy said I could crunch numbers from wherever I was and encouraged me to find a place and buy it. When I found the perfect property in Bethlehem, he let me telecommute. My parents are elderly now. They live with me. But I have a home healthcare nurse come in to help."

"Nice," she said. She would need to find out more about his place in the country. Especially where he got the money to buy it. She wished she had insisted on going out to see him and knew she hadn't only because she didn't want to be stuck in a car with Duffy for an hour.

Kari swiveled slightly in her chair and placed her hand on the stack of documents on the table. "Agent Duffy and I have been reviewing the Foundation for New Visions in Giving's records. We understand that you're the foundation's chief financial officer."

"Who told you that? I'm not the CFO. I'm just the guy who balances the books." McCullough laughed uneasily. "I started working with Cuddy years ago when he was running a substance abuse clinic in Kensington. You know, both his and his wife's families had major drug problems. I admired what he was doing in the community and offered to help him fill in the financial section of his grant proposals."

"As a volunteer?"

McCullough nodded.

"Where were you employed at the time?" she asked.

"I worked for a large accounting firm for several years. I'm a CPA. And then, for a brief period, about eighteen months, in the SEC's securities enforcement practice group."

"Really?" she said, not divulging she was already aware of his resume.

"I left there to come work full-time for the foundation."

"Take us through how your role at New Visions changed over the years," Duffy said.

"I first met Cuddy twelve years ago, that's when I started volunteering for his nonprofit. And based on his command and technical knowledge of the charitable community, five years later, he began sharing those skills with nonprofits through his groundbreaking fundraising symposiums."

"The ones funded by Sir Alistair Middleton?"

McCullough nodded. "Yes. That's when I started being paid for my services, a modest payment from Sir Middleton's grant. And then four years after that, Cuddy expanded the program from teaching nonprofits how to fundraise to actually providing funding from..." McCullough's voice trailed off.

"From?" Duffy circled a hand to encourage McCullough to finish his sentence.

"From anonymous donors," McCullough said, his tone sounding slightly defiant. "I understand from the news that you guys are saying they never existed, but I wouldn't know anything about that. I don't know who they are, and I've never met any of them."

"Did you ask Cuddy about them?" Kari asked.

"No." McCullough paused and gave her and Duffy a perplexed look. "They were called the *anonymous* donors."

"When did Cuddy Mullins first tell you about them? Were you volunteering at the substance abuse clinic or was this the Middleton Symposium time period?" asked Kari.

"The symposium. One day, about three or four years ago, Cuddy told me that he had been introduced to several wealthy donors who wished to remain anonymous. He said that based on his reputation as a fundraiser, those benefactors trusted him to use their funds to match worthy causes."

Agent Duffy tapped his pen on the metal table's surface. "And you believed him?"

"I didn't have any reason not to. I saw the money come in—there were several fifteen thousand dollars checks. Plus, he knew Sir Alistair Middleton. I assumed he was the one who had made the introductions."

Duffy shook his head in disbelief. "Mr. McCullough, didn't you just tell us you're a CPA?

"Yes."

"Well, so am I, and I believe you owed your clients a tenacious examination of this anonymous donors' claim."

"My client was Cuddy Mullins and the Foundation for New Visions in Giving. I asked all the questions I needed to know." McCullough began to move his hands in front of him in a wave-like motion. "I saw the money flow in, and I saw it flow out to hundreds of worthy organizations."

"There were lots of irregularities you obviously didn't see. You may have worked for the foundation—which by the way was never a real foundation with a permanent endowment—but as a CPA, you seemed to miss a lot of red flags, huge, waving in the wind, red Ponzi scheme flags. And the fact that you did not see what was flapping right in front of your face makes you a possible accomplice or, at the least, a disgrace to the profession."

McCullough's face turned bright red, and Kari saw a vein on the side of his neck start to throb. "An accomplice?" he sputtered.

Duffy began to spread out on the table a number of spreadsheets and investment documents he had not bothered to share with Kari. She was tempted to suggest that they step out of the room, so she could find out what they represented. Instead, she took one from the stack and scanned it.

"Mr. McCullough, what exactly happens to the funds donated and held by New Visions before they're matched?" Duffy used his finger to direct the accountant's attention to one of the investment statements. "Were you also handling the foundation's investment portfolios?"

"Yes. I have my Series 6 license."

"It sounds like you wore many hats at New Visions. You said you weren't the CFO. What was your official title?" Kari said.

"I was financial adviser slash"—McCullough made a cutting gesture with his hand—"broker, but I take…er, took care of numerous finance needs. I accepted sales orders for stock; I recommended mutual funds, and purchased equities and annuities. New Vision's operational expenses were generated from interest earned from those investments. I was very successful. I'm considered one of the county's most profitable brokers."

"In Bethlehem?" said Duffy with a smirk.

McCullough's face closed down and his bravado deflated for a beat, but he rebounded quickly. "Yes, in Bethlehem," he replied.

Silence descended until Kari spoke up. "It's always fulfilling to be proclaimed best among your peers," she said, pretending that Duffy had not insulted him. "I'm sure your colleagues and family are very proud of you and your accomplishments."

"Thank you." He sat up a little taller. "I was actually honored at the Knights of Columbus's awards banquet last June. It was a wonderful event."

"I'm sure it was," Duffy said. "When Mullins asked you to be all things financial for the 'foundation'"—he made air quotes with his fingers—"why you?"

"I assumed he thought I had earned the position. I had been volunteering my services for years, and I believed in his mission. He claimed that other accounting and brokerage firms would be too impersonal, too cold and officious."

"How did he describe the purpose of his new foundation to you?" asked Kari.

"Just as the name indicates, he said it was a new vision of philanthropy. An opportunity to… Let me think for a moment." McCullough paused and gazed up at the ceiling as if the answer were there. "An opportunity for donors to participate in giving. He called it 'participatory philanthropy.'"

"What did that exactly mean to you?"

"It was a new term for me, but I came to learn that it was basically a matching program. The same type of matching program that many businesses and corporations offer to their employees."

"And how did that work?"

"It was brilliantly simple. A donor would pledge a certain amount to donate to his or her favorite cause, and Cuddy would have their donation matched."

"And the matching funds came from…?"

"The anonymous donors," McCullough said as if the existence of the anonymous donors was not in debate.

Kari nodded. "Have you ever met any of them? Do you know who they are?"

"The only one I know for sure is Sir Alistair Middleton. I have my guesses about the others."

"And how do you know that Sir Middleton is one of the anonymous donors? Did Cuddy Mullins tell you that?" asked Kari.

"Not directly. But I know he was on the board of directors of Middleton Symposium."

"Have you ever actually spoken to Sir Middleton about him being an anonymous donor?"

"No, never. But I did speak with his special assistant over the phone. She had a British accent. I can't remember her name."

"And she confirmed to you that Sir Middleton was one of the nine anonymous donors?"

"Nine? There are nine of them now? I heard more had signed on, but during the time I spoke to Middleton's assistant, there were only six."

"And did Cuddy Mullins tell you who the others were?"

He shook his head. "But I always thought that Marian Feinstein might be one."

"Did he tell you that?"

McCullough shook his head. "Not exactly, but Feinstein and Middleton both share the same Judeo-Christian philosophy and often pool their wealth to support philanthropic projects."

"What you mean by 'not exactly'? Did Cuddy Mullins tell you that Marian Feinstein was one of the anonymous donors or not?" Duffy's frustration was palpable.

"He mentioned her name and Middleton's name together all the time. But no, he never told me that either Marian Feinstein or Sir Middleton was an anonymous donor."

"Anonymous donors," said Duffy with a smirk.

"Yes. Anonymous donors."

"Mr. McCullough," said Kari, "I think we're gonna be here for most of the day. We have a lot of things to discuss. Can I get you some water and some coffee?"

"A bottle of water sounds great, and if you don't mind, can I take off my jacket? It's warm in here."

"Please do. I'm gonna make myself comfortable too." Kari stood up, slipped off her jacket, and hung it on the back of her chair. "One of the things I'm really interested in learning more about is the escrow account and how the foundation utilized accrued interest. I'm gonna go get us some waters, and when I get back, we can dig in."

"Sure. I'll flip through these documents"—he glanced over to Duffy for permission before he pulled the spreadsheets closer to him—"and refresh my memory while you're gone." Kari stood and opened the door.

Duffy called after her. "You didn't ask me what I want. Can you bring me back a cup of coffee?"

"I tell you what—come with." She beckoned to him with her finger. "I'll need help carrying everything, and there are a few things I want to go over with you. Mr. McCullough, could you excuse us for a few minutes?"

She let Duffy walk out ahead of her, and before she shut the door, she tucked her head into the room and gave McCullough a smile, "You're doing great. Just tell the truth, and everything will work out fine."

He swallowed hard and returned a forced smile. They both knew that in reality, things would probably not end well. He would have to pay for his blind loyalty.

***

After Kari's lecture during their coffee run about being snarky, Duffy had managed to keep his sarcasm and contempt in check and the rest of the interview went smoothly. Their interview lasted six hours, which included a thirty-minute break for lunch in the cafeteria on the second floor of the federal building. But now that McCullough was gone, the old Duffy was back.

"I'll dictate my notes from the interview," Kari said. "When I get the rough draft back from the transcription service, I'll make the corrections, and you can review it before I finalize. This one could end up being twenty pages long."

"Twenty pages?" Duffy held up his notebook. "I got, at the most, four pages of notes."

"Yeah, I noticed that. That's why I want to write up the interview."

"Knock yourself out, sweetheart."

"I am not your sweetheart."

He looked at her as if he wanted to start something. "That reminds me. What's up with your girl Becca?"

"I advise you not to call her sweetheart either."

"No seriously, what's her deal?"

Kari gathered up her papers and tapped the bottom edges on the table until they were neatly stacked. She glanced up at him. "Are we done here?"

"Yeah, we're done."

"Good. I'm going to go brief Becca on what we learned from McCullough."

"You want me to stay and help you go over everything with her?"

"No. I got it."

"So, I'm being dismissed? Just like that? I thought we were a team."

"I'll brief her and let her know what she missed."

"We did good, just the two of us. Who knew you could do an interview without having to hold Becca's hand?"

"Excuse me?" said Kari, fully aware that he was insinuating they were more than just partners on the job. When he raised his hands signaling his innocence, she sighed loudly. "Never mind." She picked up the files on the table. "You know the way out. See you later."

"Let me ask you a question." He didn't wait for her response or permission. "You're married, right?"

She showed him the ring on her left hand.

"Just curious, you and Becca seem very close—you know, like really good friends."

"What are you asking me?"

"You know. Is she gay?"

"Why is that any of your business?" She felt blood rushing to her face as she grew hot with anger. "Seriously, why do you always have to be such a prick?'

"Me?" He chuckled to himself and headed out, turning back just before he crossed the threshold. "I can understand why that would be a problem for you. My guess is that neither you nor Becca like pricks."

Kari was barely able to stop herself from flinging her notebook at the back of his head. "Go to hell, Duffy," she snapped. The only way this was going to work was for them to divide up the interviews. She refused to be alone with him ever again.

CHAPTER 26

Cuddy watched his wife with indifference and weariness. She sat at her dressing table and with a practiced motion, pinned and weaved blond extensions in with her own hair. She wore the extensions no matter where she was going because she thought the extra volume made her look like all the women she admired on TV, always camera ready. He knew her beauty regimen would also dictate that a layer of foundation be applied, then powder, blush, eyebrow pencil, and whatever other makeup she wore every day. CeCe believed that, without these embellishments, she looked like the skinny, white-trash girl she used to be. It was the same routine every day. She never left the house without her mask.

The prettiness of the little woman-child he had met more than twenty years ago and had immediately determined he would rescue had initially been disguised by the dull pallor of her skin, her waiflike body, and her thin, stringy hair, all the result of being raised on a steady diet of soft pretzels and Tastykakes washed down by cans of orange soda and Yoo-hoo. CeCe came from a long line of Walmart beauties and had to overcompensate for generations of poor nutrition. That's why, when they met, he was attracted first to her vulnerability before he noticed that she was, indeed, a beautiful, young woman too.

What he feared the most was CeCe losing confidence in his ability to protect her. Having grown up in a dilapidated row house near

Kensington and Allegheny that smelled like cat piss, even though during the time they lived in their place her family never owned any cats, she was aware early on that she was on the bottom rung of life, which has significant implications for someone from K & A. And although she had fierce survival skills, she was conditioned to react instead of strategize. CeCe and her younger brother, Kurt, had been raised by her single-parent mother. The identity of her father was anybody's guess. Her mother earned money any way she could. Nothing was too demeaning for her to do to support her kids. Nothing. And when their mother thought they were old enough to take care of themselves, she succumbed to a life of drugs and alcohol to forget all the unimaginable things she had done to keep food on the table when they were younger. Cuddy vowed to take CeCe as far away as possible from that life. And he had done that—but at what cost?

He stood in the middle of the bedroom with his hands in his pockets. His attorneys had called and asked them to come in for another planning meeting.

As if she could tell what he was thinking, CeCe spoke to his reflection in the mirror. "I don't understand why I need to go to this meeting. "

"Jillian said she needed to speak with you."

"Why can't they come here again?"

"They came to the house for the public relations meeting only because Olivia wanted to film the Facebook Live video from our home.

"But why do I need to go? I didn't have anything to do with the foundation's business. Didn't you tell them that?" She pushed back from the dressing table and, without waiting for him to answer her, entered her walk-in closet.

"Jillian didn't say why," he said, raising his voice so she could hear him. "And I didn't ask because I didn't think it would be a problem." *Maybe they want you there because I'm your husband and need your emotional support,* he thought. "All I know is that the legal team wants to speak with us both and then we're going over to the United States

Attorney's office to meet with prosecutors and the FBI again."

She came back out with a selection from the blue section of her closet.

"Everyone in the room will have a college education except me," she said wistfully, as she held a navy-blue dress in front of her and admired her reflection in the mirror. "I think this Donna Karan dress and matching jacket will convey that I'm a prosperous professional just like them."

"No one there will be judging you."

"Really? Seems to me lately everybody is judging us. I saw those comments on Facebook. People who were supposed to be our friends are starting to turn their backs on us," she said.

"We still have lots of supporters. But the people you're talking about were never friends."

"Yes, they were. They made contributions to the foundation. They invited us to all of their events. We were in their homes."

"CeCe, they were using me just as much as we were using them."

"Using them? Why would you say that?" Her eyes widened with indignation. "And anyway, no one's returning my phone calls, and when I went over to the Union league for lunch today and sat down with the ladies who lunch, they all ate quickly, made excuses, and left as soon as they were finished."

"The news is full of reports about the bankruptcy." He sat on his side of the bed and lowered his head into his hands. He could feel his facade of strength cracking. "And the FBI is running around town interviewing everyone."

"What about loyalty? What about being innocent until proven guilty?"

At that moment, he couldn't hold back his emotions. He bit his lip and closed his eyes for a moment, picturing the effect of what he was about to reveal. He whispered it first: "But I am guilty." He felt instant relief, so he said it again. This time loud enough for CeCe to hear. "I am guilty."

He raised his head and turned to look at her. At first, she just stared at him. And then she got up and walked around the bed, staring down with an almost clinical detachment. She grabbed his shoulders with both her hands. "Don't ever say that again. Do you hear me?"

"But, CeCe, it's true. And there's something I need to tell you, the anonymous—"

Before he could finish his sentence, she came in closer, her face inches from his. "I said I don't want to hear it." She increased the pressure on his shoulders. "We kicked and clawed our way out of the gutter. We escaped a life in Kensington that only seemed to lead straight to prison or death. I'm not going to end up in jail, and neither are you. Do you hear me? We are not going down like that."

She released his shoulders, put her arms around him, and held him close as she whispered into his ear, "Are you a con man? Did you intentionally scheme to defraud people of their money?"

Cuddy shook his head.

"Were you trying to do God's work and make the world a better place?"

Cuddy nodded.

"Then how can you say you're guilty? Guilty of what? Caring too much, wanting to help others too much? That's the only thing you're guilty of and don't you ever forget that."

"But I messed it all up. The way things have turned out was never God's plan."

Her refusal to let him speak the truth was poignant. He had promised to rescue her, to give her the life she deserved, a life of luxury and no worries. She didn't want to hear anything to the contrary.

She smoothed his hair and kissed his forehead. "Can't we talk about something else?"

"CeCe, the FBI searched our home. They're going through every one of the foundation's files and interviewing every person I've ever discussed New Visions with." He gave her a puzzled look. "What else is there to talk about?"

"I don't want to think about that stuff."

"That stuff?" He leaned forward, elbows on his knees and a pleading look in his eyes. "Don't you understand? It's just a matter of time."

"You are God's messenger." She yanked his Bible from the nightstand and held it high. Her mouth quivered with the force of her passion. "What could they possibly discover to change that fact?"

He stared back at her with the undeniable knowledge that CeCe would never be prepared for whatever fate was coming to him and, consequently, her. He sat on the edge of the bed with his head bowed. He couldn't bear to look into her eyes.

"Cuddy," she said softly.

His heart skipped a beat as he cast a desperate gaze upward at her.

"Please don't wear that." She pointed to the tie lying next to him on the bed. "I've never really liked it. Wear the new blue-and-gold one I just got you."

And just like that, the brief moment of truth and clarity between them dissipated as though his words had never been spoken.

CHAPTER 27

Cuddy and CeCe had been shuffled to the conference room as soon as they arrived at the law offices of Smith, Stevens, Keller, and Goldberg. Due to CeCe not being able to decide on what shoes to wear with her outfit, they had been more than twenty-five minutes late. Now, the legal team was pressed for time to prepare for one of the most important meetings of Cuddy's life.

"We have only ten minutes before we need to head out to the United States Attorney's office, but the main thing you need to remember is to tell the truth," said Jillian Stevens. "If you lie or even if you leave something out, it can all be used against you if you go to trial."

"We discussed the parameters of the proffer session on the phone," said Cuddy.

"Yes, but I want to make sure neither of you have any questions or concerns."

"I don't." Cuddy turned to his wife. "Do you, CeCe?"

"Questions or concerns about telling the truth?" CeCe placed a hand on his arm and addressed everyone in the room. "Cuddy always tells the truth."

"It needed to be said out loud to assure that we're all on the same page. The same goes for you too, Mrs. Mullins."

"Me? I have nothing to say to the FBI. I'm here for moral support."

"Our understanding was that you assisted your husband with the expansion of the foundation."

"No, that's not true. I told you Melinda Tribble should have been asked to attend. She's New Vision's vice president. She knows more about the foundation's operational procedures than Cuddy."

"This meeting is to discuss pre-indictment, pretrial options. Cuddy's options may not line up with Ms. Tribble's options."

"Options. What kind of options?" CeCe leaned forward.

"As counterintuitive as it may seem, considering a guilty plea would—"

"What?" CeCe smacked the table. "Nobody said anything to me about this. No. No way is Cuddy going to plead guilty."

"No one's expecting a decision about a plea deal today. Let's use this time to go over the list of anonymous donors and the list of the foundation's and your personal assets and investments."

"What? Why do they need information about our money?"

"The government has the right to ask for restitution in these types of financial matters."

"Tell them they can't have it. We need to fight them," CeCe said.

"Let me be clear that it is to our advantage to cooperate with restitution. The judge will look positively on Cuddy's willingness to cooperate. Turning over assets and investments, forfeiting the house, cars, and other assets will result in significant downward departure during sentencing."

CeCe asked, "A downward departure?"

"It's when the judge departs from the normal sentencing guideline and considers a lower sentence, in other words, less time in jail, based on the forfeiture of assets earned or acquired during the commission of the crime."

"And we would have to give them all of our money for the judge to do that? Sounds like a pay-off to me." CeCe folded her arms across her chest. Her face was clouded with suspicion.

Cuddy shifted in his chair. He had known that this would be a bitter pill for her to swallow.

"What kind of attorneys are you?" she said, pointing at Jillian. "It sounds like you're not even trying to put up a defense. Cuddy's not pleading guilty, we're not forfeiting any of the hard-earned property or investments we've acquired, and nobody is going to jail."

"Mrs. Mullins, Cecelia, we need to look at all of the options and be prepared for the real possibility that your husband will be charged with fraud—mail fraud and wire fraud."

"Maybe we need to get ourselves some new attorneys."

"Any law firm with any experience in federal criminal matters will tell you the same thing and will advise you to do the same thing that we're advising you do."

"Cuddy," said Jillian. "I didn't get the list you were supposed to email me. Did you bring it with you."

Cuddy took out several sheets of paper from inside his suit jacket pocket and handed them to her.

She scanned the documents. "House valued at $695,000; 2018 Lexus; 2017 BMW; $320,000 in a PNC savings account; $51,000 in a checking account; and $1.7 million in your stocks and mutual funds investment account. Is that everything?"

Cuddy nodded.

CeCe rose from her seat and pointed to the papers Cuddy had given Jillian. "What the fuck? So that's why they wanted me to come with you."

He grabbed the sleeve of her jacket and pulled until she returned to her chair. "Sit down and listen to what Jillian has to say."

"You knew about this all along and didn't tell me." CeCe glared at him.

He ignored her and turned back to Jillian. "So, what do you think?"

"It's not an insignificant amount, but it's only a small percentage of the $450 million they are accusing you of misappropriating and the resulting $130 million loss. Nevertheless, I think it is enough for us to request a downward departure from the mandatory twenty-four-year sentence."

Both Cuddy and CeCe gasped and the conference room was eerily quiet for a beat. It was as if their gasps had sucked the air from the room.

"Twenty-four years?" said Cuddy in a shaky voice.

Jillian nodded. "That's without forfeiture. I'm pretty confident that we will get our request for a reduction down to twelve years' incarceration if you surrender significant assets." The attorney smiled as if she was doing a good thing.

CeCe's reaction to hearing the numbers was visceral. Her face flushed and sweat prickled at her hairline. She lowered her head into her hands. "I can't believe that this is happening. I can't believe they're trying to take away our hard-earned savings."

Cuddy looked up and searched the expressions of the three attorneys in the room—they had heard it too. CeCe was upset because of the forfeiture. Not because of any jail time he may have to serve. And then, if there was any confusion about what was most important to her, she asked her next question.

"That's an eight-year reduction for returning all of the property and money we have. What would happen if he just turned in the Lexus and the money we have in the bank? How much time would he get if we gave back only some of the money?"

Cuddy's heart sank and for a moment he couldn't breathe. He placed his hand to his chest where sadness and humiliation twisted together.

"CeCe, you understand that there's no doing this halfway," said Jillian. "Cuddy needs to turn over all of his assets to show the court that he's willing to cooperate fully."

"And that's what I'm trying to tell you—the house and the investments are in my name, not Cuddy's," said CeCe. "The only thing we own jointly or has Cuddy's name on it is his car and the money we have in our savings and checking accounts. I can tell you right now I have no intention of giving away assets that are legally mine."

Cuddy blinked in disbelief. "CeCe, do you understand what they're saying?" He cast his eyes at his wife and then desperately around the room.

"Let me be clear—your husband could go to jail for a very long time if you refuse to cooperate with forfeiture," said Jillian.

"I may not have gone to law school, but I know that an individual is innocent until proven guilty. Why don't you worry about defending my husband, instead of worrying about forfeiture?"

Jillian checked her watch. "We need to know what to tell the prosecutor and the FBI when we get into the proffer."

"When it comes to taking everything we have and leaving me penniless, you can tell them to kiss my ass."

At that moment, Jillian's administrative assistant knocked on the door and entered the room. "You're gonna be late for the proffer if you don't leave now."

"Thanks, Kelly." Jillian stood, gathered the papers laid out on the conference table, and stuffed them into her briefcase. "Let's head over now. We can go over the list and continue this discussion on our walk over to Chestnut Street."

As they stood and left the room, CeCe reached out to take hold of his arm. He couldn't bear her touch and gently disengaged, moving quickly to catch up with his attorney.

***

On the way to the meeting at the U.S. Attorney's Office, Cuddy couldn't stop thinking about what CeCe had said. Money was something he had never cared about. But he had always known that CeCe's opinion vastly differed from his. Because she had never had it, once she did, money became her security blanket. What he hadn't known until now was that she valued money more than she valued him. The attorneys wanted to continue talking as they walked three blocks west and two blocks north from their law office on Locust Street to the United States Attorneys' office, but he couldn't think. The only thing on his mind was the devastating things CeCe had said.

He could end up living the rest of his life in prison. And his own wife didn't seem to care. How had he missed this cold truth about his own wife's priorities? And now that he knew about it, how could he ever overlook and forgive it?

He walked in silence a few steps in front of her. The only thing that played out in his head was CeCe's words: *How much time would he get if we gave back only some of the money?*

CHAPTER 28

What a waste of time. Kari discreetly pulled her phone onto her lap and tapped out a text message to Becca. *Are you picking up a weird vibe here?* They had been sitting in the large conference room on the twelfth floor of the United States Attorneys' office for more than ten minutes of pleasantries and chit chat. Cuddy and his attorneys were talking, but Kari questioned how much valuable information would actually be provided today. They had not yet said a word about the identities of the anonymous donors. Wasn't that what they were here to discuss? Unknown to Cuddy and his legal team, she had the list of anonymous donors retrieved from Melinda Tribble's computer. Federal prosecutor Mitch Whitmore had agreed with the strategy not to reveal their hand. They would wait to see what Cuddy Mullins offered regarding the list.

However, the text she had sent to Becca addressed the odd tension in the room between Cuddy and his wife. It seemed as if he wouldn't look her in the eye. He barely acknowledged her presence. Kari gave the woman sitting across from her a thorough assessment. Her Goldilocks-like tresses were too luscious, too long, and that caused Kari to question what else about Mrs. Mullins was fake, such as her loving attitude and support for her husband. Next, Kari sent a text to Whitmore. *This is painful. Aren't we done, yet?*

When this second proffer had been scheduled, Whitmore had told

Kari, Duffy, and Becca that Mullins was coming in to discuss the anonymous donors and a possible guilty plea. However, nothing close to an admission of guilt had passed through Mullins's lips. His attorney had offered to turn over Mullins's luxury car, a Lexus, and a little less than $400,000 he had in his checking and savings accounts. But if he wasn't pleading guilty, what was that supposed to be—a donation to the Justice Department? Plus, the forfeiture team back at her office had tracked substantial investments in an account under Cecelia Mullins's name. Even with his best efforts to charm and convince them that he was innocent, he was going to be charged with multiple counts of mail fraud, wire fraud, money laundering, and filing false tax returns. The team had already begun preparing the indictment. Now that they knew for sure that Mullins was not going to assist them, they could get back to work pulling all of the information and interviews together to complete the document.

Kari's mind had wandered. When she returned her attention back to the conference room, Cecelia Mullins was speaking.

"And it doesn't seem fair to demand that we turn all our savings over to the government. What about all of the nonprofits who benefited from the foundation's generosity? Many of them established endowments with the money provided by New Visions. Have you spoken to any of them?"

"The bankruptcy court will be asking the victims with a net gain to give back the dirty money," Duffy replied.

"Dirty money?" asked Cuddy in an indignant tone.

"Victims?" snorted CeCe. "Who are you again?"

"Special Agent Duffy with the IRS," he said with a smirk and a condescending tone.

"You think I'm scared of you?" CeCe's instant hostility signaled that she had quickly sized up Duffy and his misogynistic leanings.

Jillian Stevens patted the table softly to get the attention of her clients and calm their insulted egos. "That's clawback. Remember? We discussed it. The nonprofit victims in the black are being asked to return their profits in an attempt to make those in the red whole."

"How dare you call them victims," said CeCe. "Many of those nonprofits would have gone out of business long ago it wasn't for Cuddy sending them a lifeline. Victims my ass. You know why we're here?"

Kari hoisted herself forward in her chair. "I thought I did. But why don't you enlighten us?"

"I guess you think you're smarter than me because I didn't go to some fancy college. But I got street smarts, and those boojie donors are full of—"

Both Jillian Stevens and Cuddy immediately reached out to quiet her, but she jerked and flung off their hands and continued her tirade.

Kari thought to herself, *Oh boy. Here comes that Little Flower Catholic girl's edge Cuddy Mullins had told her about. This should be good.*

"You better take a close look at those damn donors. True altruism? I doubt it. And their choices of charities weren't so sanctimonious either. It don't matter, cuz who they give to and why they give is irrelevant. They're just greedy, greedy givers addicted to power."

"I think what Mrs. Mullins is talking about is the concept of cause marketing; we discussed this with a public relations consultant a few weeks ago. It's where a prominent person lends his name and star power for promotional purposes and provides a percentage of profits to the charitable cause." Jillian Stevens glanced over at CeCe and swallowed hard after seeing the intense scowl CeCe gave her. Stevens appeared to lose track of her words and did not finish her thought.

Mitch Whitmore gave Kari a sidelong glance before picking up the thread. "Speaking of donors, do you have the list of anonymous donors with you Mr. Mullins?"

Cuddy cleared his throat and clasped his hands in front of him. "I feel a profound obligation to protect them. When we created the concept, we agreed that their identities would never be revealed. I've taken extensive measures to ensure that I keep that promise."

"I take it that means that you are still refusing to share that list with us." Whitmore turned to Jillian Stevens. "Have you seen it yet?"

She gave a slight shake of her head.

"The Philadelphia FBI's Computer Analysis Response Team, CART, has had a chance to look over all the electronic records obtained during our search of New Visions' offices and your home computers. Remember that password-protected file you told us about?"

Cuddy turned pale and his face was clouded with confusion. "You were able to access the file?"

"Not exactly." Kari raised her eyebrows, but otherwise made sure her expression remained flat with no indication that they had a copy of the anonymous donor list. "There was no file. As a matter of fact, it appears that your CPU's hard drive had been wiped clean." She rubbed her hand above the surface of the table. "Or removed and switched out just a few days before the search was executed. Any idea how that happened?"

"Did you ask Melinda Tribble?" said CeCe. "She's the office manager."

Cuddy corrected her. "Chief of staff and administration."

"Whatever. Isn't she's the one in charge of records, digital or paper. Did you ask her about missing files?"

Cuddy stared at his wife and with a subtle shake of his head seemed to indicate displeasure.

Kari studied them both. *Good idea*, she thought. That was the plan. To confront Melinda Tribble about the anonymous donor list found on her computer.

CHAPTER 29

After the unproductive meeting with the Mullinses, Kari returned to the office and collapsed into her desk chair. The callous attitude of CeCe Mullins had unnerved her. Mrs. Mullins was the exact opposite of her husband, and although they had both claimed that she had no involvement with New Visions, Kari wondered if that was true. Compared to her husband, she was the one with the con man swagger and impertinence.

Although Duffy had taken on the task of scheduling and reviewing the foundation's financial and investment records, Kari still had in her possession bank records that went back several years subpoenaed from Cuddy Mullins's personal accounts. Duffy had decided these personal accounts weren't worthy of his CPA-level energy and left them for Kari to schedule and review using her basic white-collar crime agent accounting skills.

Based on instinct, she decided to spend the rest of the day reviewing the Mullins' pre-foundation personal accounts. Kari was looking for evidence of CeCe's connection to the Ponzi scheme. She figured that the best place to start her financial search would be during the time when the matching program was initiated, approximately three and a half to four years ago.

The first thing she noticed was that during this period, the Mullinses had multiple checking and savings accounts. The second thing she noted was recurring volatile activity in the accounts. Monthly statements showed extremely low ledger balances with frequent debit withdrawals and charges for bounced checks and insufficient funds. One of the accounts would be reconciled with a biweekly automatic transfer, probably Cuddy's paycheck, and then several immediate debit transactions to retail stores and transfers between the accounts. They would all be back in arrears within days. This erratic banking practice continued for several months until one account was finally stabilized later in the year with six deposits of $15,000 each. The others were then closed.

Kari reviewed the document index contained with the bank records and was pleased to read that all supporting checks deposited and withdrawn had been supplied under the subpoena request. She scoured the outgoing checks first and wasn't surprised to see that most of the checks had been written to retail stores and that they had been executed by CeCe. The majority of the expenditures appeared to be used to pay for furnishing their new home in Fishtown. She consulted the related bank statements and confirmed her suspicions; the checks had been written when the balance contained insufficient funds. CeCe had been running a check-kiting scam where she was intentionally writing worthless checks drawn on fictitious balances she created by moving money from one account to another account. These manipulations artificially inflated the account balances. The fact that the accounts were closed shortly after she started the scheme was a strong indication that the bank had detected her fraudulent transaction manipulations and restrained the accounts until all uncollected funds were cleared. But where did the Mullins get the sudden influx of capital to clean up their act?

She continued to scroll through the check images until she found the checks she had been looking for. *Bingo!* There was the $15,000 check Lennie and Tanya Adams said they had given Cuddy Mullins for the first anonymous donor match, along with five other checks for $15,000 each deposited within the same week as the other donors Kari knew had been supporters of the Foundation for New Visions in Giving since its inception. She continued to trace the funds and discovered half of the money was used to balance the accounts, pay bills, and pay off personal debt, and the remaining funds were deposited into a newly opened foundation account.

Kari glanced at the time listed in the lower right-hand corner of her computer screen and was amazed. She had been working for hours. She sat back in her chair, clasped her hands behind her head, and sighed with satisfaction. She would hand off the records to a financial forfeiture analyst to complete the tracing of funds, but there was no more giving Cuddy Mullins the benefit of the doubt. What Kari had discovered that afternoon was the intentional and calculated birth of a Ponzi scheme.

Cuddy Mullins needed to re-introduce himself to the Ten Commandments—especially the one about thou shalt not steal.

CHAPTER 30

He had barely spoken to her on the ride home from the attorneys' office. She tried to explain why she had said the things she had, but he refused to engage in the conversation and was content with allowing silence to settle between them. When she reached over to rub the scar on the back of his head, he jerked away from her touch. He had spent the last seventeen years of his life loving this woman, caring for this woman, making sure she had everything she needed, and now he wasn't sure if he had ever known her. Were her material possessions that valuable to her? More valuable than he was to her? He placed his hand on his stomach, where resentment and hurt continued to coil together, producing a burning ache in his gut. This was more than just her love for pretty, expensive things. This was who she was. How had he missed this?

He pulled the car into the driveway and entered the house through the side door. Potter, as always, was there to greet him. He picked up his dog and nuzzled his face with his own, whispering to him, "You're the only one whose love I can depend on."

CeCe entered the door behind him.

"Cuddy, please let me explain. I was just asking the question. That's not the way I really feel. You know I love you. Let's fight this together. You've done nothing wrong. You should not have to go to jail for something you didn't do."

"But I have done something wrong. Hundreds of nonprofits and donors have lost millions of dollars. Someone is going to have to answer to that. And that someone is me."

"Can't you call the anonymous donors? Won't they come to your defense and make the foundation solvent?"

Cuddy stared at her and wondered if he really needed to say out loud what was so obvious to everyone but CeCe. No matter how much her comments and behavior had wounded him, he knew what he had done was an even greater disappointment. "CeCe, it's over. I tried to be a positive force in this world, to do God's work. But I failed. And that means we're going to have to give the money back, along with everything that we bought with it. I need you to cooperate with the investigators."

She shook her head.

He turned away, walked up the stairs into the bedroom, and locked the door behind him.

She jiggled the door handle and then kicked it. "Cuddy. Unlock the door," she begged.

He laid himself on the bed and didn't answer her. Several minutes passed. He could tell she was sitting on the floor in front of their bedroom door. As far as he was concerned, she could sit out there for hours. He didn't want to see her, and he definitely didn't want to hear anything else she had to say. He looked around the bedroom with all of its fancy furnishings and linens—four-poster bed frame, brocade curtains, and chaise lounge. Who needed all of that crap? He certainly didn't. He had allowed her to change who he was and what mattered most to him. He thought that he had been helping her and, until now, had not recognized what it had done to him.

"How can you ask me to give up all of this? What about me?," she pleaded through the door. "Do you want me to do what my mother did to earn a living? Is that what you want me to do?"

He could hear her crying on the other side of the door. It wasn't her fault that she was so screwed up. He got up and turned the knob to unlock the door. He took her in his arms. "God will make sure that everything works out in the end. Pray and the Lord will tell us what to do."

CeCe pushed herself away from his embrace. "You've got to be kidding. This is not something you can pray away. This is our lives, and we should be fighting to preserve everything we worked so hard for." She waved her hand around the room as if to indicate that her silk draperies, her 800-thread-count sheets, the artwork on the walls represented their lives.

"That's the problem—all this crap we have. We don't need it. Never did." He reached into his pocket, pulled out his Bible, and recited the verse he had been thinking about ever since she'd uttered those materialistic words at the proffer.

"'Beware, and be on your guard against every form of greed; for not even when one has an abundance does his life consist of his possessions.'" He looked at her and shook his head slowly. "Don't you get it? It's stuff. It's all just stuff."

"Cuddy, please don't ask me to give up everything you gave me, everything you promised me." She pounded his chest with the palms of her hands.

"That's the problem. You're worried about losing your stuff, and I'm worried about losing our souls."

Her sad eyes displayed a look of desperation, and she repeated the words that always cut through him like a knife. "I'll kill myself before I'll be poor again," she said.

He knew that the days of darkness and despair would soon engulf her again. She had suffered from depression since her high school days, when he had first met her. When things got rough, she was always threatening suicide, and when that happened, he would do just about anything to save her from herself. But this time, he didn't know if he had the strength or desire to keep her off the ledge.

CHAPTER 31

"Immunity?" Melinda Tribble looked at them with confusion. "Why would I need immunity?"

Kari watched as Tribble's eyes darted around the room and gave each agent a perplexed look. Kari, Becca, and Bryant Duffy. Three on one. They agreed that making their interviewee feel a bit intimidated wouldn't be a bad thing. Was she innocent or was she complicit in the charity Ponzi scheme? That's the question they were trying to determine. After the last proffer, when CeCe Mullins had implied that much of the blame for the Foundation for New Visions in Giving should be placed squarely on Melinda Tribble, they'd made a quick phone call, and Tribble had agreed to speak with them. She did not ask, and Kari had no obligation to suggest Tribble bring her own attorney along for the interview.

"This is a criminal matter, and we would assume that you would want some assurances that you would not be charged," said Kari.

"Oh my God." Tribble placed a hand on her chest and looked around at the three agents sitting across from her.

Kari was surprised at Tribble's reaction. The SEC and the bankruptcy court had boarded up the office, the FBI had confiscated and searched the files. Cuddy Mullins had hired a team of attorneys to meet with federal prosecutors and the FBI and IRS investigative team, and Melinda Tribble was surprised she too might be implicated in the scam?

"Did you see the Facebook Live video? According to Cuddy Mullins, the administration of his concept was the problem," said Becca. "Aren't you the chief of staff? To us, that sounded like he was blaming it all on you."

Tears began to flow down Tribble's face. She reached into her purse, pulled out a tissue to dry her cheeks. "I didn't want to believe that things were this bad. But here I am being interrogated by three FBI agents. I don't know how things could get any worse."

"I'm not FBI. They are." Duffy flicked a thumb in the direction of Kari and Becca. "I'm with the IRS."

"In addition to money laundering and bank, mail, and wire fraud charges, Mr. Mullins is also facing serious tax consequences," said Kari. "We're here to determine your role in the scheme."

"What about the anonymous donors? I was hoping to find out from you today if you've spoken to any of them and if you think that they would be willing to continue this work with our staff and me."

"Why don't we begin at the very beginning." Kari clicked her gel pen and hovered it over her notebook. "When did you first meet Cuddy Mullins?"

Tribble explained that Cuddy Mullins was operating in a different capacity when she first met him six years ago. At that time, his service business was called the Center for New Visions in Giving. There was no foundation with endowed funds. The center's purpose was to provide training seminars for not-for-profit organizations, such as food banks, day care centers, drug rehab programs, churches, and adult literacy programs, to assist them in fundraising and general management skills. They called the training sessions institutes, and these institutes lasted for approximately two and a half days. Outside consultants hired by Cuddy would come in to teach the classes. In addition to the face-to-face training, the participants were encouraged to access the center's video library and were provided with updates via a monthly email newsletter. Tribble, who had a master's degree in business administration from Drexel University, was hired by Mullins as director of the center. The center operated under a grant from the United Way.

"You know about the United Way, don't you? It's where donors from around the region contributed to their favorite charities," said Tribble. "Our center was established to make sure the funds the nonprofits received were spent as efficiently as possible. We also began working with donors to show them how to maximize their charitable giving."

"And their charitable tax breaks," added Duffy.

"Yes. That's true," she said with a slight tilt of her head and continued her explanation. "About four years ago, Cuddy told me that he was moving the center in a new direction. The grants for the program from the United Way had started shrinking. We began using the same techniques we were teaching in the classroom to go out and supplement our grants through direct donations from community benefactors. In some ways, our fundraising efforts were competing with the efforts of the very nonprofits we were trying to serve. We were actually struggling to stay operational—our administrative expenses were substantial—so Cuddy started looking outside of this region for funding sources. He was quite successful. That's when he first told me about the anonymous donors."

"What exactly did he tell you?" said Kari

"I was already aware that he knew Sir Middleton, and I always assumed that Sir Middleton was one of the first anonymous donors and that he introduced the concept to his other wealthy friends."

"The concept...?" asked Kari.

"Participatory philanthropy, where nonprofits are not just given funding but work to raise it and then have it matched by donors. It's the 'teach a man to fish versus give a man a fish' philosophy. You've heard about that haven't you?"

They all nodded.

"But you're saying he never told you that Sir Middleton was an anonymous donor?"

"No."

"And he never told you the names of any of the other alleged anonymous donors?"

"No."

Kari pushed the paper in front of Tribble. "Could you please take a look at this list of names? Are these the individuals that you came to believe were possibly anonymous donors?"

Tribble took the list and read it over carefully. Her mouth was a tight line. Her hands began to shake so much that the paper made a rustling noise. "Where did you get the list?" Tribble's eyes were wide with excitement.

Duffy smacked his hand on the table. "Seriously? We retrieved it from your computer files."

Tribble, who just moments ago had seemed to be filled with hope, looked like all hope had been sucked out of her body. She bit her lip, but that didn't prevent a sad, weak moan from escaping her mouth. "He allowed me to peek at the list once. After he left the building, I snuck into his office, searched his desk, and scanned it into my computer files." She glanced up and gave them an apologetic smile. "I'm sorry I lied to you. My plan was to use the list to connect with the anonymous donors after things cooled down."

"And so you believe that these individuals were providing undesignated donations to the foundation to be used to match the funds the nonprofits and benefactor donors gave to New Visions?"

"Yes." She glanced at the list she was holding, let her hand fall slack, and released the paper. "I wanted to believe Cuddy. He told me they existed. I did believe Cuddy."

"Melinda, someone erased the hard drive on Cuddy's computer. All of his files are gone. We weren't able to find this list or any files on his CPU." Kari tapped her pen on the paper in front of Tribble. "Do you know how that happened? Who would've been responsible for destroying evidence?"

"Not me." Her eyes widened. "Is that why you asked me here? Do you think I did it?"

"Someone did," said Kari.

"It couldn't have been Cuddy. He doesn't know anything about computers. He wouldn't know how to do that."

Kari believed Melinda Tribble wasn't responsible, but wasn't convinced she knew what the Mullinses were capable of doing. Kari had asked the question. "How about CeCe?"

"No. She knows less than Cuddy about computers. She knows Facebook, Instagram, and Pinterest. That's it. Plus, she would have no reason to destroy documents on his computer. She knows nothing about the foundation."

"Well, if Cuddy didn't do it, if CeCe didn't do it, if you didn't do it, then who did?" said Duffy.

At that point, Melinda Tribble became inconsolable. Her shoulders shook with each sob. The agents gave her time to collect herself and then debriefed her about everything she knew about the foundation, Cuddy and Cecelia Mullins, and the anonymous donors. She agreed to meet with Cuddy and wear a wire to record the conversation. If Tribble was to be believed, it appeared that the Ponzi scheme was operated right under her nose.

Tribble was right. She didn't need immunity—she needed a clue.

CHAPTER 32

Cuddy had been ecstatic when Melinda called and asked him to meet her for lunch. He had not seen her since the last proffer, when she had asked the attorneys if they represented her too and had learned that they did not. He missed his old friend. Melinda was the one who supported his dreams, who stood by him and encouraged him to do God's work, even more than CeCe had. It had been several weeks since he had last seen her, and as he walked up to the entrance of the hip and flashy Mexican restaurant on the corner of Thirteenth and Sansom and saw his dear friend waiting outside, he was consumed with joy.

She stood with her hands on her hips in the bright afternoon sun. He hadn't realized how much he'd missed her. When she greeted him with a kiss on the cheek, she smiled, but he could tell she was upset. He pulled her in close and held her for several seconds.

When the silence was broken, Melinda was the first to speak.

"Why?" She cocked her head quizzically.

"You think I'm guilty?" Cuddy stared into Melinda's eyes. They glistened with tears. He instantly realized that if his most loyal friend and supporter had doubts, he had no hope of convincing twelve jurors he was innocent.

Melinda stared down at her hands and couldn't look him in the eyes. "I have real doubts. I know your intentions were always in the right place. I don't know what happened or how to explain it, but something went wrong along the way."

"Let's sit down, and I'll do my best to explain everything to you."

They stepped inside the restaurant and followed the hostess to their table. After ordering, they avoided talking about the foundation and Cuddy's status for a bit and settled into an easy conversation about everything else, just like old times. Melinda asked about Potter and told Cuddy she knew what a comfort the dog was for him. But eventually the topic at the forefront of their thoughts had to be addressed.

"I've never felt the need to ask you this question, but under the circumstances, I have to ask you now." This time she looked him directly into his eyes. "Were there ever any anonymous donors? Did New Visions ever receive undesignated funds?"

He did not immediately answer her, but he didn't look away.

"Cuddy, I need to know the truth. You said we were changing the world for the glory of God. How did this happen? So many people have been hurt. All of the good that we did has been destroyed." She allowed an awkward silence to descend between them and waited for his response.

Dejected, he stared out the restaurant window at the people hurrying up and down the block. He realized that it would be harder to confess to Melinda than it had been to reveal himself to CeCe. He took a sip from the water glass their waitress had just filled. In his nervousness he spilled a little on the red tablecloth.

"I wish you could have trusted me. I've been in your corner. I have had your back from the very moment I heard you talking about the concept of participatory philanthropy. I've been reading the stories in the paper, and it doesn't look good."

Cuddy remembered that morning's *Inquirer* headline: "Donor's New Vision about Swindler." The article featured an interview with Roger LaMott. LaMott had always been one of the foundation's biggest supporters. LaMott's change of heart was profound. "Since when do you listen to rumors? People believe what they want to believe," he said.

Melinda flinched. "People don't believe in words. They believe in the person who is saying those words. They believed in you. I believed in you."

"Believed?"

"What am I supposed to think? I saw the Facebook Live video. The FBI told me what you and CeCe said about the missing files."

"You've been speaking to the FBI? Did you let Jillian Stevens know this?" This time when he looked into her eyes, the tears were gone and in their place was a dark and wary disenchantment.

"Your lawyers aren't looking out for me," she said. "And now that I'm no longer receiving a paycheck, I can't afford my own legal team."

He could feel a nervous tension building up between them. He had had his hand on her hand. He removed his and let it drop to his side. "It sounded to me like you're trying to blame this whole thing on me," she said.

"Melinda, you have to know that's not true. I don't blame anyone for any of this."

"But you should."

"Who?"

"CeCe."

He shook his head vehemently. "How could you say that?"

"Cuddy. Don't be a fool. She has been the cause of all your problems from the very beginning. You may have been doing this for the glory of God, but CeCe has been in it for the glory of CeCe. The spending, the trips, the loft in Fishtown, the houses—all of that is why you are where you are today, and until you wake up and see what she's done, you're going up in flames. And may God save you."

"Melinda, CeCe's just trying to find the happiness she was denied growing up."

"Where's your Bible?"

Cuddy reached into his pocket and pulled out the weathered book. "Did you want to pray with me?"

"You need to stop pulling out Bible verses for other people and start pulling out a Bible verse for yourself. Find one about loyalty and trust." She reached across the table, placed her hand softly on his cheek and stared into his eyes. "You're going to have to pay the price, but this is not all on you. You need to ask yourself if CeCe's going to pay too."

"She's already paid more than any human being should have to pay. Her mother was a drug addict who was too high to stop the strange men she brought into the home from abusing her kids. Her brother, Kurt, died of an overdose a few months before their mother. CeCe has been under treatment for depression for most of her life and can you blame her? After what she's been through, and—"

"Stop it, Cuddy," she snapped. "That's her story. I've heard it all before. Why do you keep telling it as if it were yours?" She reached across the table and placed her hand on his. "Do you realize how much of your life is dictated by her past?"

He blinked but couldn't answer.

"Let me remind you of your story, the one you've mentioned only a few times." Melinda leaned in close and stared into his eyes. "When you first met CeCe, she was thrilled that you were majoring in pre-med at Temple because she had always dreamed of being a doctor's wife. She wanted to get married right away. No way was she going to risk you leaving her ass once you became a rich physician. But you had to change your major because of the blinding headaches from the head injury you received after she convinced you to go down to the railroad tracks to El Campamento, the epicenter of the heroin epidemic, all by yourself to look for her mother and you got cracked over the head with a lead pipe, robbed, and left for dead. Remember that? And then you wanted to break up with her and become a Catholic priest, but CeCe was able to persuade you, with a fake pregnancy scare, that the priesthood was your mother's dream, not yours. Remember that?"

He started to speak, and she cut him off.

"I'm not done yet. That woman is a user, just like her mamma. But she is addicted to wealth instead of drugs. CeCe clung to you, to your future, and projected all her dreams and hopes on you. You were supposed to be her savior, her knight in shining armor. But you can't keep letting her mental and emotional instability drive you crazy."

Cuddy felt the weight of her words flatten him. He hung his head, but she used her index finger to gently lift his chin so he was looking into her eyes, which shone bright with passion.

"One last thing. Late at night, when you're in bed, and you can't sleep because you're trying to figure out how in the hell you ended up in this mess, I suggest you look at the woman sleeping beside you. And if you are tempted to grab your pillow and smother the life from her, I won't blame you."

***

After Cuddy left the restaurant, he walked to the garage where he had parked and sat in his car for several minutes before feeling steady enough to drive. He had been deeply disturbed by the things Melinda had said about CeCe. At that moment, he wondered if he had ever really loved her. Had she been his first major charity project? The question saddened him. Was Melinda right? Were the mistakes he had made created by his desire to please CeCe more than his commitment to God's work?

The sound of a car's horn blaring brought him back to reality. He glanced in his side-view mirror and saw a middle-aged woman leaning her head out her window inquiring whether or not he was going to pull out of the space. He had no idea how long she had been sitting there, waiting for him to move. He pushed the ignition button, put the Lexus in reverse, and pulled out. When he neared his suburban neighborhood, he realized he had driven from Center City onto the Vine Street Expressway, then the treacherous Schuylkill Expressway and didn't remember anything about the car ride.

His mind was fully occupied with thoughts about what he was going to do. In the months since he had learned that the FBI was investigating him, he had put the matter into the hands of God. But although his faith had not wavered, he now knew that good people could make bad decisions, and that part of being devoted to God was learning from the lessons He presented. For the first time, Cuddy asked himself what were the lessons he was supposed to be learning from this experience? What was God trying to tell him?

The crossing gate came down at Conestoga Road, and Cuddy sat in the idling car as the early rush-hour Paoli-Thorndale Line train rumbled along the tracks and through the intersection. After the train had passed and the gates were raised, he sat until alerted once again by the blaring horns of the impatient drivers behind him. It was as if he was in a trance. He knew for sure he didn't feel like himself. He could feel everything slipping away and himself losing control. It was as if he had been living in a dream and was suddenly awakened.

He left the car in the driveway, not bothering to pull into the garage. He walked in through the side door and passed CeCe, who was in the kitchen preparing dinner.

"Did you see Melinda? Did you tell her I said hello?"

"CeCe, I'm not feeling very well. Can we talk later?" He picked up Potter and continued walking as he spoke. "I'm going to go lie down."

"Dinner will be ready in less than an hour," she said.

"Eat without me. I'm not hungry."

He didn't bother looking back, even as he heard her calling out to him. He was not ready to deal with her. He needed to figure out the next chapters in his own story first.

CHAPTER 33

He slept for fourteen hours. And during that time, God came to him in his dreams and told him what he needed to do. The first thing he did when he got out of bed was apologize to Potter who was laying on the floor beside the bed, as if he knew something was wrong and not to bother him. He had to assume that CeCe hadn't fed him or walked him the evening before. She lay beside him in a self-induced sleeping-pill coma. A bottle of Ambien rested on her nightstand. With the two of them swept up in their own personal crises, Cuddy was concerned that his little buddy wasn't getting the care he needed. He hugged the dog to his chest and kissed the top of his fluffy head. He would ask Melinda if she would adopt him. She'd always liked Potter.

Cuddy took the dog for a quick walk around the block and hurried back inside to feed him and give him fresh water. Once he made his amends, he sat with the pup on the steps of the backyard deck and called his attorney.

"I need help, Jilllian," he said as soon she came to the phone.

"That's what I'm here for, to help get you through this," she said.

Her response indicated that he had failed to express his true needs. He repeated his admission, "I think I need help."

"Cuddy, I'm not sure what you're saying to me. What kind of help?"

"I need to see someone—a shrink, a psychiatrist." He lowered the phone from his ear and placed his head in his hands and began to weep.

The words began to sputter out through his fingers. "I was only trying to do good. I was only trying to glorify God."

"Cuddy, I can't hear what you're saying. Are you speaking into the phone?"

He was holding his cell so tightly that his hand cramped around it. He loosened his hold and placed the phone to his ear again. Letting out a deep breath, he said, "It became an obsession, and then it became a delusion."

"What do you mean delusion? Like hearing voices?"

He nodded.

"Cuddy, did you say yes?"

"The anonymous donors, they spoke to me."

"Tell me exactly what's going on, so I can figure out what kind of help you need."

His stomach was a tight mass of fear and self-loathing, but as soon as he said the words, he felt instant relief. "I don't think that the anonymous donors ever really existed."

"Are you saying you imagined they were real?"

"Yes," he said, nodding soberly. "I heard them. They were speaking to me."

Cuddy talked with Jillian for a few minutes more before she told him she wanted him to meet with a psychiatrist immediately. While she placed him on hold, Jillian called in a couple of favors and scheduled him for an appointment that afternoon.

"Once the indictment is filed..." Jillian paused for a beat before continuing. "Cuddy, you need to know that I heard from the Assistant United States Attorney today and you're going to be charged sometime this week. Once that's done, we'll enter a plea of not guilty and request that the court order a mental health evaluation."

"I'm admitting to you that there were no anonymous donors. Doesn't that make me guilty?"

"No. Far from it. But let's talk about that after we get you some help. Did you tell CeCe? Does she know about the voices?"

"No. Not yet." He looked up at the bedroom window, where he knew CeCe was inside, dead asleep. He only felt pity and anger for her now, but he couldn't tell Jillian that. Instead, he said, "I don't want her to worry."

CHAPTER 34

Kari and the investigative team waited until Mitch Whitmore hung up the speakerphone to make sure the line was disengaged. The latest communication from the foundation's defense team was major news to everyone gathered in the prosecutor's office. Stevens had called Whitmore to let him know that they would be considering an insanity defense. As soon as the indictment charging Cuddy Mullins with operating a Ponzi scheme was filed, they would ask the court to have him undergo a series of mental health evaluations.

"She was kidding, right?" Duffy shook his head in disbelief. "What a bunch of bullshit. Is that the best they could come up with? Cuddy Mullins was hallucinating each time he met with anonymous donors. What? Like they were his imaginary friends?"

"We all laughed when he used this crap during his Facebook Live video, but to use it as a legal defense is ludicrous," said Becca.

"The burden of proof is on them. How are they going to prove that?" Kari spoke to no one in particular and did not expect an answer.

Whitmore paced behind his desk. "You heard what she said. Cuddy Mullins suffered a serious head injury that caused him to develop an attachment to the Bible and become a religious zealot intent on saving the world through the glory of God."

Duffy stood. "More like he was intent on scamming the world through the glory of God. How can they say the guy was mentally incompetent? He was sane enough to dupe hundreds of people out of millions of dollars. Insane my ass."

"Look, guys,' said Whitmore. "Let's not let this distract us. This scheme was not a delusion. Based on the work Kari did scheduling the Mullins' personal finances, we now know exactly how the matching donation scheme started."

Becca held up the flow charts and exhibits prepared by a forensic accounting analyst that illustrated the movement of checks deposited and withdrawn from the overdrawn accounts.

"Whitmore's right. Let's continue reporting our investigative updates first, and then we can discuss how the evidence contradicts an insanity defense." Kari turned to Duffy. "So, Mr. CPA. What's the bottom line? Is this still a $450 million Ponzi scheme?"

Duffy used his middle finger to push his glasses farther up the bridge of his nose and said, "Technically, because that's how much the Foundation for New Visions in Giving took in. But after doing a reconciliation of deposits and withdrawals into the foundation's banking and investment accounts, the actual loss is about $130 million. Still a significant loss. I already provided that loss number to the defense."

"Yeah, not too shabby," said Becca.

"It's certainly one of the most damaging schemes ever to hit the charitable world," added Whitmore.

"Can I take a look at your spreadsheet?" Kari reached for the ledger-style bound spreadsheets. She flipped through the pages. "Nice job. I like how each page reflects each victim's deposits into the foundation and any expenditures returned back to them."

Duffy nodded. "The tab next to the philanthropist's or donor's name is color-coded. As you can see—"

"The black tabs are for participants who were in the black, ahead of the game when the foundation filed for bankruptcy, and the red tabs indicate those who didn't make out so well. Did I get that right?"

Duffy gave her a weak round of applause.

Kari tilted her head to the side and smiled. "Accounting 101."

Whitmore pointed to a stack of identical, bound spreadsheets on his desk. "Duffy has provided each of us with our own copy of his ledger and Becca has distributed the records related to the personal accounts. I know you guys have already conducted a number of interviews."

"Yeah," said Kari. "They all are telling pretty much the same story—donors were practically fighting to be the top dog, to be recognized as the most generous, get their names mounted on a hospital wing or new building. They all agree that after the initial solicitation, he never asked anyone to give him a dime. As a matter of fact, the more rules and restrictions he set up, the more people wanted to be let into the club. The exclusivity was irresistible."

Becca nodded. "But it grew too large too quick. And soon, he needed to collect more donations before the whole damn pyramid toppled down on him."

"Even if they're singing the same tune, we need to document them. Each one will be a separate count for the indictment. If this case is really going to trial, how do you want to go about contacting the rest of the victims?" Whitmore raised his hands, palms up and threw out the question to the investigators.

"Between Duffy, Becca, and me, we've conducted"—Kari wrinkled her nose while she performed a bit of mental math—"a total of about thirty-four interviews to date. So what are you looking to clear? Twice that number?"

Whitmore paused for a moment. "Yeah, that sounds right. That would give us a total of around seventy face-to-face interviews."

"If that's what you need, you got it." Becca saluted no one in particular. "I'm just a foot soldier in this army. But so far, we've had an opportunity to meet some pretty interesting people."

"It's your call, Mitch," said Kari. "Is that enough to prove the fraud? Perhaps we could just mail the rest a questionnaire and then connect directly with the best ones?"

"Yeah. Fifty supplemented with the responses from the questionnaire, that should work. How many victims in total do we have?" Whitmore asked Becca.

"Three hundred and eleven—that's counting individual people and businesses—gave money to Cuddy Mullins. Some of them multiple times. Since the whole thing was a fraud from the beginning, I consider every one of them a victim."

"I agree. What about you two?" Kari flicked her finger between Mitch and Duffy.

Duffy and Whitmore nodded in agreement. Whitmore said, "I really like your idea about the questionnaire. Why don't we send one to all of the victims and concentrate on interviewing the higher-dollar ones or those with compelling stories of loss? You know, a pity message to tug at the heartstrings of the jurors."

"Who's gonna work on the questionnaire? I don't have the time to write up essay questions," said Duffy, taking in a frustrating breath.

"We got this." Kari poked her thumb in Becca's direction. "We'll work with one of the analysts to develop a list of questions that will trigger an actual face-to-face interview if the response deems one appropriate."

"In addition to victims with substantial losses, let's also make sure to interview the earlier investors to confirm how this scheme started," said Whitmore. "We still have to tackle our most difficult problem of trying to prove a negative."

"That the anonymous donors never existed," Kari said, elaborating.

"Exactly. Where do we stand on that issue?"

"Even with this new development, which I'm guessing is an admission that the anonymous donors were a big fat lie, we should still demand a list of names from Cuddy's attorneys."

"Of the folks on the list we got from Melinda Tribble's computer, how many people do we still need to talk to?" asked Whitmore.

"We've talked to seven of the nine people on the list, and we haven't come across anyone who provided New Visions with undesignated funds. They all were directing their donations to specific charities," said

Kari. "However, Sir Alistair Middleton is the most significant donor we have yet to speak with. I've been in contact with several people who say they have spoken to Middleton's personal assistant who they claim confirmed he was a donor."

"Who's that?"

"Brooke Warner. They either say they spoke to her on the phone, FaceTime, or Skyped with her when she confirmed that Middleton was one of the anonymous donors."

"That's a key interview we have to nail down. What's the plan?" asked Whitmore.

"I think Agent Wheeler and I should fly down to Aruba to meet with Sir Middleton and his assistant as soon as possible." Duffy grinned. "Right, Kari?"

Kari gave Becca a sideways glance.

"What? Why did you look at her that way? I hope you and your girlfriend don't think you're going to slip down to the islands together without me?"

"Excuse me?" Kari straightened up and leaned forward. She could feel her chest tightening.

Whitmore shot her a reproachful look. "I don't think Duffy meant what you thought he meant by that question."

"Careful before you defend him so quickly."

"Whoa," said Duffy. "Whitmore's right. Don't be so sensitive,"

"That's not the first time you've made a comment like that. I know what you're implying and I'm not going to let you get away with it." Kari jabbed a finger toward Duffy.

"I just thought the two of you—"

"Okay. Now I am getting a little peeved too." Becca glared at Duffy. "What exactly are you insinuating?"

Whitmore stood up. "Come on, guys. We were all making nice, and all of the sudden things have gone a little haywire."

"We have been managing to be cordial and professional and getting this job done, but I have no desire whatsoever to go anywhere with you.

If you want to go to Aruba to interview Sir Middleton, enjoy yourself. I'm not going with you."

Becca looked at Kari. "You want to tell me what's going on?

Kari pointed at Duffy. "Ask him what he said when we were interviewing Nick McCullough, New Vision's corporate accountant."

Whitmore, who was still standing behind his desk, placed both hands down and leaned forward to address the three agents. "I don't know what was said, but I do know that it's nothing I want to get in to right now. Why don't we reconvene after the questionnaire has been drafted? We'll assess our progress and then figure out who's gonna get the questionnaire."

"And what about the interview with Sir Middleton?" Duffy stood up and pushed back from his chair. "If there's any possibility he's one of the anonymous donors, I will be at that interview."

"Kari, you're the one who has a problem traveling with Duffy. So what should we do about this? I'm not interested in spending any of my time engaged in couples counseling with you two."

"Mitch, I'm not going to allow him to harass us or you to ignore it."

Duffy jumped to his feet as if Kari had taken a swing at him. "Harass you? Here we go again with that 'hashtag me too' shit." He pointed at Whitmore. "So what's it going to be? Who's going to Aruba?"

"I don't give a damn about going to Aruba," Kari snapped at Duffy. "Someone needs to interview Sir Middleton and his assistant. I'm okay if that's you."

"No, you two can go," Duffy said with a rueful but equally smug smile. "I hope you have fun. Don't forget the suntan lotion."

Kari went stiff and felt blood rush to her face. "Was that a racial dig?" Kari turned to Whitmore. "Now do you see what I mean? You still want to defend this guy?"

"Duffy." Whitmore's eyes widened in indignation. "Come on, man. This is unacceptable. You need to think twice before you say another word." He shook his head in disgust. "I think you need to apologize to the agents."

The rebuke seemed to take the wind out of Duffy. He hesitated for a beat and then extended his hand. "Sorry. I got carried away. I meant no harm."

Neither Kari nor Becca extended their hands in return nor did they verbally accept his apology. The silence in the small room grew. After several awkward seconds, Duffy stuffed his papers into his briefcase and stomped out of the office without saying another word.

***

It took Kari a moment to compose herself. When she finally found her words, she told Whitmore and Becca, "No way am I going on an overnight trip with that sexist prick."

"What just happened here? One minute, we were talking about donors and financial accounts, and next thing you know, I was in the middle of an intervention," said Whitmore.

"Some guys can't deal with strong women."

"What was it that he said to you and when was that?"

"When we were conducting the interview with McCullough, the New Visions CPA. Duffy asked if Becca was gay and made some homophobic remark about the two of us."

Becca held a hand up. "Why is this the first time I'm hearing about it?"

"He's an ass. Don't worry about it."

"I'm not worried about it. I am gay."

"I told him it was none of his business."

"I guess I'm going to have to report this to EEO." Whitmore pulled out a slip of paper and began jotting down notes.

"No." Kari shook her head. "Don't bother. I've run into his type too many times, and no one ever does anything about them and we women face the backlash for speaking up."

"Things are different now."

Kari looked at him with skepticism. "Really? Because a few actresses wore black to an awards show?" She bit her lower lip. It's just not worth the drama."

"So where do we stand? Can you both continue working with him?"

"Nope. I told you that first day when he was sitting in your office that he was going to be a problem. I'm just surprised he didn't reveal himself as a major asshole before now."

Concern clouded Whitmore's eyes. "How do you expect me to get him off the team without reporting him?'"

"You're the one pushing on that door of cynicism. That's for you to figure out."

"Great. Thanks a lot."

Kari grabbed her jacket and purse off the back of her chair and with a slight tilt of her head and a wry smile said to Becca, "Ready to go, honey?"

Becca laughed and flipped her middle finger.

As they left the room, Whitmore called after them, "Middleton and Warner still need to be interviewed. Are you two going to Aruba?"

Becca locked arms with Kari, and as they walked out of the office, she said, "Hell yes!"

CHAPTER 35

K ari and Becca came into the house straight from the US Attorneys' office and hung their coats in the hall closet. Auggie wagged his tail and nudged them with his nose, demanding to be petted. Kari knelt and scratched his thick hairy chest.

"I've never heard this house so quiet," said Becca. "Where are the rug rats?"

"It looks like Kevin and the kids aren't home yet. Which means he didn't make anything for dinner."

"Not fair. You promised me a home-cooked meal. Kevin's cooking is the best part of being partners with you."

"Thanks a lot," said Kari with a smirk. "Top chef Kevin usually throws something together." Kari tried to remember what was going on that evening. Where was her family?

She certainly did not feel like cooking. She was still seething from dealing with Bryant Duffy. It had been a mistake to acquiesce to Whitmore about bringing the IRS into the case, at least not that particular IRS agent. She was just about to pull out her phone and send her husband a text when the back door banged opened and the house instantly filled with laughter. She greeted Kevin with a peck on the cheek and rubbed the tops of her children's heads as they passed by her.

"I'm hungry." Carter sniffed the air like he was a lion stalking prey. He gave Kari an accusatory frown. "You didn't cook anything."

"We just walked in too. Everyone say hello to Aunt Becca." Carter gave Becca a high five while the girls gave her a group hug. Kari looked at her husband. "You guys didn't grab something on your way home from wherever you were?"

"I ran the girls to the store for some stuff they said they needed for a class project due tomorrow. Did you know about it?"

"Dad," said Morgan, "I told you the social studies teacher just assigned it today. We're not slacking."

"I think Daddy was checking on whether Mommy was slacking." Kari took Morgan's jacket and helped her hang it up. "What did you need to get from the store?"

"Poster board. We have to make a timeline."

"You should have called me. There's extra poster board downstairs in the basement."

Kevin walked over and put his hands on her shoulders. "Check your phone, sweetie. We texted you."

Kari took out her phone and looked at the screen. "Sorry. I didn't see it," she said with a rueful smile.

The girls flew past them on their way down to the basement rec room. One of them yelled up the stairs, "Where is it? Do we have colors? Daddy made us get white poster board. I wanted yellow. Do we have yellow? Morgan said she doesn't see it."

Kari walked to the top of the staircase and yelled back, "On the second shelf from the top. There should be at least three large pieces. I think there's a yellow one." She shut the door, then opened it again to shout out more instructions. "Don't pull everything out. Don't make a mess."

When she turned around, Carter was standing next to her.

"When are we going to eat?"

"Why don't you go upstairs and start working on your homework? I'll call you when dinner is ready."

"What are you making?"

"I don't know. It will be something edible. Now go do your homework?"

Kari turned back and shouted down the basement staircase one more time to the girls. "Did you find it?"

"Yeah, got it," Casey said. "We cleared off the big table, and we're gonna work on it down here."

Kari closed the rec room door and almost bumped into Becca. "I'm sorry. I forgot you were here."

"Apparently," she laughed. They walked into the kitchen together. Kevin was staring into the refrigerator, and Becca took a spot next to him. "Anything in there to eat?"

"Well, Aunt Becca, there're leftovers from yesterday, but not enough for everyone."

Becca turned to Kari. "Looks like I've been uninvited to dinner."

"No. Stay. I'll order a pizza."

"No thanks. I can get pizza myself."

Kevin reached into the fridge, took out two beers, and handed one to Becca. "I'm sorry," he said as he closed the refrigerator door, opened his can and took a sip. "I usually have a hot meal ready for my warrior princess when she gets home from locking up bad guys." He sat his beer on the counter and stepped in between Becca and Kari, placing his hands on their shoulders. "How are my favorite crime fighters doing?"

"Ugh. Don't ask," said Becca with a shake of her head and a swig of her beer. "It was one of those days at the office."

"What happened?"

"Thanks for asking, but I know you really don't want to know," said Kari.

"Don't say it like that. It's not like I bore you by rehashing my day on the job." He sighed heavily. "I'm home now. I try to leave that stuff at work."

"I can't always do that."

"Yeah, I know." Kevin came up behind her as she was rummaging through the kitchen junk drawer for the flyer for Salvador's Pizza, the kids' favorite. He grabbed her around the waist and nuzzled her neck.

"So what happened? I'm dying to hear all about it," he said with mock excitement.

Kari leaned into his embrace and teased him back. "You don't really care," she said with a giggle.

Becca cleared her throat. "Don't mind me. I just wanted to remind you I was here before you got carried away."

"It was that IRS agent I told you about. The one that we were practically forced to work with. I did mention that he's homophobic?"

"Did he say something to you, Becca?"

"He made some crude remarks about Kari and me."

"Like what?"

"He's pissed that we might fly down to Aruba to interview one of the donors. He insinuated that we're... more than coworkers and friends."

"You're mad at him for that? I'm sure that lots of guys in your office fantasize about you two together."

Becca picked up a dish towel and whacked him across the butt. "Not you too!"

Kevin shook his head vigorously. "Never," he said with a lopsided grin.

"Well, neither Becca nor I appreciated him expressing his thoughts out loud. What an ass. I would never cheat on you with another woman. Because, ah, sorry, Becca, I'm not gay."

"Why are you apologizing to me? You're not even my type."

Kari playfully punched her in the arm.

"Look, guys, I don't want to 'not eat and run,' but..." Becca stood in front of Kevin and pretended to look over his shoulder. "You sure you don't have your world-famous jambalaya on the stove?"

He shook his head. "Come back tomorrow, and I'll make you something good."

She made a pouty face and playfully stomped her foot. "But I'm hungry now."

***

Kari was relieved when Becca left. The last thing she wanted was to continue talking about cheating. But while they were discussing what toppings and sides to include with their pizza order, Kevin, with a goofy grin, returned to their prior conversation.

He smacked his forehead with the palm of his hand. "Sorry, babe, but I can't get the image of you and Becca out of my head. Make it go away," he said with a chuckle.

"You're a sick puppy. She's my best friend." Kari placed her hands over Kevin's eyes. "Stop visualizing that. Stop it now."

"Would you rather I start picturing you with your IRS asshole guy?"

"Now I'm going to throw up," she said, bending over and pretending to stick her finger in her mouth. "He's the last person on earth I would cheat on you with."

"Who's the first person? Is there a list?" He had a confused expression and seemed to be watching her with knowing intensity.

She wondered what her face revealed. She tried to smile, but inside, panic mounted. Her heart was hammering, and she lost track of her words for a second. She had promised herself that she would not lie to Kevin if he ever asked her if she had ever cheated on him. But he hadn't actually asked her the question. Masking her fear, she finally answered, "That hot actor on *This Is Us*. And if you want to know if I mean the white brother or the black brother, my answer is yes." She then picked up the phone to call in the pizza order.

While she was on her cell, Kevin went upstairs to change out of his work clothes. When he came back downstairs, to Kari's relief, the topic of cheating did not come up again.

CHAPTER 36

Sir Alistair Middleton's house was a sprawling, beachfront property located in the island's exclusive Malmok community. Kari drove the rental car through the gated entrance and up a beautifully landscaped, private driveway paved with crushed shells. The house featured several decks and terraces providing lavish panoramic views of the Caribbean Sea.

Becca let out a long, soft whistle. "So this is what a few million dollars can buy in Aruba."

As Kari pulled the car in front of the house, she had only a second to wonder where she should park before a young man wearing an untucked white shirt over cobalt-blue shorts approached the driver's side window.

"If you leave the keys in the ignition, I will park your vehicle for you," he said. His accent was as smooth and gorgeous as his looks. He opened the door and motioned to the front of the house. "Please go in. Mr. Middleton and Brooke are expecting you."

As the handsome, bronze-complexioned man drove away, Becca remarked, "Valet service? Yep, we are talking big money here."

Kari and Becca knocked on the front door but, after a few seconds, turned the polished handle and, as instructed, let themselves inside. "Hello?" Kari walked into the open foyer, which went straight through to floor-to-ceiling windows and looked out onto the beach and water.

Ornate grand staircases bracketed the foyer. She had never seen anything so beautiful. She glanced over toward Becca, but the only thing she could say was, "Wow."

Becca shook her head in disbelief. "Ah, yeah. Wow."

When a female voice with a hint of a British accent called down to them, they both looked toward the staircase. "Sir Middleton and I will be down shortly," the voice said. "We're not quite prepared to receive you yet."

"We were told to let ourselves in."

"Yes, of course. Please make yourselves comfortable out on the veranda. I had the chef set out some beverages and a few snacks."

Kari could see that out on the huge back deck was a table covered with a white tablecloth blowing and flapping gently about in the wind. Kari shrugged and motioned Becca to follow her outside as she took another long look around the beautifully decorated interior before stepping across the threshold into the warm Aruban breeze. She helped herself to some fresh mango and a glass of water, while Becca loaded her plate with fruit, shrimp, and finger sandwiches. "Does this look like chicken or tuna to you?" she asked as she sat down at the table and began stuffing her face. "I could see myself working here. Do you think they have an FBI satellite office?"

"No such luck. The whole Caribbean is covered out of Barbados. You'd probably end up being assigned to chase drug dealers and human traffickers all day, not hanging out at luxurious resorts being served exotic meals."

"Good point."

Kari enjoyed the time she and Becca had to sit and catch their breath while waiting for Sir Middleton and Brooke Warner. They had arrived on the island that morning and would be leaving the following day.

Kari thought about how different the short trip would have been if she had been required to come down with Bryant Duffy. He had bowed out without explanation. When she had contacted the legal attaché for host-country clearance, he told her they did not have the manpower to assign someone to accompany her on the interview. With their high-profile interviewee, two-agent corroboration was prudent, so Becca was given the green light to assist with the interview. Kari teased Becca that since she owed Kari for the trip, she would have to take notes and write up the interview.

Sitting out on Middleton's veranda, Kari and Becca were enjoying the food and the view so much that they almost forgot why they were there. Nearly fifteen minutes after they arrived, their host was guided onto the patio in a wheelchair by a lovely, beautiful, deeply-tanned woman in her mid-thirties with shocking orange-red hair. On the other hand, Sir Middleton was not what Kari had expected. He was at the least in his late nineties and appeared to be feeble and weak. He smiled at them as his assistant Brooke maneuvered him closer so he could stick out a thin, age-spotted hand. Kari was surprised at how soft and delicate it felt, and shook it with just the right amount of firmness not to insult to his manhood nor shatter any delicate bones.

She introduced herself and Becca and, in more detail than when she had called to schedule the appointment, explained why they had come all the way from Philadelphia to interview him and Brooke Warner.

"So, Sir Middleton, before we start asking you a bunch of questions about Cuddy Mullins, I want to get straight to the million-dollar question, no pun intended. Are you one of the foundation's anonymous donors, and do you know the identity of the others?"

"I could have told you that answer over the phone." Like his handshake, his voice was thin, but his eyes were full of vigor. "No. I am not one of the foundation's anonymous donors. I've provided the Foundation for New Visions in Giving with numerous grants for the good work they have done in the area of fundraiser training, but I have never given them undesignated donations to be matched with gifts from other donors or nonprofits."

"That was rather clearly stated," said Becca, taking notes.

"My attorney briefed me on what was being said about me in Philadelphia, and I wanted to be sure to put the rumors to rest," said

Sir Middleton. "I am not one of the foundation's anonymous donors." He repeated his statement again before continuing. "You mentioned that you also wanted to speak with Brooke because her name has somehow been connected to this rumor too?"

Kari explained to Sir Middleton and Brooke that several donors had indicated they had spoken to her via phone or Skype and that she had confirmed Sir Middleton's involvement.

"Skype?" said Brooke.

"You know what Skype is, right?"

"Yes, but I've never contacted anyone, not even a relative, using Skype. I don't even have an account."

"You never used Skype to conduct business transactions for Sir Middleton?" asked Kari.

"No." Brooke touched Sir Middleton's arm. "You do know that I'm his personal assistant, not his administrative assistant. I don't schedule his business appointments, nor do I assist him with his business transactions. That's Dana's responsibility."

"Dana?" Becca looked up from her notes.

"Dana Knoop. Dana's away in New York this week."

"Maybe the people we spoke with got you two confused. Could Dana have been the one to contact the donors we spoke to via Skype?"

"Dana is a man. I hope they didn't confuse me with him." Brooke laughed at the thought.

"Do you know who else it could have been? We've interviewed several people who claimed to have spoken to you. They described your accent and..." Kari tugged a few strands of her own hair. "The color of your hair."

"Well, I can see why you're confused. Not many people were born with this shade of red. But it wasn't me."

"Actually, there used to be a trainer at our gym who..." Becca tilted her head to the side, seemingly remembering something. Kari gave her a questioning look and then an image also popped into her head—the photo of Becca with an orange-red wig standing in CeCe Mullins's closet.

"Is everything okay?" asked Brooke.

"Have you ever met CeCe Mullins, Cuddy Mullins's wife?"

"Yes. They attended the Philadelphia Ball in New York together several years back when they were operating the Middleton Symposium. Before all of this matching foundation stuff."

"Interesting," said Becca.

"Why don't we start at the very beginning?" said Kari. "We'd like to ask you a few specific questions about Mrs. Mullins."

CHAPTER 37

Cuddy scanned the most recent story posted online about the ongoing federal investigation of him, his beloved foundation, and one of his closest allies: **New Visions' Accountant Faces Lawsuit.**

The article reported that McCullough had kept quiet about financial irregularities he discovered while handling the foundation's accounts and investments. Cuddy placed both hands on his churning gut; his friend was, most likely, also exposed to criminal charges along with this civil claim. Cuddy was also sick that his former supporters were reading this incriminating headline.

It was becoming harder and harder for Cuddy to recall the last time someone other than CeCe, Melinda, or one of his attorneys had called him or come by to visit. It was as if every friend and associate had been infected by the virus of distrust. The news had spread slowly through the philanthropic community, infecting everyone he knew. At first, they had told him that they refused to believe the news reports that New Visions in Giving was a Ponzi scheme. Some had contacted Sam Shiffler, the *Inquirer* reporter, directly to complain and provide their on-the-record comments about his good deeds. But soon the virus had morphed into a variant that killed all hope. Now, all he wanted them to believe was that he had never meant to hurt them.

He was a good person, and his past good deeds should be reason enough for them to continue to support him, to give him a chance to fix the mess he had made.

CeCe stirred restlessly next to him in the bed. She slept a lot lately. He lay awake most nights unable to sleep and could see how much his legal troubles weighed on her too. He watched as she tossed and turned and murmured to herself. Whatever she was dreaming of was causing her discomfort. When she unconsciously moved her leg during the night, and her thigh touched his backside, the warmth of their physical connection no longer gave him comfort. He felt himself recoiling from her touch. He knew that they were slipping away from each other. They had always had disparate viewpoints about the world, but with these recent problems, their differences were even more apparent.

But despite everything that was happening, he still had hope. He still believed that everything happened for a reason and it would all work out for the best in the end. CeCe had a more fatalistic view. Based on her sad childhood, she believed that she needed to protect herself from unseen forces that were determined to take her down. He lived by the words "do unto others as you would have them do unto you." Her motto had always been "get them before they get you."

Cuddy looked over at the digital clock on the nightstand and was shocked to see that it was already past eight o'clock. Now that he had no reason to set the alarm—he had nowhere to go—he remained in bed longer and longer each morning. Thank God he needed to get up to walk and feed Potter. Otherwise, who knew how long he and CeCe would hide in their bedroom feeling sorry for themselves?

He stretched his legs and wiggled his toes under the covers and then swung his body upright, planting his feet on the floor. He could hear Potter starting to move around right outside the bedroom door. "I'm coming, buddy. Sorry to make you wait."

"What?" CeCe asked, startled by his voice. "What's going on?"

"Nothing. Go back to sleep. I'm going to take Potter out."

"If you didn't have that dog, you wouldn't have to get up. You could stay here with me."

"Yeah, but then I wouldn't have my dog," Cuddy said soberly.

"I know you think I'm joking, but I'm not. If you had a choice between that dog and me, I'm sure you'd choose Potter."

He looked back over his shoulder at the woman he once loved. "Let's hope that I never have to make that choice," he said as he walked out of the bedroom. Once on the other side of the door, he picked up Potter, hugged him tight, and sighed. Truth be told, he wasn't capable of abandoning either one of them. He could never abandon her. Everyone in her life who had meant anything to her had done that. He now knew what that felt like.

***

When he returned from walking Potter and approached the house, he saw a strange car in their driveway and wondered who would be visiting them unannounced. Instead of going through the back door and into the kitchen, he entered the house through the front and encountered Agent Wheeler and the other female agent who was always with her. CeCe stood beside them looking frightened.

"Mr. Mullins, Kari Wheeler," she said, shaking his hand. "And this is Agent Becca Benner."

"Of course, I know who you are. What's going on?"

CeCe was in her nightclothes. Her thin blond hair was limp and disheveled, and she had a childlike sadness in her eyes.

"Why are you here?" he asked.

Contrary to the somber atmosphere in the room, Potter bounded over to the agents and with a playful wag of his tail invited their attention.

"Hey, puppy. Do you remember me too?" Agent Wheeler bent down to pet Potter. She looked up to answer his question from her kneeling position. "We have an addendum to our prior search warrant. Your wife has a copy of what we're looking for." She pointed to the paper CeCe held in her hands. "We won't be here long."

CeCe, holding her pink robe with one hand, passed him the paper she was holding in her other hand. A confused expression spread across his face as he read over it. "What's this about?" He directed his question to both the agents and CeCe. "What in the world would you want with her wigs and her personal electronic devices. CeCe is not an employee of New Visions. She had nothing to do with the operation of the foundation."

"We have reason to believe otherwise," said Kari.

Cuddy stared at his wife. "Honey, are you all right?"

Tears were brimming in her eyes. She used her fingers to flick the teardrops away.

"When I heard them knocking, I thought it might be one of the neighbors and that something had happened to you when you are out walking Potter. I mean, who else would be at our door at this hour?"

"It's not really that early." Becca glanced down at her watch. "It's after nine o'clock."

Kari pointed to the search warrant he was holding. "We need the items listed, and we'll be on our way."

CeCe escorted them up to her walk-in closet, where Becca located the wig box where she had last seen it. She looked inside and nodded to Kari. "It's in here."

Becca asked CeCe for her iPad and cell phone. Cuddy watched with shock as CeCe silently turned over the items. It was obvious to Cuddy that his wife knew why the agents were there and what they were looking for. Agent Wheeler completed an evidence receipt and handed it to CeCe. Then the two investigators walked back down the stairs and let themselves out. As soon as the door closed, CeCe collapsed at the top of the stairs.

Cuddy stood frozen on the landing.

"CeCe, what have you done?"

CHAPTER 38

In another life, the one he dreamed about when he pretended this one never existed, he would be singularly focused on helping others and spreading the word of God. In that world, people still respected and admired him, including his wife. But recently in this world he was often lost and confused.

"I don't understand. Why would they seize your phone and iPad? And the red wig?" He ran his fingers through his hair. "Where the hell did that come from?"

CeCe opened her mouth to speak, but no words came out. Cuddy could see that the agents' visit had had a devastating effect on her. Her complexion was pale, and her eyes were filled with fear. He walked up the steps toward her, and when he reached the top, he placed his hands on her shoulders and gently shook her.

"CeCe, you have to tell me what's going on. If you did something wrong, I need to know what it is and we need to tell Jillian Stevens." He stared at his wife.

"I... I think it has something to do with the anonymous donors."

"What?"

It was obvious to him that she was holding something back. Perhaps, he would go first. Before he had time to change his mind, he blurted out, "CeCe, there are no anonymous donors." He took in a big breath. "There never were. They never existed."

He waited for the shock and horror to sink in, to appear on her face. He waited for her to slap him or push him away. He waited for her to scream, to curse him. But she didn't do any of those things. Instead, she calmly said, "I know. I've known that since the very beginning."

This time, it was he who was speechless. His blood pressure slowed, and he felt light-headed. He sat down on the step beneath her and placed his head in his hands. He couldn't believe what she had said. The shock made him gasp, made it hard to catch his breath.

She lowered herself to the step above him and rubbed his back and stroked the ugly scar at the top of his head that, for her, symbolized his devotion to her. But as her words soaked into his consciousness, he swatted her hand away and scooted down a few steps, where she couldn't reach him.

"You knew?" he said, looking back at her.

"Why are you so surprised? I know you better than anyone on this earth."

"So why didn't you say anything? Why didn't you stop me?"

"Stop you? I thought it was brilliant. My mother and brother schemed and lied all their lives to scratch out a living. Look what you were able to achieve. This was nothing like my family's con games."

"Con games." He stood up quickly and almost lost his balance. He caught himself just before he took a tumble down the stairs. "This isn't a game. I wanted to do good things. I wanted to honor God."

"Cuddy, you wanted to clean up our banking accounts. Be real. You just told me that the anonymous donors never existed. It was one giant con game from the very beginning, starting with the check-kite scheme the banks discovered."

"No no no no." He started down the stairs. By the time he reached the landing, she was standing in the middle of the staircase. "I wanted to do good. I am a good person. I never meant for any of this to happen. I only needed twenty-five thousand dollars to satisfy the bank and keep the symposium open, but the initial donors started spreading the word, and things just got out of hand. I didn't know how to stop it. But you knew? Even then?"

CeCe nodded. "I was your sales support, encouraging donors to send in their checks."

"What are you talking about? You think I wanted all of this to happen?" He waved his hand in the air, a small gesture of denial.

She nodded again. "You created a lie to justify all of this. I simply pretended to believe it too."

"But you knew I didn't want any of this to happen."

"Really?"

"If you're questioning that, then I guess you never really knew me—and I guess I never really knew you."

"You could have stopped this at any time."

"I tried. I was only asking for enough to clear the debt. But the word spread and the Foundation for New Visions in Giving began to grow and grow. I didn't know how to stop it."

"You didn't want to stop it. You convinced yourself that you did this for God, but you have to admit that you love the power and the recognition. 'Cuddy, please let me become a member of your foundation, please let me give you money.' You loved how all those wealthy people absolutely adored you."

"You loved it more."

"And at least I'm honest enough to admit that."

"I wanted to help the poor and the homeless and the addicted and the illiterate and the…"

"I know that, Cuddy. I'm not saying that your intentions weren't good. But come on, honey, at some point, you knew it was going to come to this."

"But I was doing God's work."

"No matter how many times you say that, it doesn't make what you did right. Have you read the paper lately? You're accused of orchestrating and operating a $450 million Ponzi scheme.

"That's not true—"

"Stop kidding yourself," she snapped. "You did this, but you had help. Every one of your donors and recipients has to share part of the blame. Anonymous donors? They wanted to believe that bullshit because they were greedy. Damn greedy givers. Greedy takers. Everybody always wanting more, more, more."

Her angry words cut through him like a knife and his despair morphed to anger. His heart began to beat faster, and he clenched his fists. "I did this for you. I wanted to be a priest, but instead, I married you."

"You're fucking blaming me?" She threw her head back and laughed. "I guess you expected me to believe that you thought the anonymous donors were real. That all that crap the lawyers are telling you to say about your delusions is true." There was not a trace of compassion or love in her voice. "Be real!"

"I felt that…"

"That what?" She peered at him with disbelief, as if she was daring him to lie to her.

"I'm telling you the truth. I felt like God knew what I was doing, and he somehow sanctioned it because of all the good that came from it. The grants and donations were real. The foundation has helped people—lots of people. We did good things. *We did great things.*"

"Yeah, and what about the three million dollars that we spent?"

He took the stairs two at a time and yanked her roughly onto the steps, his hands were around her neck before he realized what he was doing. "I did that for you," he said as he squeezed her windpipe. "I would have been happy living a chaste life in the rectory. *I did that for you!*" He squeezed her neck harder. He could have been a different person. He could have had a different life. He could have been a better man. If only he had never met her. He shifted his unbalanced weight onto one knee to direct most of his body weight into the task of eliminating CeCe from his life.

Potter's yapping pulled Cuddy out of the fog. All of a sudden, Potter was on his back, pawing Cuddy's shoulders and face. It was the pup's persistent barking in his ear that brought him to his senses. As he released his hold on CeCe's neck, he recoiled in horror as she fell limp against the staircase wall, her face pale blue and bloodless. Relief flooded over him when she began to gasp for air and cough violently, her entire body heaving and jerking as she attempted to fill her lungs and brain with oxygen once again.

Cuddy looked down at his wife. How long had he known she was no good for him? How long had he known she was too damaged to fix? She was the force pulling him away from his true calling. He hated her. He wondered to himself how long had he known that.

CHAPTER 39

Violently red, angry welts instantly materialized on CeCe's neck. Cuddy stared at them with regret but couldn't allow himself to ask her for forgiveness. He had never even snapped at her before, let alone laid a finger on her. Sadly, she didn't expect him to be sorry for what he had done. She waved her hand as if what had happened was nothing. She ordered him downstairs to fill two Ziploc bags with ice, and when he brought them to her, she placed them in a damp towel from the bathroom and wrapped it around her neck.

"I may still have to wear a scarf or a turtleneck for a few days, but this should keep down the swelling and lessen the bruising." She motioned for him to show her his hands. She turned them palms down, and for the first time, he noticed the deep cuts and scratches made with her fingernails in her frantic attempt to remove his hands from her throat. "Oh, Cuddy," she said. "Look what I did to you. I'm sorry." She smiled sweetly and took one end of her towel and tenderly patted away the drops of blood that had dried on his skin.

He started to cry. At first, the tears streamed down his face, but within seconds of releasing his shame, he was sobbing at her feet. Here was a woman who had suffered so much abuse and neglect growing up that she believed she owed him an apology. He knew she was using his humiliation to manipulate, but that didn't excuse the fact that he had just tried to kill her. And yet, she was apologizing for clawing at his hands as he attempted to crush her throat. He had married her to protect and keep her safe from harm, and he had ended up mistreating her like all the other people in her life who were supposed to love her— her mother and her mother's many boyfriends. She seemed to accept his attacking her as if it had been inevitable.

"I'm so ashamed," he said. "The one thing I promised was that no one would ever hurt you again." He adjusted the cold compress draped around her neck. "And look what I've done."

"Don't. I'll be okay. You know that worse things have been done to me."

"Not since we've been together… and not by me."

"I don't want to talk about this anymore. We need to figure out what to do about the FBI. I guess they learned that I made some calls."

"To whom?"

"Potential donors who were hesitating when you first started the foundation."

"And the red wig?"

"I made a few of the calls on Skype or FaceTime disguised as Sir Middleton's assistant, Brooke Warner."

"Jesus Christ, CeCe."

"They won't be able to prove anything. I deleted the Skype account. I'll show you." She reached into her pocket to get her phone and remembered it had been confiscated. "Dammit, they have my phone. But they won't find anything. They're just speculating that it was me because of the red wig. They can't prove anything."

"I hope you're right. The last thing I wanted was for you to be pulled into this mess. Even if you knew about it, I am the person who did this."

"Now that everything is out in the open, we'll deal with this together." She touched his face and leaned in to smooth his hair away before she kissed his forehead. "I love you, Cuddy Mullins."

"I love you too, CeCe," he said and pulled her in close. He felt empty inside and wondered if she recognized that he had said the words with an almost clinical detachment. He was sincerely sorry for what he had done but he felt no love for her, especially now after what she made him do. Cold water from the wet towel dripped around her neck and onto his shirt and pants. Even though he knew he no longer loved her, he was worried about what would happen to her. Because one thing he knew for sure: he was going to jail for a very long time.

Cuddy made her some hot tea and was able to convince her to eat half an English muffin. As she held the cup, her hands were visibly shaking. Her sad eyes held the knowledge that something between them was irreparably broken.

They sat together quietly in the atrium, looking out at the kidney-shaped pool in the backyard covered by a dark-green tarp. It triggered more resentment and anger in him. CeCe had insisted they needed a pool so they could invite inner-city kids out for a swim. What a joke. The pool was seldom used. They hadn't even bothered to open it this past summer. She must have seen him looking at it and guessed what he was thinking. When he turned to her, she immediately looked away. Soon after, she told him she was exhausted and wanted to crawl back into bed. He went up with her, and as he pulled the covers over her, he could not believe that his anger had caused him to react the way he had. It frightened him that he was capable of such rage, especially since he could detect it still simmering deep within.

He went back downstairs and let his eyes glide over the beautiful, expensive furnishings, the contemporary art, all of the things that were supposed to symbolize their success and wealth. CeCe had filled their childless home with stuff, and it all seemed colder and lonelier than usual. The lack of laughter was what bothered him most—he was isolated and emotionally adrift.

He thought about calling Melinda, the only person who might answer his call, and then he thought of another—Tracy Cordoza. He chastised himself. He had been so consumed by his problems he had not thought about how the young woman was adapting to her new prosthetic. It had been weeks since he had visited her at the rehab center.

"Hello," the cheerful voice of Tracy's mother answered the call.

"Hi, Mrs. Cordoza. It's Cuddy Mullins. I'm calling to check in on your daughter's progress. Is she there?"

"Who is this?" she asked. He thought he detected a hostile edge in Mrs. Cordoza's voice.

"Cuddy Mullins. I came by to visit Tracy when she was at Magee. I'm assuming she's been released. How's she making out? Is she walking on the new leg yet?" He knew he was rambling, but he was detecting palatable tension from the other end of the phone. He paused a beat for a response, and when none came, he repeated, "Is she there?"

"Tracy and I read the articles in the paper about you. Don't call her anymore," she said and then hung up without saying another word.

If she had stayed on the phone, he would have struggled to squeak out a word. His throat was constricted with dread. He felt like he couldn't breathe. Is this what things had come to? Now he was a pariah, shunned by the very community he had dedicated his life's work to help.

He suddenly felt claustrophobic inside his house that was never really a home. He grabbed Potter's leash and a jacket and headed out to take a walk in his woodland sanctuary. Once they arrived at their favorite clearing, he released Potter, so he could bound off to explore. Cuddy had hoped that being outside would make him feel better, but despair continued to weigh heavily on his heart. Potter returned, dragging a stick that Cuddy absentmindedly picked up and flung for the dog to chase and retrieve. His attention was fixed in the direction where the stick had landed when he jumped at the jarring sound of the SEPTA Regional Rail train flying past. The noise of the blaring horn reverberated inside his brain—he hadn't heard its approach until it was screeching past him. He thought once again about Tracy and her own despair. He wondered how she was doing with her recovery and was embarrassed. She now knew that he was not the person who could bring her salvation and help her find her path. He couldn't even save himself.

He thought about how easy it would be to throw himself in front of the next commuter train that roared by. He could run out in front of the train on its next scheduled trip. Knowing that the midday train only ran every hour, he climbed up the embankment and boldly balanced on the thick wooden ties that fastened the steel rails together. He looked up and down the railway and wandered along the tracks until he came to the bend in the line, where the approach of the train would be hidden. He wondered if he had the courage to allow the train to slam into him and end it all. What had the SEPTA safety manager said back at Somerset subway station? That if you were going to commit suicide by train, this was how to do it. With a head-on collision with a commuter train, there was no chance of surviving. What would be left would be gathered up in trash bag. He crouched on his haunches, touched the welded rail, and then lowered himself onto his back across the tracks. He couldn't understand what had gone so wrong. All he had ever wanted to do was help others, to be of service. Connecting those who wanted to give to those who needed their gifts. He looked up at the blue sky and spoke to God, asking for a sign that ending his life was not the answer to his pain and shame. A cool breeze blew over him, and he felt the gravel beneath his body and the warm sun on his face. He was a good person. Why had things gone so wrong? Was this the way to fix it all?

The next thing he knew, Potter started licking his face and bouncing around on his chest. How could he have forgotten about him? He grabbed the pup by the collar and rolled off the tracks, Potter securely in his arms. They landed with a thud on the walking path below. Sprawled out on the ground, Cuddy hugged the little dog. "Thank you for coming to save me, Potter, but the next train is nearly an hour away." He laughed out loud, stood, hooked Potter back on his leash, and brushed the leaves and dirt off himself. He reached into his pocket and pulled out his Bible, flipping through pages until he visualized the one he was looking for. He felt it more than read it. A scripture selection for himself.

No temptation has overtaken you that is not common to man. God is faithful, and he will not let you be tempted beyond your ability, but with the temptation he will also provide the way of escape, that you may be able to endure it.

Yes. He could endure this. He could use the time during his incarceration to reset his life, to cleanse his soul. To minister to the other inmates. He would endure this.

But what about CeCe? He had no idea what the FBI had on her or if they planned to charge her. No matter what, he was determined that everything they had acquired would be forfeited. But if the government took their money and property, what would CeCe do? Where would she go? Even considering the best-case scenario, where he would be sent away but she would avoid prison, he wasn't sure if she would be able to survive on her own.

CHAPTER 40

With a morning of psychological excavation ahead of him, Cuddy Mullins settled into the comfy chair in the psychiatrist's office and felt strangely relaxed. He was surprised how much he was pleasantly anticipating the opportunity to explore his thoughts and perhaps discover what made him do the things he did.

In the three weeks since an eighty-two-count indictment had been filed by the United States Attorneys' office formally charging him with bank fraud, mail fraud, wire fraud, money laundering, false states, filing false tax returns, and, for good measure, impeding the administration of revenue laws, the defense team had started submitting the motions needed to launch their diminished-mental-capacity defense. He had already sat for a battery of brain scans and psychological tests to detect possible brain damage, as well as an evaluation by renowned forensic psychiatrist from the University of Penn Medical Center, Dr. Dwight Park. This morning's appointment was with the court-appointed psychiatrist for the prosecution.

"Mr. Mullins, as you are aware, the court has appointed me to meet with you and submit a psychological evaluation. I have read the brief provided to the courts containing mitigating circumstances your attorneys would like the court to consider, as well as responses from the prosecution side.

"I was hit in the head with a lead pipe and suffered a major concussion," Cuddy said. He had enjoyed his session with the psychiatrist his attorney had him see first. He understood what would be expected of him during this court appointed session.

"Okay. And you think that had an effect on your ability to determine right and wrong?"

"The other doctor said it might explain my delusions. You know, about the anonymous donors?"

"I assume you're referring to the psychiatrist chosen by your defense attorney. My evaluation will be independent of his. Why don't we start by reviewing your history? All I ask is that you be open and honest so that my evaluation can be as accurate as possible. Relax. Take as much time as you need. I blocked off the morning for our session."

"Will we be able to take care of everything today?"

"I believe so, and I'm willing to work through lunch if need be. Why don't you sit back and relax? Begin wherever you want to begin."

Cuddy remained upright in the brown leather recliner opposite the psychiatrist's chair. "Aren't you going to ask me questions?"

"Yes. But first I want to hear what you think the issues are. Why do you think you ended up here?"

He shifted uncomfortably in the recliner. He did not want to recline, but he kept sliding backward on the smooth, brown leather seat cushion. He wanted to simply tell the appointed psychologist what he had been saying all along. That he had been trying to make the world a better place. To do God's work. He had decided to say nothing about what he had done to CeCe. That had been an abomination.

"So basically"—he pointed to the notepad the psychologist held in her hand—"I'm supposed to tell you things about me that prove to you that I'm a mental case so the judge will go easy on me?"

"You're just supposed to tell the truth."

"Well, the problem is I'm not sure I know how to do that anymore." She raised her eyebrows.

"Because of the delusions. My head injury."

"Do your best," she said and motioned with her right hand for him to lie back in the chair.

"These accusations have been devastating for me. It's all been very depressing."

"I believe it's important to address one concern up front: Are you having or have you had in the past any thoughts about causing harm to yourself or others?"

"No," he said. He pushed the button to lower the back of the chair into a reclining position. "Never."

***

They had spoken for almost two and a half hours before Cuddy told the psychologist about the turning point in his life when he was attacked and developed the special gift of knowing the Bible. He pulled the New Testament from his inside jacket pocket and offered to select a perfect passage for her. When she didn't immediately answer him, he lifted his head to look at her. Instead of being intrigued by his offer, the doctor seemed to be disturbed.

"Do you ever copy these selected passages and hand them out to people?"

"Always." He nodded. "I feel obligated to share my gift with those in need. I get this sensation, and I see—I know the right page and the right passage. It just happens."

He waited for the doctor to say something and when she didn't, he continued. "I would be honored to select a scripture for you, but I can't force it. It just comes to me naturally."

She said nothing. And although he couldn't actually see her from his prone position, he could tell something was wrong.

"Excuse me for a moment," she said. He heard her get up from her chair, walk over to her desk, and pick up her phone. After a few seconds, he overheard her leaving a message. He detected in her voice what he thought might be concern. "This is Dr. Patel." She spoke softly, as she left a message. "I need to cancel our one o'clock appointment for this afternoon. Please call me later so we can reschedule." She hesitated and then repeated her message. "This is Dr. Patel." This time she spoke deliberately into the receiver as if to guarantee that the message would be heard. "Our one o'clock appointment is canceled. Do not come to my office."

Cuddy sat up and watched as she turned around. She smiled, but Cuddy could tell it was fake.

He leaned forward. "Is everything okay?"

"Yes, of course." The psychologist moved from behind her desk and returned to her chair. She crossed her legs, picked up her notebook, and said, "I want to make sure that we have enough time for me to complete my evaluation today. I thought it wise to reschedule my afternoon appointment just in case."

"Just in case what?"

"We need more time." Her posture was rigid, and she was drumming her pen on her knee.

"Was it something I said?" He held up his Bible. "Was it about the scriptures? If you thought my offer was inappropriate, I apologize. I certainly didn't mean to make you uncomfortable."

She didn't answer his question. Instead, she waved for him to resume his reclined position. Soon they had returned to their previous easy conversation, and the interruption was forgotten. They talked for another hour.

"Mr. Mullins, I believe we can finish up this evaluation today if we power through for another hour or so. Since my afternoon appointment is canceled, do you want to continue?"

"Is it possible for us to get something to eat first?" As if on cue, his stomach let out a loud growl.

"I was hoping you would say that. There's a little deli that serves really good sandwiches nearby. I can call in an order, and we can take a short break. Does that work for you?"

"That works for me," he said.

"I'll have it delivered."

"If you have something you need to do, you know, like make a call, I'd be happy to stretch my legs and go pick it up. Is it the one on the corner?"

She nodded.

"I could use a quick break. I would never have imagined how tiring it is to talk about yourself." They both laughed politely.

"What do you want?"

He gave her a quizzical stare.

"To eat," she said, and they laughed again.

"I thought you were asking me a philosophical question." He chuckled. "I'll take a hoagie."

She tore a piece of paper from her notebook and looked up at him. "Oil or mayo? Onions and peppers?"

"Oil, onions, and sweets."

"Got it. I'll call the order in."

Cuddy nodded. "Where's your bathroom?"

"The men's room is to the left of the elevator."

"I'll excuse myself and then walk over to pick up the food."

"Let me get you money."

He waved his hand.

She shook her head. "I can't do that."

"I'll get it. Pay me when I get back," he said as he left the office.

***

He searched for Dr. Patel's name on the bags resting on the pick up counter and made his way through the lunch crowd to pay for the order at the register. While he waited to be rung up, his eyes were focused through the storefront window at the people walking by on the street. He did a double take. He thought he had spotted Agent Wheeler walking past the deli. He paid and quickly pushed his way through the patrons still waiting for their orders. When he got outside, he didn't see her. Maybe he had been mistaken. But if it had been Agent Wheeler, she was nowhere to be seen now.

Returning to the office building and riding up in the elevator, he thought about what was left for him to share with the psychiatrist. He had tried to emphasize all the great work he had accomplished. He hoped she would see the connection between his brain trauma and all of the bad decisions he had made afterwards. There had to be a connection. As far as he was concerned, nothing else could explain it. He was not the Bernie Madoff of the charitable world. He had not intentionally created this mess. When the elevator door opened, he stepped out into the hallway and could hear Dr. Patel speaking to someone around the corner, out of his view.

"As soon as I realized that he was the subject of your case, I knew you would not want to bump into him and have him find out you're one of my patients too."

"It's not your fault. I should have checked my phone before I came."

"You better go. He's probably right behind you."

"I'll take the stairs."

Cuddy immediately recognized the voice of Agent Wheeler. So he had seen her out on the sidewalk. Interesting that she was here. Why did she need to see a psychologist? He could hear two doors shutting, presumably Dr. Patel going back into her office and Agent Wheeler slipping through the stairwell exit. He jogged down the hall and followed her, catching up with her on the next floor's landing.

"I thought I heard your voice." She jerked around abruptly and grimaced when she saw him.

"I know what this looks like," she said, "but I'm not here checking up on you."

"I wasn't thinking that. You were Dr. Patel's one o'clock that she tried to cancel."

"I'm not going to have a discussion with you about why I'm here or why you're here."

"We know why I'm here." He laughed, hoping to put her at ease. As he looked closely at her, he felt the same connection he got the first time they had met, as if they had something in common.

Agent Wheeler turned to continue walking down the stairs.

"Please wait."

She paused.

"I keep getting this strong vibe every time I see you, and I'm struggling to figure out what it is." She shrugged, but he could tell that she was curious about what he meant. Maybe she could feel it too.

"After you showed up at my house a few weeks ago, a passage came to me that I thought I would give you the next time I saw you." He searched his jacket pocket and pulled out his Bible and removed a slip of paper. "Who knew it would be so soon?"

"I don't want it."

"Why not?"

"I don't believe in it. Your gift," she said. Her voice had a slight waver.

"Is that really what you think? That it has no meaning? Why so resistant, so afraid of what's written on a little piece of paper?"

"I'm not."

"Well then, take it." He handed her the folded paper. "It's from Romans 2, God's righteous judgment."

He watched her hesitate for a beat before taking it and slipping it under the outside flap of her brown leather handbag.

"Read it later. Read it never," he called out to her as she hurried down the stairway.

CHAPTER 41

It was late by the time they had helped with homework, cleaned up the dinner mess, and settled side by side in the family room, in front of the TV. The kids were up in their rooms, getting ready for bed, and Kari and Kevin were alone. Kari was thinking about running into Cuddy Mullins at Dr. Patel's office earlier that day and unconsciously let out a heavy sigh of annoyance.

"What's wrong now?" said Kevin.

Kari shook her head. "Nothing." She stared at the TV.

"You're a million miles away."

"I'm right here, watching this stupid show." She pointed at the screen. "A real cop would never do what he just did. You know that, right?"

"Today's Thursday. Didn't you go to see your shrink today? I thought seeing her was supposed to make you feel better. It doesn't seem to be working."

"It's working." She watched him roll his eyes at her. "Something weird happened when I got there today. I was thinking about it. That's all."

"Something weird?"

"The Ponzi scheme guy we're investigating was ordered by the court to have a psych evaluation. Dr. Patel got the assignment, and I ended up bumping into him there."

"Awkward?"

"Definitely."

"You didn't want him knowing that you're both lying on the same couch?"

"Of course not. Remember I told you he passes out those Bible verses like they're fortunes?"

"What's wrong? He gave you another one today, and you didn't like yours?"

Kari scrunched up her nose.

"Let me see it."

"It doesn't make any sense."

"Let me see it. Maybe I can help you figure it out."

She didn't move.

"Seriously, Kari. If it's bothering you that much, I want to read what it says."

Dread and regret settled over her like a cloud. Why had she mentioned the slip of scripture to him? She removed it from her pocket and read it out loud.

"Romans 2. Therefore you have no excuse, O man, every one of you who judges. For in passing judgment on another you condemn yourself, because you, the judge, practice the very same things. We know that the judgment of God rightly falls on those who practice such things. Do you suppose, O man—you who judge those who practice such things and yet do them yourself—that you will escape the judgment of God?'"

Kevin motioned with two fingers for her to hand it to him.

"It's a joke," she said. "He doesn't know anything about me or my life."

He read it over several times. He glanced up at her each time, as if doing so would help him discover its meaning.

"It has nothing to do with me."

"Did you do something that warrants the judgment of God?"

"Me? No."

"Then why does it bother you so much?" He reread the scripture.

JERRI WILLIAMS

"What are you afraid of being judged about?"

"Give it back. I should have thrown it away without reading it. It's a joke."

Kari avoided looking directly at Kevin. She was scared of what he would see in her eyes. She gave him a sidelong glance and saw suspicion and distrust in his expression. Her heart began to beat faster. A desire to flee took over, and no matter what she did to try to hide it, she knew Kevin could sense her fear.

"I've wanted to ask you something, and I think this is the perfect time to get a straight answer from you." He picked up the TV remote and lowered the volume.

Kari stood and pointed upstairs. "Let me check on the kids first, and I'll come back down so we can talk."

"No." She could tell he was agitated. He was jiggling his leg, like he always did when he was disturbed about something.

"Remember when you and Becca were leaving to go to Aruba, and we were talking about that IRS agent who accused you of having a thing?"

"Oh, come on, Kevin. You can't possibly believe I'm having an affair with Becca."

"No, not with Becca."

She knew he was waiting for her to say something, but she was afraid to speak, afraid where this conversation would take them.

"When I said something to you about it, you didn't deny having an affair."

"What do you mean?"

"I remember it clearly. You said you would never cheat on me with a woman because you were not gay." He leaned in closer and looked her directly in the eyes. "Why'd you qualify it like that?"

"I didn't."

"I hope you wouldn't cheat on me with anyone, male or female." Kevin laughed uneasily and poked her with his finger. "That's what you should have said."

When she didn't respond, he stared at her in a way that seemed like he was burrowing into her thoughts, digging for the truth. Kari began to shake uncontrollably, her body physically expelling her secret. The pained look on his face made her lips quiver and tears begin to pool in her eyes.

He shook his head in disbelief. "No, Kari, no" was all he said.

"I didn't know how to tell you," she said, her tears now turning into sobs. "And it's been destroying me each day I didn't say anything."

"All this time in therapy…" He looked so hurt. "It wasn't about the shootout. It was about the affair."

"It wasn't an affair. We had consensual sex"—she stabbed her index finger in the air—"one time."

"Oh, only once," he said, his tone dripping with sarcasm. "You cheated on me, had sex with another man, but only one time."

"It was twice. But the second time he raped me." Her released anguish produced a cry that was ugly, raw and ragged.

His eyes remained full of anger. Her revelation inspired no pity. "And all this time you let me believe your guilt was about the shooting incident."

"It was both." She shuddered in anticipation of the bomb she was about to drop. "I had sex with the man that I shot. I had sex with Joe Wilson."

"What are you talking about?"

"He assaulted me." She clutched at Kevin's arm, but he pushed her away. "He raped and blackmailed me. But I didn't want to kill him; I just wanted him to leave me alone. He was staying at the Sheraton with a woman, and Everett and I just happened to be there, and her husband arrived and shot her, and I was protecting the people. It was self-defense. The review team said it was a good shooting and…" She knew she was rambling, but she couldn't control herself. She wiped tears and snot from her face with the back of her hand.

"Stop it." He shook her hard. He looked at her as if he didn't recognize her. "Stop it."

"You have to forgive me. I was faithful before I made this horrible mistake. Fifteen years." She buried her head in her hands.

"Isn't that how many times you shot him? Jesus Christ, Kari! You emptied your weapon into him—fifteen times. A shot for every year of our marriage."

"He wouldn't put his gun down. I had no choice."

He was breathing heavily, and his words came out slow and deliberate. "And we all thought you were a hero."

"Mom's not a hero?" The kids were standing on the stairs, looking down at them. How long had they been listening? How much had they heard?

"Apparently not," Kevin answered after a beat. She could see that he immediately regretted his remark, but not because of her—because of hurting them, scaring them. Kevin looked up at the top of the stairs, where Carter and the twins stood.

"Your mom and I need to talk. Please go back to your rooms. We'll call you when we're done."

Kari could not look at them. She did not want to see the disappointment and confusion in their eyes. "I'll be up to check on your homework when we're done," she called out. "Do as Daddy said. Go to your rooms and shut the door." As an afterthought, she added, "Everything's gonna be okay."

Kevin spent the next hour grilling her, only stopping once to allow the kids to come down and get a snack and reassure them that they were having a serious discussion, but that they would work through it.

The kids—and Kari—knew he was lying.

With the kids sequestered away in their rooms, she told him everything. How when she was working the strip club corruption case, she had met Joe Wilson while conducting an interview at one of the clubs. How in one regrettable moment of weakness she went back to his hotel room with him. How he had found out her true identity and tried to blackmail her into providing information from his FBI file to help him beat a federal drug case. How she was determined to stop him.

And how when she discovered Joe Wilson was having an affair with his codefendant's wife, Everett helped her install cameras in Wilson's hotel room and make a sex tape, which she threatened to show Wilson's codefendant. Wilson knew his violent partner would kill him if he found out. The following day, when Kari and Everett returned to the hotel to pick up the camera equipment, Wilson's codefendant arrived at the same time and shot his wife. Wilson returned fire and killed his codefendant. When Wilson spotted Kari, he probably assumed that she had showed his partner the sex tape and told him where to find them, and though she called out for Wilson to drop his gun, he raised his weapon, and Kari had no choice but to shoot.

"Everett had no knowledge of Wilson's criminal background. He thought he was helping when he contacted the codefendant." Her jaw quivered from the power of her confession. "I was protecting Everett as much as I was protecting myself when we agreed to conceal the underlying blackmail scheme. Since we had a cooperative witness living nearby, we were able to convince everyone that we just happened to be at the right place at the right time."

"I feel like a fool." Kevin held up a finger to silence her when she started to correct him. "You've been lying to me for almost a year."

"You have to give me another chance," she said barely above a whisper.

"I don't have to do shit." He abruptly rose up from the couch and took a step back. He pointed at her but said nothing. His face was flushed, but his eyes were vacant. He turned away and climbed the stairs two at a time to their bedroom, essentially suspending the discussion. They both had work the following day.

She followed him up to bed, wondering if she should offer to sleep on the pullout sofa in the basement. But instead, she lay down next to him in their bed. She couldn't sleep and lay there, listening to Kevin breathing in the dark. Everything that she had dreaded was happening now. And she had no indication from Kevin what he was going to do about it. They would need help with this.

First thing in the morning, an hour before the alarm was set to go off, Kari got up, went into the bathroom with her cell, and left a text for Dr. Patel. After she hit send, she climbed back into bed. Her mind settled just enough for her to finally fall asleep.

***

When the alarm went off, Kevin was already up and in the kitchen brewing coffee. She hurried downstairs to speak with him before the kids woke up.

"Were you able to get any sleep? I was awake for most of the night." Kari walked over to Kevin, who was at the sink, and placed her hand on his back. He disengaged with an awkward jerk as if he were burned by her touch.

"I couldn't sleep either. Sometime during the night, I realized how ridiculous it was." Kevin stared at her.

She couldn't read his facial expression. "What's ridiculous?"

"The fact that I was sleeping in the bed next to you. That was pathetic. I don't want to share a bed with you." He spat out *you* as if it were a bug that had landed in his mouth. "I'm moving down to the basement tonight."

"I understand. I've had more than nine months to prepare myself for the day when I would tell you about what happened. And you—"

"And I had no clue until you gut punched me."

She was saddened by what appeared to be animosity in his tone. "I thought we would need help processing everything. I sent a text to Dr. Patel. Maybe she can fit us in today. We need to figure out how to move forward."

"Move forward? I'm not sure we're going to be able to move forward."

Her throat tightened as she started to panic. "But you seemed willing to work this out last night," she said with a pleading pitch.

"Kari, I think I was in shock last night. I didn't know what to think or how to react."

"And this morning…" She dreaded his response.

"This morning, I'm angry. I'm angry with you, and I'm angry with myself. I should have known there was more."

"That's why I think we should get in to see Dr. Patel as soon as possible." Her voice was full of desperation.

"No. You can go. And maybe I'll go to someone too, but I'll get my own shrink and my own attorney."

Kari's heart skipped a beat. She felt the blood draining from her face. "Your own attorney?"

"I don't know if I can ever"—he made air quotes—"'get over this.'"

Kari suddenly remembered Cuddy's scripture. She now knew what it meant. She and Cuddy were both cheaters who were going to have to pay for their sins.

CHAPTER 42

Before the meeting in the main conference room of Smith, Stevens, Keller, and Goldberg had begun, Cuddy helped himself to the Danishes, bagels, fresh fruit, and coffee laid out on the long credenza in the rear of the room. A paralegal had been tasked to collect press clippings about the legal troubles of Cuddy Mullins and the Foundation for New Visions in Giving. When Cuddy saw how thick the folder was, his mood sank. He glanced down at his plate and put down his fork. He was no longer hungry.

He and CeCe sat together with all the members of their legal team to strategize what came next. As concisely as possible, Jillian had dissected the indictment for them. Cuddy was concerned to learn that there had been an addendum to the original indictment and his accountant and friend Nick McCullough had also been charged in the scheme with one count each of wire fraud and aiding and abetting, as well as impeding the administration of revenue laws for allegedly accepting bribes in the amount of $510,000 from Cuddy to discourage him from asking difficult questions when reviewing New Vision's books and investments. Thank God CeCe and Melinda had been spared—for now.

"Obviously, we can still proceed with a diminished-mental-capacity defense, but based on Judge Sterling Benedetti's recent ruling, we recommend that you enter a plea," said Jillian. She wore a sober expression and placed her palms flat on the table in front of her. "This type of charity fraud case has zero jury appeal. As I advised you earlier, it would be prudent to present your statement to the court and request a downward departure based on acceptance of responsibility and the voluntary forfeiture of assets."

"What?" CeCe rose from the table. "I told you Cuddy's not pleading guilty and we aren't giving them our money."

"He wouldn't be pleading guilty. Not exactly. A nolo contendere, or no contest plea, is where Cuddy would proclaim he is innocent of the crime while nevertheless admitting that the prosecution has enough evidence to prove that he is guilty beyond a reasonable doubt. The judge has indicated he would rule against our use of psychiatric experts. Cuddy's conditional plea would allow us to take the issue to the Court of the Appeals. We can't do that without him being sentenced first."

"CeCe, Jillian has explained the other benefits to this nolo contendere plea."

"It's a strategy where Cuddy doesn't have to admit guilt and his plea, therefore, can't be used against him in the civil lawsuits that have been filed and will be filed in the future."

Cuddy placed his hand on her arm and directed his wife to return to her seat. "It's an option, sweetheart. It sounds like it's the right thing to do, but for now, it's just one of many options."

From the corner of his eye, he could see Jillian raise an eyebrow and give a slight shake of her head.

"What about me?" said CeCe, her voice cracking a little. "Are they planning to charge me too?"

"No." Cuddy spoke up quickly. He wanted to answer the question before anyone else could give one of their abstruse legalese-laden responses. He wanted her status clearly stated. "No, you won't be charged," he said. "The legal team has worked all of that out."

"There's something you're not telling me." She looked at him suspiciously.

Jillian reached across the table and grabbed CeCe's hand gently.

"The investments and house must be signed over."

"Absolutely not!"

"That's the only bargaining chip we have to keep you out of jail."

"That's everything we have. I'd rather go to jail and have something waiting for me when I—when we get out." She turned to Cuddy and made what he determined was an insincere apologetic face. "I'm sorry, Cuddy, but where would I live? What would I live on? Please don't ask me to do this."

"It's a good thing," said Jillian. "The assets will be liquidated and go back to the victims as part of a victim restitution pool."

"Good for them. Not for me."

"You don't understand," he said. "If we give up the assets, they have agreed not to charge you as a coconspirator. If you say no, they'll charge you and take them anyway. The money and property belong to the government either way."

"That's blackmail," said CeCe.

"When it comes to you, the feds may be throwing their weight around," said Jillian. "But what Cuddy isn't telling you is that his exposure could amount to twenty-five to thirty years in jail, with no parole. The forfeiture of all your assets could reduce that exposure by half, as will our downward departure request based on a diminished-mental-capacity defense."

Cuddy closed his eyes, let out a deep breath, and slammed his hand on the table. The room grew eerily quiet. As he spoke, he felt a measure of control come back to him. "That's not what's important to me. I deserve whatever I get. If we give everything back, He will forgive us."

This time, the silence in the room was weighted with uncertainty.

"He who?" CeCe asked, but then, her face slowly registered understanding. "You mean God?"

Cuddy nodded.

"God was there when I was going through my shitty childhood and did nothing to help me. You told me I went through all of that so I would appreciate love and wealth more when it was finally provided.

Now, He's going to snatch it all away? Why should I give a damn about what God thinks?"

Cuddy reached into his inside jacket pocket, took out his Bible, and laid it on the table in front of him.

"Don't!" CeCe's chair scraped the hardwood floor as she pushed herself up from the table, grabbed the Bible, and flung it across the room barely missing the paralegal as it whizzed past her head. "I don't ever want to hear another fucking reading from that damn Bible!"

Embarrassed by her outburst, he flinched at her crude reference to the word of God.

CeCe cast a defiant gaze about the room. "I'd rather be dead than be poor again."

CHAPTER 43

It had been two weeks since Kevin had learned the truth about Joe Wilson, and Kari desperately needed to speak to someone about the fallout. She'd had several sessions with Dr. Patel, but what she really needed was to talk to a friend. Due to the career-ruining implications of the situation, she couldn't lean on Becca. But Everett knew about everything. He shared her story. She stuck her head in the computer analysis office to look for him. He wasn't there, but she bumped into him in the nearby corridor.

"Everett. I need to speak with you."

"What's up? Did you find out more about the hard drive missing from your subject's CPU?"

"It's not about that." She moved in closer as she could whisper. "I told Kevin the truth. I think he's going to take the kids and leave me." She spoke in a wheezy voice caused by keeping her voice low and by the heavy lump that had settled in her throat.

As she stumbled over her words, Everett backed away. He shook his head and touched a finger to his mouth, panic registering on his face.

"I needed to talk to someone about this. I know we agreed but..."

Everett kept shaking his head and looked up and down the hallway. He motioned for her to follow him to closed files, where he pushed the button for the automatic shelves to open and he walked into the secluded aisle. He again pressed a finger to his lips, grabbed a pencil from the shelf, and wrote something on the back of one of the green file-removal slips. Holding on to the pad tightly, he held it up for her to read. The note read, *We agreed to NEVER talk about it.* He ripped off the piece of paper he had written on and tore it into tiny pieces, which he then placed in his pants pocket.

"Oh my God! You think I'm trying to set you up?" She could feel the heat of embarrassment and disbelief rise up from her neck onto her cheeks. She was shocked that he would think that she would betray him.

His expression turned from distrust to contrition. "I don't know what you want from me, why you want to *talk* about it," he whispered.

She could tell he was allowing himself time to consider her motives. He wrote another note: *Meet me across the street outside of the Visitor's Center. 10 minutes.* He tore up that note and tucked the tiny pieces in his pocket too.

"Thank you, Everett," said Kari. He left the room without responding.

***

She was positive that he had left the office before she had, but when she crossed Sixth Street and walked around the Independence Visitor's Center, he was nowhere to be found. She wasn't sure where to meet him. She hurried to the grassy mall and then headed back toward the building. Finally, among the families and tour groups venturing in and out of the building, she saw him pushed up against the brick wall near a lesser-used entrance. As she got closer to him, she saw compassion and concern on his face. She was relieved and grateful to see him. He was the only one she could talk to about this.

"Kari, I came out here against my better judgment. Once we made the decision to withhold info, we knew we could never go back. We could lose our jobs."

Kari realized that Everett had no idea how much he still didn't know about her connection to Joe Wilson. That's why it had been so easy for him to accept the pronouncement that he was a hero. And maybe he was, even if she could never see herself that way.

"After my suspension, I had a terrible time accepting that I had messed up. But I got help and moved on. I feel terrible that Kevin found out about Joe Wilson." He held up both hands in front as if to push away the knowledge. "But the only thing I need to know is how this will affect me."

"I don't know what to do."

"This may sound cold, but the only reason I came out here was to find out what you told Kevin about me."

"He already knew you were there."

"So he has no idea that I knew there was something going on between you and Wilson?"

She knew he was going to go ballistic when she told him the truth. "I told him everything. He knows everything," said Kari. Everett's eyes widened and he clutched his stomach as if he had been kicked. "I had to tell him. I couldn't lie to his face."

Everett stared at her with a look of anger and fear. "*Oh My God*. But we promised never to tell anyone not even our spouses." He pounded his head with both hands as he scowled at her. "What have you done?" he said, his words fraught with despair.

"He won't tell anyone else." Even as she said the words, doubt overwhelmed her.

"Really? You don't know what he'll do if he decides to divorce you. He might do anything, say anything to keep you from getting custody." The muscles in his jaw were clenched. "What were you thinking?"

She opened her mouth to speak, but he shook his head. "I care about you, Kari, but if you need help, I'm not your guy. I have to think about my future, my career, my family."

He stepped toward her as if he was going to hug her, but suddenly turned away. She watched as he walked quickly back toward the federal building.

CHAPTER 44

Kari entered the gym and waved at Carter, who was sitting on the team bench tying his shoe. As she walked toward the home team's section, she continued smiling and waving at her neighbors and the parents of her kids' friends, who were also there to watch the rousing after-school competition. She wondered if they had any idea what was happening behind the doors of the Wheeler-Jackson home. How the family unit was barely holding on. It had been two weeks since Kevin had learned about her betrayal. He had not kicked her out of the house, for the good of the children, but they barely spoke and continued to sleep in different beds. She was devastated. But now that everything was out in the open and she no longer had to hide the truth, her shame had stopped nibbling away at her insides.

Kevin and the twins were sitting in their usual spot opposite Carter's team bench, strategically in the middle of the bleachers. The girls stood up and gleefully waved at her. When he spotted her, Kari thought she detected a smile on Kevin's face too—it didn't stay long, but it had been there. She apologized to those she had to maneuver past as she climbed up into the bleachers. When she reached her family, the girls instinctively moved and created a space for her to take her seat next to Kevin.

"What? Carter's not starting?" she said as five of her son's teammates ran out onto the court for the tipoff.

"Settle down, momma bear." He absentmindedly patted her knee. "This is an intermural game; they all have to play the same number of minutes. He'll get his time on the court."

She was unable to pay any attention to what he was saying; she was fixated on his touch as a wave of adrenaline surged up her thigh. It seemed like it had been ages, not just a couple of weeks, since there had been any physical contact between them. He caught her looking at where his hand was resting and abruptly removed it, looking away.

During the first two quarters, they didn't speak. The noise level in the small space didn't allow for conversation at a non-ear-shattering decibel. The yips and yelps of the spectators, the screeching sound of rubber shoes scuffing along the highly polished wooden floor, the constant whistle of the referees, and the blaring game buzzer made up an adequate excuse for them to avoid small talk. They both kept their eyes straight ahead and concentrated on the action on the court. These sporting events were the only time they spent together since the big revelation.

Toward the end of the first half, she could feel him studying her, and she realized that she was pushing her tongue against the inside of her lower lip, an old nervous habit that always got on his nerves.

"I'm sorry," she said. "Was I doing that thing again?"

"Yeah, but it's okay. It just makes you look weird." He shrugged. "It's okay with me if you if you want to look weird in front of a whole gym full of people."

This time, he didn't tone down his expression—he smiled broadly at her, a teasing glint in his eyes. But before she could engage in an attempt at their first civil conversation in weeks, he excused himself, saying he needed to use the restroom, and escaped with the crowd leaving to grab halftime snacks.

She felt silly having any hope that the coldness between them was thawing or would soon; nevertheless, she placed her hand on her knee where his had been earlier and smiled.

CHAPTER 45

A month after Cuddy Mullins entered a nolo contendere plea, he was scheduled to return to court for sentencing. The Honorable Sterling Benedetti would hear the testimony of expert witnesses, victims, and investigators before he decided to accept and render his sentence. His attorneys anticipated the sentencing would last from several days to a week. The issues at stake were Mullins's mental health and capacity, and his intentions. After testimony had been entered on record, it would be up to the judge to determine whether Mullins was legally sane or not.

Prosecutor Mitch Whitmore stood behind the lectern, adjusted his notes, and waited while the court officer swore in Dr. Nina Patel. They had already heard from Dr. Dwight Park, the forensic psychiatrist from the University of Penn Medical Center hired by the defense to examine Cuddy Mullins and present a report to the court. Dr. Patel placed one hand on the Bible and the other she held high, her palm facing outward. She repeated the oath to tell the truth and took her seat on the witness stand.

"Dr. Patel, are you aware that several years ago, Mr. Mullins was assaulted and suffered a severe brain injury?" asked Whitmore.

"Yes, determining if that incident had cause and effect related to what he is accused of and his claims of being a religious zealot are what I was asked to determine."

"Dr. Patel, would you consider Mr. Mullins to be a religious zealot?"

"There is not a clinical definition for what makes one a religious zealot. However, if you are asking if it is my expert opinion that Mr. Mullins is overly occupied with religious scriptures and sacraments to an extreme or fanatical degree?" Dr. Patel placed her forefinger to her nose and adjusted her glasses. "No, he is not. His attachment to the Bible is more fervent than most Christians, but not to a point where it is destructive to him or others."

"You say that even though he is here in court today accused of operating a scheme that took in more than $450 million that primarily targeted Christian-based institutions."

"That's correct. I'm not here to assess Mr. Mullins's motivation to target the faithful, but his crimes were not caused by his unchecked devotion to God."

"And could you explain to the court how you made that determination?"

"I engaged in several hours of evaluation and analysis with him and then compared his responses to case studies of individuals with fanatical and zealot tendencies."

"So when Mr. Mullins' attorneys indicate that he acted out of unchecked religious fervor and not greed, that would be incorrect in your professional experience?"

"Yes, I disagree with that assessment."

"Do you have an opinion regarding his mental health?"

"I diagnosed Mr. Mullins as having a personality disorder commonly known as narcissism."

"And could you tell us more about how narcissism works as it relates to the charges filed against Mr. Mullins?"

"It is my belief that Mr. Mullins created the Foundation for New Visions in Giving in order to promote himself and that the scheme expanded as he exploited others in this attempt to obtain approval and admiration."

"Let me understand what you're saying." Whitmore tapped his pen on the base of the podium. "Is narcissism a mental illness and impairment that would cause Mr. Mullins to have delusions about anonymous donors?"

"No. Narcissism is a trait that many leaders and important people have. When directed in a positive manner, it can sometimes allow these visionaries to create extraordinary products and accomplishments."

"And delusions about anonymous donors?"

"Again, it's my opinion that a diagnosis of narcissism does not present with delusions."

"What about hallucinations? Mr. Mullins claims he had meetings with these anonymous donors. Could he have been hallucinating?"

"No. Hallucinations do not involve complex conversations with recognized characters, such as anonymous donors."

"So when Mr. Mullins claims to have had delusions or hallucinations once a month on Sundays." Mitch Whitmore looked down at his notes for a moment. "Sometimes several times a month. When he says he had these meetings and that he now realizes that they were delusions, in your professional experience, is he telling the truth?"

"No, he is not. I would say it's impossible to have hallucinations that occur on selected dates at scheduled times," said Dr. Patel. "And such delusions would be a complete novelty in psychiatry. That's not how the brain works."

"And so your conclusion about whether or not Mr. Mullins had delusions or hallucinations about the existence of the anonymous donors is…"

"I would have to conclude that Mr. Mullins is making this all up, that he is pretending."

"Would it be correct for me to interpret your polite answer to mean that Mr. Mullins is lying to the court about this?"

"Yes. That would be correct." Dr. Patel turned to look at the judge and nodded. "When it comes to whether or not Mr. Mullins could have legitimately believed that the anonymous donors existed based on any type of perceived delusions, I believe he is lying about that possibility."

"Did you also have a chance to review Mr. Mullins's performance on a battery of psychological tests that Dr. Park, the psychiatrist retained by the defense team, had him undergo?"

Yes, I did."

"And your conclusions about those tests?"

"My review of the tests indicated malingering."

"And would you explain the term *malingering*?"

"The results indicated that Mr. Mullins was trying to appear to have brain damage when he does not. I believe that any crimes the defendant may have committed were not the result of diminished mental capacity."

"Thank you, Dr. Patel." Whitmore turned and nodded at the judge. "Your Honor, I have no further questions."

Judge Benedetti smiled at the attorneys sitting at the defense counsel table. "Ms. Stevens, do you have any questions for Dr. Patel?"

Kari wasn't surprised when Jillian Stevens nodded and stood. "Yes, I have a few questions." She took her place behind the lectern. "Dr. Patel, you indicated that Mr. Mullins did have a personality disorder. Is that correct?"

"Yes, that's correct. Narcissism."

"You also said that in some leaders, this narcissism could be a good thing. But I would imagine that means that, in some cases, it could lead to negative behaviors. Is that correct?"

"It is a mental disorder that can affect conduct."

"To include how Mr. Mullins operated the Foundation for New Visions in Giving?" asked Jillian.

"That could be possible. How significant those effects would be, I would not be able to tell you."

"Have you had the chance to review the conclusions presented to the court by your colleague Dr. Park?"

"Yes, I have."

"And do you agree or disagree with their conclusion that Mr. Mullins's disorder negates or at the least explains his intent to commit a crime, in this case, the alleged Ponzi scheme?"

"I'm not sure if I understand what you're asking."

"I'm asking if you are one hundred percent sure that the charges filed against Mr. Mullins were not exacerbated by Mr. Mullins' personality disorders, which you confirmed he had, and that based on them, he could not form criminal intent."

"Objection." Whitmore leaped to his feet. "Dr. Patel was retained to provide an evaluation and insight to the court. She should not be asked to make decisions about guilt."

"Overruled." Judge Benedetti leaned his body in the direction of Dr. Patel and nodded. "The court would like to hear Dr. Patel's educated thoughts on this matter and promises not to rely on that opinion when the court makes its final determinations. Continue, Dr. Patel."

Kari watched intently as Dr. Patel clasped her hands in front of her and answered definitively. "I can tell you with one hundred percent certainty that, whether Mr. Mullins had a brain injury that caused him to have visions and a photographic memory of the Bible or not, it is my professional opinion that he understood the difference."

"The difference?" said Jillian.

"Between right and wrong. After examining Mr. Mullins, I have no doubt that he understood the consequences of his actions."

***

On the fourth day of the sentencing hearing, Whitmore advised Kari that she would be their last fact witness before he submitted victim statements and the defense presented character witnesses. He and Jillian Stevens would then make their closing statements.

"Your testimony will complement and illustrate what Dr. Patel testified about yesterday."

"Are you sure you don't want Becca to introduce the last bit of evidence instead of me? Won't the defense bring up the fact that I'm also a patient of Dr. Patel?"

"I doubt it. Think about it. If they bring it up, you'll testify that you see Dr. Patel in regard to the heroic shootout you were in last year. By bringing up the therapy, they would be pumping up your credibility and authenticating your bona fides." Whitmore knocked on his forehead with a knuckle. "It would not be a smart move on their part to give your testimony added credence."

"Okay." Kari shrugged. "I just want to help the case and not hurt it."

"If this were a trial with a jury, I might hesitate to put you on the stand. But in this situation, I'm good. No matter what happens this week, it's going to be appealed. The defense is still fuming over the fact that the judge ruled to limit the testimony from the psychiatric experts." Whitmore shrugged. "Ergo the no contest plea."

"So much for acceptance of responsibility," said Kari.

"The main thing I need you to do is authenticate where you found Cuddy Mullins's calendar, so I can enter it into evidence."

"I got it."

Before heading to the courtroom, Kari dropped by the war room next door, where they were temporarily storing the metal utility carts holding the evidence they rolled over from the U.S Attorneys' office every day. She located the box containing items obtained from the foundation and removed the burgundy Moleskine calendar Cuddy Mullins kept that listed all of his scheduled conference calls and meetings with the anonymous benefactors.

Later that morning, when Whitmore called her to take the stand, she was ready. Kari had been sworn in and was sitting in the wooden box next to Judge Benedetti. Whitmore had her recite her name, title, and credentials before beginning his questions.

"Are you a doctor, Agent Wheeler?"

"No." She shook her head.

"Were you in the courtroom when Dr. Nina Patel and Dr. Dwight Park gave the court the results of their independent evaluations of the defendant's mental health?"

"Yes."

"And you heard that Mr. Mullins claimed to both of these mental health professionals that he experienced psychotic episodes where he thought he met with anonymous donors."

"Yes."

"Agent Wheeler, let me show you an item marked as evidence in this matter." He handed her the calendar. "Can explain to the court what you're holding?"

"It is a calendar that was collected by me during a search of the Foundation for New Visions in Giving." She opened the hardcover book and flipped through the pages. "The handwriting inside has been identified as being that of Mr. Cuddy Mullins."

Whitmore turned to address the judge. "Your Honor, may I remind you that defense counsel has stipulated that this calendar belongs to and that the notations inside were made by the defendant."

Judge Benedetti nodded. "Yes. Please continue."

"Agent Wheeler, could you please turn to the page dated Sunday, July 22?"

Kari turned to the page and waited for Whitmore to continue. "What does the handwritten notation on that page say?"

"It says conference call with anonymous donor at three p.m."

"How many similar notes did you find in the calendar?"

"During the calendar year, there were twenty-two such notations where Mr. Mullins wrote down when he would be attending a meeting or conference call with the anonymous donors. At the beginning of the year, they were every second Thursday of the month and then changed to every third Sunday. We seized the calendar in October, but appointments were scheduled until the end of the year, excluding the weeks before and after Christmas."

"And what is your professional investigative opinion about that notation, Special Agent Wheeler?"

"Based on the testimony this week, that the anonymous donors never existed, and Dr. Patel's testimony earlier that people can't schedule their delusions, and based on my investigative experience, it is my opinion that this calendar is evidence of Mr. Mullins's deliberate intention to lie and defraud his victims."

Whitmore walked back to the prosecution table and picked up a color-coded diagram printed on eleven-by-seventeen paper. "May I direct your attention to these flowcharts that were entered into evidence earlier this week."

Kari leaned forward and scanned the documents he handed her. "Yes, this is a chart reflecting several bank accounts under the control of Mr. Mullins several years ago, where approximately fifty thousand dollars were in arrears."

"You mean the accounts were all overdrawn?"

"Yes. That's correct." She placed documents in front of her on the wide edge of the witness stand and used her hand to smooth them, so they laid flat. "The banks demanded their money and Mr. Mullins began soliciting funds from benefactors promising a double-your-money return after several months. The donors were apparently more forthcoming with donations, and within weeks, he was able to pay down the overdraft. He applied for a grant and used those funds to double the money of the initial donors. Once the word got around about this new concept in philanthropy, 'participatory giving,' the scheme was off and running."

"Thank you, Agent Wheeler." Whitmore turned to the judge. "Your honor, the prosecution believes that these flow charts and this calendar are proof that the Foundation for New Visions in Giving was nothing more than a Ponzi scheme and that Cuddy Mullins is nothing more than a consummate con man. We respectfully request your consideration of the government's recommendation for the maximum sentence with significant jail time."

CHAPTER 46

Late that afternoon, after the sentencing hearing had been adjourned for the day, CeCe and Cuddy were once again in the large conference room of the law offices of Smith, Stevens, Keller, and Goldberg. A powerful feeling of déjà vu suddenly came over CeCe, and she knew exactly why they were there and what was about to happen. She was ready for them. She had thought it over, and no way was she going to change her mind. The doors of the conference room swung open, and even though Jillian Stevens and her legal assistant walked in with smiles on their faces, CeCe did not believe they were happy.

Jillian placed a red folder on the table in front of her and opened it to display several documents with colorful tabs that read *Sign Here*.

"CeCe." Jillian leaned over and gestured to a document. "It's time."

CeCe's heart began to race, and she could feel beads of sweat forming all over her body. "You don't understand what you're asking me to do."

Jillian cocked her head as if she was surprised. CeCe couldn't imagine why—she had been telling the attorneys and Cuddy for weeks that she would not turn over all their assets to the government, especially their home. They obviously thought she would eventually cave to their pressure.

"If I did sign away all of our assets, where am I supposed to live and what am I supposed to live on?" she asked.

"The feds aren't going to keep the money," added Cuddy. "It will be used to provide restitution to the nonprofits who lost money."

Jillian let out a loud sigh. "We don't have any more time to discuss this. Judge Benedetti set aside a full week of his calendar for these proceedings, but this is not a trial. It's a sentencing. Had the case gone to trial, the expert testimony we heard today would not have been admissible as evidence. You understand that don't you?"

"I have faith that the judge believes that Cuddy wasn't motivated by greed and that all he wanted was to do God's work by raising funds for charity," said CeCe. "I know he'll find it in his heart to consider all that he heard today before he sentences Cuddy. I know he'll be merciful."

"There's no need for deliberation; the judge could actually sentence your husband as early as tomorrow morning, after Cuddy reads his statement to the court. The only thing left before that is victim testimony. We'll wrap up with our character witnesses, and then Cuddy will address the court. The judge will have heard everything he needs to make up his mind." Jillian pushed the papers and a pen closer to her. "Cuddy has signed over all of the property in his name. It's time for you to relinquish your rights to the investments and property in your name."

"Cuddy?" She turned to face him, but his head was down, and he wouldn't look her in the eye. Instead, he was focused on the documents in front of her.

"CeCe, this isn't just about hoping to get the court's sympathy and a lighter sentence based on the forfeiture of funds." Jillian said it softly, as if she were speaking to a child.

CeCe did not appreciate her tone and could feel her resolve hardening. She didn't appreciate being manipulated this way.

"The stakes changed once the feds discovered that you impersonated Sir Middleton's assistant to convince donors to contribute to the scheme. If you don't sign, all the government needs to do to obtain those assets is to charge you as a coconspirator. So either way, the money and the house will end up with them."

Jillian's legal assistant added. "And you would end up in jail."

"Maybe I should let that happen," CeCe said defiantly. "At least then I'd have somewhere to stay."

She was startled when Cuddy suddenly pushed back his chair and stood. "Stop pouting and feeling sorry for yourself. Time to grow up, CeCe," he snapped. "I'm not going to be around to take care of you."

"I can take care of myself." She spoke with confidence, but fear grabbed ahold of her and a sickening wave of despair weighed her down.

"I know you don't believe that," he said. "You're like a stray that nobody wanted that I picked up on the street. I found someone who will care for Potter, but I have no idea who's gonna take you home and feed you."

Cuddy was staring at her with all-consuming hate. She had seen such hatred in his eyes before—when he had his hands around her neck several weeks prior. The lawyers were staring at her and Cuddy, and their eyes were bright with excitement, as if they were cheering and willing him to finally speak up and demand that she do the right thing. She felt herself buckling under their condemnation, and the embarrassment and humiliation of the moment got stuck in her throat. She couldn't speak.

"If I hadn't been so concerned about giving you everything you wanted," Cuddy continued, "there's a good chance none of this would have ever happened."

She felt like she had been slapped in the face. It seemed so real that she raised her hand to touch her cheek and feel the heat of the sting. She looked up at all of the faces staring at her. Not one of them held sympathy. Not one of them was on her side. It was as if all of their hands were around her windpipe, choking the life out of her. She took shallow breaths while she waited for her panic to subside.

"Sign the papers, CeCe. That's not our stuff. We didn't earn it legitimately. You have to turn it over."

"I would safeguard the things in my name until you got out of jail, so you would have a place to come home to."

"What we had together was never a home. You didn't even want to have kids. You never wanted to have sex."

"You know what I went through as a child." She backed herself against the wall. "Why are you saying these things in front of them?" She pointed an accusatory finger at the lawyers. "Why are you trying to humiliate me? You kept telling people you wanted to be a priest, so celibacy shouldn't have been a problem for you."

Cuddy walked over to where she was standing and placed his arms around her, in what she knew was an embrace without passion. After a moment, he took her arm and led her back to the table. He handed her a pen and pushed the papers closer to her. Her body was cold and she felt empty inside.

She picked up the pen and held it above the papers. Her eyes met his. She found only pity and pain in his. She knew he hoped she was feeling surrender and relief. But she was only stricken with fear. She needed the money. She looked around the conference room, defiantly shaking her head, and let the pen drop. Cuddy and the attorneys watched as it rolled off the table and to the floor. She couldn't be poor again. She couldn't do it. Not even for Cuddy.

If the government wanted her money, they would have to pry it from her cold, dead hands.

CHAPTER 47

The courtroom was packed with Cuddy's former friends and associates. He knew many of them were there to witness his demise. When he caught the eyes of Lennie and Tanya Adams and they looked away, his heart clutched, and he almost lost his already shaky composure. As part of the sentencing phase, the judge had reviewed more than one hundred letters filed by not-for-profits, institutions, and donors who were now struggling to make up the millions lost in the Ponzi scheme. The statements from organizations and donors caught in the scheme directly blamed Cuddy for program cuts, layoffs, legal bills, financial woes, and personal betrayals, stating that their organizations had been economically handicapped and publicly humiliated through their connection with the New Visions scandal.

There were also a handful of true believers who appeared before the court as character witnesses for Cuddy. When they spoke of his commitment to God and recounted his past good deeds, he gained a measure of resolve to convey his regrets when it was his turn to address the court. Just knowing that there were people present who were not looking to pummel him with stones would get him through this next stage. He would seek out their encouraging faces in the gallery.

Soon, Judge Benedetti signaled that it was Cuddy's time to speak. His emotions spiked, and he lifted his face skyward, secretly gnawing on the inside of his cheek to stifle a sob. It worked. The emotions settled just beneath the surface. He rose from his chair and began to walk over to the witness stand. Before he got too far, Jillian Stevens grabbed him by the arm.

"No, Cuddy. Stay here." She waved her hand over his side of the defense table. "You can address the court right from here."

"Mr. Mullins," said Judge Benedetti, "are you ready to enter a plea?"

"Yes, Your Honor." He swallowed hard. "I plead no contest." And with that announcement, his days of proclaiming his innocence were over.

"Thank you, Mr. Mullins. The court accepts your plea and acknowledges that, by pleading, you have saved the taxpayers the expense of a two to three-month-long trial." Judge Benedetti held out his hands, palms opened. "Do you have a statement you would like to read?"

Cuddy nodded and cleared his throat. He held the prepared words in his hand but chose to speak from his heart. "Your Honor, every day for most of my life, I have said a prayer for others in need, and today, I made a rare prayer to God for myself. I prayed for your leniency." He placed his hands together. "I've always considered myself a good person who tried to do the right thing. But my mother would tell you I was a lapsed Catholic who hasn't gone to mass for years. I remember well my childhood pilgrimages to Sunday school, where I dropped my pennies and dimes into the collection plate to save the pagan babies. My brothers kept their change and brought candy from the corner store on their way home. And they teased me mercilessly for giving mine to the church, but I wanted to make my mother proud. Bless her soul; she was an angel." He made the sign of the cross.

"I was lost for a few years. But, later, after my injury"—he stopped for a moment, closed his eyes, and touched his scar—"I became a born-again Christian, and it was my aim to honor God through service to others. When they came to me, I believed the anonymous donors were a sign from God that I was to help as many people as possible in what I envisioned to be a financial ministry. Unfortunately, I'm a disaster when it comes to handling finances, mine and others." He shrugged and continued.

"I tried to do what God wanted of me. I was and forever will be his servant. Even now, when I close my eyes, I can see the anonymous donors sitting around the conference table. I now realize they only existed in my imagination. With a heavy heart, I admit to everyone in this courtroom that my irresponsible actions have hurt thousands of innocent people." He turned to acknowledge the spectators in the gallery.

"With no disrespect to the court, I must declare that I will face a more powerful judge than you one day, and, at that time, I could be condemned to a greater prison and my sentence will be an eternal one. All I want is to be useful now, while I still live and breathe in this life. I pray that I will have the opportunity to be of service wherever I end up and for however long I'm there."

As soon as Cuddy was finished, as predicted by Jillian Stevens, Judge Benedetti recessed for lunch and informed them all that he would be ready to render his sentence when they returned.

Knowing that in one hour, his fate would be sealed, he doubted, even if he had had an appetite, he'd be able to keep anything down.

***

By 1:01 p.m., all interested parties had gathered for the last time in Judge Sterling Benedetti's courtroom. Cuddy took his place at the defense table next to Jillian Stevens, who gently patted his knee under the table. CeCe, who had been ostracized by the defense team, sat stoically in the first row, dabbing her eyes with a handkerchief, but for the most part, everyone, including Cuddy, ignored her during the marathon sentencing. Cuddy was ready to accept the consequences of his transgressions.

Judge Benedetti took his place on the bench, called things to order, and charged ahead. "I've listened to the testimony presented to me this week and reviewed the evidence and motions submitted and also reviewed the presentencing report I received from probation. The bankruptcy trustee has provided me with the preliminary settlement agreement between the victims of this scheme, wherein the winners, those who profited, have, in theory, agreed to help out those organizations that lost money. The victims' letters spoke for them, and I have taken all of this into consideration, and I'm ready to impose your sentence."

He motioned Cuddy onto his feet with a wave of his hand. "Mr. Mullins, will you please stand?"

Cuddy stood and faced the judge. He was nervous, but not in a jittery way. He felt surprisingly composed at the same time. His heart was beating a little faster, but he would not have described what he was experiencing as panic or anxiety. He had been anticipating this day, this time, for more than a year. He was ready.

"Mr. Cuthbert Mullins III, I sentence you to twenty-two years' incarceration. I believe this sentence, although a reduction from the thirty years' incarceration that could have been imposed, epitomizes and rises to the inordinate scope and enormity of the damage done in this case. Your actions have left hundreds of churches, Christian colleges, homeless shelters, and recovery centers in precarious positions, not knowing how they will pay for projects you promised to fund. With these deeds, you have destroyed the exemplary history of good works performed before you began this inconceivable scheme.

"Ms. Stevens, your client may sit down now. While you and I and Assistant United States Attorney Mr. Whitmore discuss a little housekeeping, immediately after I adjourn this hearing, Mr. Mullins needs to visit the Marshals' office here in the federal building for processing. I am giving him one week"—Judge Benedetti held up a finger—"before he has to report to prison. They'll explain where he needs to go and what he needs to do when he gets downstairs."

Cuddy's mind immediately started calculating all the projects he needed to complete. He would have to use the time wisely to get his affairs in order. Melinda Tribble had been in the courtroom. As they had previously arranged, Cuddy would have her come over to pick up Potter on his last day home. The pup wouldn't understand why Cuddy was no longer around to care for him, but Melinda would give him a good home, and he would learn to love her as much as he did Cuddy. Twenty-two years was a long time to be locked up. He'd be nearly sixty-one years old. That was almost double what they had estimated it would be if they had been able to mitigate his exposure by increasing the forfeiture. But perhaps, when they appealed the sentence, he would have more assets to hand over.

Cuddy knew what had to be done. Suicide was the only answer.

CHAPTER 48

They rode home from court in silence. However, as soon as they entered the house, Cuddy turned to CeCe and said, "I need to take Potter out for his walk, but when I get back, we need to talk."

CeCe nodded. "You hate me, don't you?"

"No." He shook his head. "But I'm terribly disappointed. I've explained to you as best I can that an important part of accepting my guilt and being good with God was giving back everything I took." He stooped to attach the leash to Potter's collar and let out a big sigh. "I'll never feel worthy of His forgiveness until I do."

"I can't do what you're asking me to do."

"I know that now. You're a stubborn woman, Cece Mullins."

"I'm a scared woman."

"We'll work on a plan as soon as I get back. I promise I know what needs to be done."

"You're not going to change my mind. And I'm so tired." She rubbed her eyes. "I just want to go lie down."

"Please don't. I won't be too long." Using a stern tone of voice that signaled that he was giving her an order, he added, "Do not go upstairs. You can nap after our talk."

***

Upon his return from walking Potter, as usual, he entered the house through the back door. She stood in the middle of the kitchen, as if she hadn't moved since he left. He could tell she was emotionally fragile and exhausted. Her eyes were filled with fear, like a child waiting to be punished.

"CeCe, you're trembling." He convinced her to sit down at the kitchen table while he made them each a cup of tea. He then scooted his chair next to her and held one of her hands, while he stroked her hair. Then, he told her everything. He told her about witnessing Tracy Cordoza's attempt to commit suicide by throwing herself on the subway tracks at Somerset Station, about the SEPTA safety manager saying that Regional Rail or Amtrak was the more efficient way to commit suicide by train, and how he had laid across the tracks behind their home but was too weak to go through with it.

"I even keep a train schedule here in the junk drawer with all the times the Regional Rail train passes through every day." He opened the drawer and held up the timetable for the Paoli-Thorndale Line. "If I were a stronger man, suicide might still seem to be a way to end all of this pain and disappointment. Even dreaming about lying across those tracks brings me peace of mind sometimes, but I still have hope that things will work out for the best. Do you still have hope, CeCe?"

CeCe didn't say a word. She just stared sadly into his eyes and gently rubbed the scar on the back of his head.

***

For the next few days, Cuddy continued to share his thoughts about suicide with CeCe. Not once did she say suicide was not the solution or offer that he should get counseling. Not once did she ask him to promise not to kill himself. She just sat there and listened to him talk about how a train traveling at a normal rate of speed could do as much damage to a body as having a bomb detonate in front of you.

Two days before he was to self-report the U. S. Marshals' Office in the Federal Court Building, he returned from taking Potter out. Cuddy was surprised to see CeCe was already awake and up. She was slouched at the kitchen table. With the exception of the remains of her bright pink lipstick leftover from the day before smeared on her mouth and face, she wore no makeup. Her hair was limp, oily and unwashed. But something else was different.

"CeCe, are you okay?" he touched her cheek and then ran his hand through her hair.

"Don't," she said. She brushed his fingers away. "I look ugly."

"What's wrong, Sweetie?"

"I can't do it."

"Do what?'

"Take care of Potter while you're away."

"Don't worry about that," he said. "Remember, I made arrangements for Melinda to adopt him.

"I should be the one to take care of him while your away, but you don't even trust me to do that," she said. "To care for a dumb animal."

Cuddy flinched. "Not true. But let's not worry about that right now. You shouldn't be worrying about stuff like that right now." He pushed a strand of hair from her face. "I'm going to go up and take a shower." He unclipped Potter's leash from his collar and hung it on the hook next to the door. "When I'm done, I'll fix us both a nice big breakfast. How does chocolate chip pancakes sound?"

As he turned to go up to shower, she called him back. She got up from her chair and stepping behind him placed her arms around his chest and held him tight in a full body hug. She didn't say a word, but before releasing him, she raised up on her tiptoes and kissed the scar on the back of his head. When she let go, and he turned to look at her, she wore the biggest smile she had in weeks.

Cuddy let the warm water cascade over him. He realized he was, most likely, experiencing one of the last private hot showers he would have for many, many years to come. He stayed in until the hot water turned cool. He dressed quickly, and when he got downstairs, Cece was nowhere to be found. He called her name and looked out the window, into the backyard and beyond the pool. The first thing he noticed when he looked around the kitchen was that the kitchen junk drawer had been pulled open and the train timetable lay open on top. He knew where she had gone. He knew what she planned to do. He dropped to his knees, placed his head in his hands, and began to pray, "Forgive me, Father, for what I have done."

Only a few moments passed before a sudden panic engulfed him and he opened his eyes. *Potter. Where was Potter?* He looked at the hook next to the door. No leash. He had not seen the note left on the counter next to the drawer. He crawled over on his hands and knees to retrieve it.

Dear Cuddy, I did not want you to be worried about who would take care of Potter and me, so we have gone to be with your God in Heaven. I will always love you, Cece.

"No. Cece. No," he cried out loud. He could not believe what he was reading. What had he been thinking? He looked at the kitchen clock as he burst out the back door. He still had five minutes before the next train came through. He could get there in time if he ran. He continued to pray and ask God for guidance as he sped through the woods and down the familiar trails.

Cuddy climbed up the embankment and out of the corner of his eye spied her lying on the tracks a few yards from the bend—the perfect spot to be sure the train engineer didn't have adequate time to react. Just like he had told her. He called out as he ran the quarter mile down the track toward her. She barely moved, but he could see that she was struggling to hold on to something. *Oh my God. She has Potter in her arms.*

"Noooo! Cece, please don't do this!" He stumbled forward, tears streaming down his face as he ran wildly down the gravel path next to the track, slipping and tripping on the pebbles along the way. "*Let him go!*"

As he got closer to her, he could see that she, so determined to go through with her plan, had used wire coat hangers to secure her neck and one hand to the rail. She was holding on to Potter's collar with the other hand. "No. Don't!" he screamed. "I'm sorry. I'm sorry."

His heart clutched when he heard the horn blast of the train. In his panic, he took a misstep on the gravel and tumbled down the embankment just as the train rounded the bend. As he lay sprawled out on the ground with the breath knocked out of him, all he could hear was the horn blasting, the screeching of steel on steel as the engineer threw on the brakes as a powerful rush of air swept over him. When Cuddy scrambled back up the embankment, he could see that the train had come to rest nearly a quarter mile up the track. He was shocked by the scene in front of him. He soon realized that the gore littering the area was pieces of his wife. He crouched within a foot of her severed hand, diamond rings still on her fingers, and unconsciously reached for it and then recoiled from the gruesome sight. Dizziness overcame him, and he fell to the ground as black dots and bright lights circled in front of his eyes.

He could hear someone running toward him, could feel the person leaning over him. Cuddy looked up to see a man dressed in jeans and a yellow safety vest, the train engineer.

"*My wife*!" Cuddy screamed, his voice high pitched and anguished. "*Potter*!" He covered his eyes with his hands. He couldn't look at the horrific scene in front of him. "Oh my God," he mumbled. "Oh my God."

"When I came around the bend, she was lying across the tracks," said the engineer. Cuddy could hear the pain in his voice. "I'm so sorry. There was no time to stop."

Cuddy tried to speak, but his anguish was insufferable. His chest tightened. He bit his lip and grimaced.

"Sir? Are you hurt?"

He was in a fog, barely conscious with despair. He heard another voice say that the accident had been reported to dispatch and the paramedics and the medical examiner were on the way. He felt hands gently laying him on his back and loosening his collar. They were talking to him, but he couldn't understand what they were saying. He continued to float away to a place he could comprehend, where he didn't have to witness the damage he had orchestrated. But then a familiar sound jolted him out of unconsciousness. A tinkling sound. He sat up suddenly, startling the engineer and the uniformed train conductor who had joined them. Cuddy pointed to the high grass nearby but fell back on wobbly legs when he tried to stand. The conductor cautiously approached the area and parted the tall grass. She knelt, and when she stood and turned around, she was holding a white mass of fur in her arms.

"*Potter*," Cuddy called out. Cece had let go of him in time, but the pup must have been hurled into the brush from the velocity of the speeding train, and had the wind knocked out of him. He raised his head, wiggled out of the arms of the conductor, and ran to Cuddy, circling his head, whimpering and licking his face.

"How's my little buddy? How's my little buddy doing?" was the only thing Cuddy could say until he had fully accepted that Potter was alive. As he hugged him tight, Cuddy looked up at the sky and said a prayer of thanks to God.

CHAPTER 49

In order to arrange burial services for CeCe and complete the necessary transfer documents to forfeit the assets and property he had inherited from her, the judge gave Cuddy an additional two weeks before he had to report to prison. He spent the time visiting every nonprofit in the region and offering to donate his furniture, cars, clothes, books, and time to those in need. Some accepted his charitable gifts; most did not. But nonetheless, it was therapeutic for him. Potter was now safely with Melinda, where he would be well loved.

Cuddy spent his last night of freedom at the Marriott in Center City. They looked at him suspiciously when he checked in with no luggage. The next morning, he placed all of his personal items, except for his driver's license, in an envelope addressed to Melinda Tribble and dropped it in the hotel's mailbox before beginning his last stroll down Market Street to the courthouse six blocks away. He loved Philadelphia and wondered if it would make sense to anyone how much he would miss his city. All he had ever wanted to do was make Philly and its citizens better. He passed a homeless man sitting on the northwest corner of Tenth Street and wished he hadn't left all of the contents of his wallet, exactly $23.89, for the hotel housekeeper. He would have liked to hand the man enough for a cup of coffee and a donut at least. He apologized to him, explaining that his wallet was empty too.

Once at the federal courthouse, he took the elevator to the U.S. Marshals' offices on the second floor. They frisked him before ordering him to remove all his clothing and submit to a body-cavity search. He bent over and coughed twice as instructed. They made him shower in a communal bathroom with other prisoners even though he had informed them he had taken one that morning. They gave him a baggy, orange jumpsuit to put on and had him sit alone in a holding cell. They said he would be taken over to the federal detention center later in the day. He would be there temporarily, until a bus was scheduled to take him and any other new inmates to Lewisburg Penitentiary, where he would be assigned permanently.

"You know you could have had someone drive you up there and self-reported," said the marshal who processed him. "You could be sitting around here for days, maybe a week. But I guess you're in no big hurry."

"I didn't want to bother anyone. I'll be okay." He sat down on the metal cot, stretched out his legs, and leaned against the concrete wall. "Would I be able to get a Bible to read while I wait?"

"A Bible? Yeah, I guess there's one around here someplace."

The marshal returned with a hardcover Bible like the ones they used to have in hotel rooms. This one was well worn. He fanned the pages with his thumb and was finally able to feel comfortable with his surroundings. He was at peace.

He had been reading for less than an hour when he heard the main door of the holding area open and was surprised to see Special Agent Kari Wheeler walking toward his cell. She held a green card in her hand.

"One of the marshals is a good friend. He called to tell me you were here. I could have asked him to make an extra copy of the final disposition card"—she waved the green five-by-eight card in the air—"but I wanted to let you know how sorry I was to hear about your wife."

"Thank you. That's very kind of you." He looked at her closely.

"I was also a little curious."

"About what?"

She hiked a shoulder in a half shrug. "I could never quite figure you out. How you could create a scheme involving millions of dollars and millions of lies but also have a resume of good deeds and charitable work."

"There's no mystery. I'm a true believer, God's servant."

"Then how did you end up here, locked up?"

He shook his head. "This is the consequence of my actions. I don't question his plan for me, and I accept my shortcomings. We all need something to believe in. I always hoped that CeCe would have found something to believe in—other than me," he added. "I tried to be a good person."

"I still don't get it. You say you're working for God, but you cheated people. That's not my definition of a good person."

"I respect your opinion, but God's is the only judgment I accept. I lost my way. But I'll have twenty-two years to do good work in His name.

"You act as if you're preparing for a new life as a monk in a monastery instead of going off to prison."

"When I get my work assignment, I hope they let me be of service to the other inmates in some way. Maybe this was his plan for me all along—to minister to inmates."

He noticed she was staring at the Bible he was holding. He patted the cover.

"They wouldn't let me bring mine. This is not the American Standard Bible version I'm used to but give me a second." He flipped a few pages back and forth until he came to what he was looking for. He read it out loud.

"'He has granted to us His precious and magnificent promises, so that by them, you may become partakers of the divine nature, having escaped the corruption that is in the world by lust.'"

"It's from 2 Peter 1:4," he said. He handed the Bible to her and pointed to the section on the page. "I believe this is his word for me, but for some inexplicable reason, I feel these words are for you too. Here's the rest of the passage."

The world of lust? she said, repeating the last few words in her head. How could he know? She didn't look up and instead fidgeted with the rings on the fingers of her left hand. It was obvious to Cuddy that the words deeply affected and disturbed her.

"Lust for power and attention, lust for money and possessions, or lust as in sexual desire," he said.

How did he know that was what she was thinking about?

"It's all the same. It's about wanting more or to be more." He took the Bible back and continued reading from the scripture.

"'Now for this very reason also, applying all diligence, in your faith supply moral excellence, and in your moral excellence, knowledge, and in your knowledge, self-control, and in your self-control, perseverance, and in your perseverance, godliness, and in your godliness, brotherly kindness, and in your brotherly kindness, love. For if these qualities are yours and are increasing, they render you neither useless nor unfruitful in the true knowledge of our Lord Jesus Christ.'" He closed the Bible.

"That last sentence brings me hope and comfort. He's not done with me yet." He looked her in the eye. "We're all sinners. But he loves us anyway. Repent and ask Him for forgiveness."

She shook her head. "I'm not religious. I haven't been inside a church in years."

He placed his hand over his heart. "Spirituality, not religion. His forgiveness. Your redemption. That's all it takes."

***

As soon as Kari exited the detention center, she pulled a notebook and pen from her bag and scribbled a note to herself before she forgot the scripture number 2 Peter 1 verse 4. She would never have admitted this to Cuddy Mullins, but maybe he was right—the verse was meant for her. Maybe there was a chance for redemption for her too.

CHAPTER 50

She was holding a tiny Bible with a worn, black, vinyl cover. She knew they had one someplace in the house. She had searched and rummaged through several places for it and had, embarrassingly, located it deep within the kitchen junk drawer. She found the verse Cuddy had recited to her earlier that day and read it again. That's what she was doing, standing in the middle of the kitchen reading the New Testament when Kevin walked in through the back door.

"So what now? You're going to start reading the good book and going to church?"

"Church? Probably not. But I don't know." She flipped through the pages. "Maybe."

"Really? You must have found something pretty powerful inside there," said Kevin.

She placed a finger on one of the thin pages and held it up for him to read. "I want to get your interpretation of this scripture."

Kevin read the passage and let out a loud sigh. "It talks about moral excellence, self-control, perseverance. These things are the beginning tools to finding forgiveness, but I'm still not sure yet if I can do that. But for the sake of our children, I'm going to keep trying."

"That's all I can ask of you." Grateful tears filled her eyes, and she patted his cheek, noting to herself that he no longer instinctively recoiled from her touch. "I will do whatever I can to win back your trust and your love."

"You'll always have my love. That's what makes this so difficult." He stared into her eyes. "But I'm not sure if I loved and knew the real you. I doubt that, until now, you knew who you were."

She smiled softly and playfully flipped through the little Bible. "There's probably a perfect passage in here about finding yourself."

He took her hand in his and returned her smile, and, for the first time since he'd learned about her shameful secret, she felt they had a real chance. It would be different, but nevertheless, they could move forward together.

And that's when she realized that, despite her best intentions, she had once again let a case change her. But this time, the change was for the better.

Thank you!

I hope you enjoyed Greedy Givers.

Please take a moment to write a short review and post it on the online sales page of the retailer where you purchased Greedy Givers. Reviews help readers find good books.

Visit: jerriwilliams.com

Join my Reader Team and I'll send you the FBI Reading Resource— books about the FBI written by FBI agents, the FBI Reality Checklist, and my monthly email digest to make it easy for you to keep up to date on the FBI in books, TV, and movies and more!

Please check out all the books in Jeri Williams'
Philadelphia FBI Corruption Squad Series featuring
Special Agent Kari Wheeler:

Pay To Play (Book 1)
Greedy Givers (Book 2)
Spoiled Spenders (Book 3)

And her non-fiction book about FBI clichés and
misconceptions in books, TV, and movies:

FBI Myths and Misconceptions: A Manual for Armchair Detectives

Jerri's books are available as ebooks, paperbacks, and audiobooks
wherever books are sold.

Acknowledgments

Many people have played important roles from the first draft to the publication of Greedy Givers. Special thanks to Burnett Jones who provided technical advice regarding train safety matters. I'm also grateful for my beta readers—Sue McCullough and Bill Iezzi— and the members of my advance reader team, especially Lisa Williams, Judy Tyler and Mike Jortberg.

Greedy Givers was inspired by a case I worked on during my FBI career. I dedicate this book to my former investigative and prosecutive team members, Loretta Hart, Brian Cosgriff, Judy Smith and Rich Goldberg.

I also express love and gratitude to my husband Keith Wert for his patience as I sequester away in my home office for hours at a time to get the words down on paper.

Thank you all for your support!

Jerri

Made in the USA
Middletown, DE
21 July 2020

12722382R00165